To the previous generation of romance authors
whose stories helped me through my darkest days.
And to the new generation of indie authors
who helped me believe I could fulfill a lifelong dream.

READY
to
Live

SHEFALI PREM

1

Luc

I HATE INDEPENDENCE DAY. Ten years ago today, I lost my freedom and became imprisoned in a pit of guilt that will last into eternity. Since then, I've spent each Fourth of July in solitude in my hometown.

Unfortunately, it's not a peaceful retreat. Rather, it's the scene of my crime.

I stand at the window of my childhood home in Fontaine, Louisiana. Watching the sun set over the treetops, I open another beer and take a long sip as I reflect on that night when everything changed.

It was the summer after high school graduation, just weeks away from the start of my college football career. I'd been so happy and free, celebrating with friends at a Fourth of July party at the nearby lake. We had gathered for the last big hurrah before everyone went their separate ways. There had been a bonfire, beer, and beautiful, willing girls. The world had been my oyster.

Everyone would say the world is still mine for the taking. I'm the highest paid Super Bowl–winning quarterback, loved by millions, with years of football ahead of me. Beautiful women are at my beck and call. What more could I ask for?

Peace. I would give it all up—every dollar, every accolade—if I could have just a little bit of peace for my tortured soul.

My gaze wanders across the small backyard to the edge of the woods, the trees blending into the dusky sky. The tiny house I'm standing in is located along a narrow, winding road. My closest neighbor is almost a half mile away, perfect for keeping my presence here on the down low.

I turn from the darkening view and my even darker thoughts when a knock sounds on the door. My scheduled visitors are early, but I don't mind. I want to get this part of my plan over so I can move on to the next.

I down the rest of my beer and set the bottle on the end table before crossing the small living room to the front door. The brisk knock comes again just as I open it to see a tall, slim blonde. My normally tight self-control slips, evidenced by the immediate reaction of my heartbeat jumping into a full gallop.

I blame the reaction on the alcohol and the importance I've placed on the night. It can't be the woman. I come across beautiful women almost every day. I've learned to be immune to them. And yet, I'm surprised at the zing of attraction that goes straight through me as I rake my glance over her body. Despite her lack of any real curves, she's a knockout. Golden hair pulled back into a high, sleek ponytail, gray eyes, fair skin, and curved pink lips.

The woman sticks her hand out. "Hi, Saint. Um, Luc. Or should I call you Mr. Saint? I'm sorry." She stops and takes a deep breath, as if nervous. I suppose it's natural for women in her profession to be nervous when alone with a strange man. But why is she alone? And why does she know my name, as if she was expecting to see me?

I'd assumed she—they—would figure out who I was, even in the backwoods of Louisiana. Sometimes when I don't want to be bothered by people, I'll admit to who I am, but with a conspiratorial wink that would make the person question if I really am *the* Lucien Saint.

"I'm sorry," she says again, letting her hand fall when I continue staring at her, trying to make sense of what feels wrong. "May I come in?"

Something definitely feels off, but I'm too curious about her to close the door in her face. Instead, I open it wider and allow her in. She walks to the middle of the room and stops, looking around. There isn't much to see—the living room is smaller than my closet at home in Manhattan.

I push the door shut, and she whirls toward it when it closes with a loud click. Okay, not a good sign. Women in her profession should be used to being alone with men. Although maybe being out in the boondocks at night is making her nervous.

I look her over again, taking my time, starting with her feet. She has on heels, but they're more businesslike than sexy, just like the loose brown slacks and rumpled linen blazer hanging on her narrow frame. A thin beige top underneath reveals the slightest of curves.

When she moves to reach into the giant leather purse hanging from her shoulder, the blazer shifts to reveal the shape of her breast, the tight point at the center outlined against the cloth. My dick twitches beneath the zipper of my jeans. It must be the anticipation of what's about to happen that's making me react, because I've had women shove their overflowing cleavage in my face and felt nothing. This one barely even has tits.

She adjusts the large purse on her shoulder and faces me, sticking her hand out again. "Hi, I'm Charl—"

"I don't need to know your name, sugar," I interrupt. "I just need to know if you're qualified to do your job."

She stares at me, taken aback. Yeah, I guess that was a dick thing to say. Before I can apologize, she blasts me with a searing look full of pride and indignation. Her outstretched hand goes to her hip, and she says with a huff, "I wouldn't have just been promoted and assigned to you if I didn't have the qualifications, Lu—Mr. Saint."

It's my turn to be surprised.

"Promoted? I didn't realize they had levels of—" I break off, impatient to move on. "Whatever. I don't really care. Would you like a drink before we start?"

2

Charlie

I STARE IN CONFUSION at Lucien Saint. He's talking like he expected my arrival. But that can't be, because I didn't even know I was going to be here until just a few minutes ago.

My thoughts go flying when he moves to stand in front of me in three quick strides. His sudden nearness causes my breath to hitch, but when he leans toward me, I stop breathing. Visions of what I think he's about to do to me—lusty things—assail me, forcing me to take a regretful step back. The images evaporate when he straightens, and I realize he was reaching into a cooler at my feet. I feel foolish as he offers me one of the two beer bottles he's holding, eyebrow raised in question.

"No, I'm on the job," I answer, then jump when a faint boom sounds outside.

"Fireworks about to start at the lake," he says, his lips quirking in amusement.

"Right. Of course." I laugh, my nerves making it little more than a breath of sound. Despite my confidence in my qualifications, I can't help feeling nervous. He's my biggest assignment, and I don't want to mess it up. But I'm not sure if it's the job that has

me on edge or my attraction to him, revived from the crush I
had on him when he played with my brother for one season. I
asked Brent to introduce me to him. Of course, my overprotec-
tive big brother refused. It didn't stop me from drooling over
Luc and having fantasies about him.

I didn't think it was possible, but the man has gotten even
better-looking since his first season in the NFL. Still, it's no
excuse for me to behave like a starry-eyed fangirl. In my line
of work, I often interact with drool-worthy athletes. While I
acknowledge their sex appeal, I've never felt a flicker of personal
attraction to any of them.

Yet there's something about Luc that pulls me in—always
has. I'm reminded of some of my fantasies as I drink him in,
from his closely cropped tight curls to his high cheekbones and
full lower lip, to his tall, lean body with just the right amount
of muscle rippling under light brown skin.

But it's his striking hazel eyes—swirls of blue, green, and
amber—offset by thick dark lashes, that seem to look right into
me, putting me on edge. Maybe a little alcohol wouldn't hurt
to help me relax before we start, I reason.

"Actually, yes, please. I'll take a beer," I clarify, holding out
my hand for one. I let my Kate Spade tote bag slide off my arm
onto the sofa next to me.

He opens the second bottle, which he'd been about to put
back down, and hands it to me. When his fingers brush mine,
I ignore the bolt of lightning that goes up my arm, coinciding
with another boom outside. I steel myself against the attraction.

I am a fortress. Impenetrable.

I take another small step back, trying to be discreet so he
won't realize how his nearness is affecting me, and take a sip of
the beer, feeling the cold glide down my throat, into my belly.
His intent stare unnerves me, but I refuse to let him know how
he's affecting me. I stare back and take another sip. Lowering
the bottle, I run my tongue over my top lip to catch the droplets.

His gaze follows the movement, his eyes ablaze with desire. With one long stride, he's standing in front of me. At five-foot-ten plus two inches of heel, I still have to raise my eyes to meet his. I lose my breath when he invades my space. Taking the bottle from me, he places both on the coffee table.

"Wha—" Before I can finish a single word, he's pulling me to him, slamming my body against his hard chest. Before I can squeak out a protest, his mouth is on mine, moving over my lips, stealing my breath. His tongue demands I open, and I'm helpless to do otherwise.

The walls of my mental fortress collapse against the surprise onslaught. It's because he caught me unaware. I would have resisted if I'd had another second to prepare.

That's my story, and I'm sticking to it, I tell myself, even as I open my mouth wider and meet his invading tongue with mine. It's not enough. I need to be closer. I raise my arms to wrap them around his neck. His hands roam over my back, making my skin feverish, the heat of his touch causing shivers to go through me when he palms my ass and pulls me closer. A desperate moan escapes me when his growing erection presses into my belly. I barely have a chance to savor the sensation of him pressed against me before his hands slip under my top. I gasp, overwhelmed by the addition of skin-to-skin contact.

He pulls away. At least his mouth does.

"Am I going too fast?" he asks, his voice deep and growly. "I'm sorry. It's just been—"

It's my turn to cut him off. I crush my mouth to his, pulling his head down to me even as I lift up on my toes. His frantic moan kicks my desire to the next level. His need, his passion, is like nothing I've ever experienced. He makes me feel like a sex goddess. No one has ever done that before.

Before I know it, he's unhooked my bra and moved it out of the way to reveal my breasts. I gasp as he covers them with his large hands, rubbing the hard points against the center of his palms. He continues kissing me, ravaging my mouth, while his fingers pinch and roll my sensitive nipples.

Oh God yes!

My knees almost give out and I moan in protest when his hands leave me to drag off my jacket. It's not until he removes his mouth to pull my top over my head that I have a brief moment of clarity. I have to stop this madness. I might have learned a lot about Luc through my research so far, but in reality, we've just met. We haven't even shaken hands yet!

A quick press of his lips against mine stops a hysterical giggle from escaping. Then all thought disintegrates when he slides the bra down my arms and plumps a breast for his mouth. He covers the entire mound and sucks, his tongue flicking against the hard point. I bite my lip to keep my moan in, but it's no use.

The sound makes its way past my lips when he rakes his teeth over the tip and bites it gently. The second nip is a little less gentle, making me cry out as the jolt goes right to my sex that's already on the verge of convulsing.

"Oh God yes!" I say the words aloud this time.

He trails his lips over my skin to the other breast, sucking and licking until I'm melting between my legs. I gasp when he puts his arm around my hips to bring me closer to his erection. My mound instantly grinds against him of its own accord, seeking relief, something, anything, to quench the fire he's started there.

His mouth switches to my neck while I tug at the button of his jeans, fumbling with it in my frantic haste to release his hard length. He makes short work of the side zipper on my slacks and yanks them down my hips. I finally free the button on his jeans but struggle with the zipper tab, eager to get to what lies beneath. He nudges my hands out of the way to pull the zipper down himself. I already have my hands inside the back of his jeans, sliding my palms over the curve of his tight buttocks, pushing the jeans down farther as I explore the taut muscles. When the silky skin and heat of his erection brushes against my stomach, I hurriedly bring one hand around to his front and stroke him.

He's kissing me again, his large palm cradling my head, holding me close. When the other hand moves to cup the wet heat between my legs, I hook one thigh around his hip to give him room and moan when he tests my readiness. I would have told him, had he asked, that I've been ready since our fingers brushed over the beer bottle.

"Luc," I gasp when his thumb glides over my clit and circles it. Overwhelmed by the onslaught of sensation, I pull my mouth away from his kiss and press it against his neck, licking and sucking while my hips take up a rhythm of their own against his fingers. My fingernails dig into his back while my other hand brushes his out of the way so I can position his erection where I need it the most.

"It's been too long. I can't wait," he murmurs. He lifts me, allowing me to wrap my other leg around him.

Then I'm falling backward. Even as my arms tighten around him to hold on, he places me on the sofa and positions himself at my entrance.

Time stops when the hot slippery tip of him nudges me. I meet his eyes and have a moment of panic when I realize what's about to happen. The feeling dissipates in the next instant when he slowly enters me, then grabs my thighs under my knees and holds them up, thrusting the rest of the way into me at the same time, pushing all air out of me along with a sound that's half moan, half sigh.

"Fucking perfect," he murmurs, staring at the place where we're joined. He raises his gaze to mine and something passes between us as we look into each other's eyes. I have no time to examine the feeling because he pulls almost all the way out and then slams back into me. My eyes close and time speeds up.

No, it's him. He's all speed and motion. I bite my lip and muffle a scream at the fullness, at the incredible sensations buffeting me as he reaches deeper with each hard, fast stroke.

"I'm not going to last. I'm sorry," he says between harsh gasps, his voice raspy.

Sorry? It feels incredible, every thrust hitting a spot inside me that makes me gasp and whimper. All I can do is hold on to him, my inner walls as tight around him as my arms around his back. He takes me to the pinnacle that is right in front of me. I reach for it, jumping over the edge—an explosion of sensations ripples through my body as he drives back in with one hard push and jumps with me, letting go with a long groan. A kaleidoscope of lights and thundering booms surround me.

"Oh God yes, yes," I whimper, my body twitching and shaking with an orgasm that seems to go on forever. He continues to pulse inside me while I spasm around him. Outside, the nonstop crackle and boom of the fireworks in the distance reach a crescendo that seems to echo where we are joined. I have never felt an orgasm so strong. Ever. He has totally lived up to his reputation.

"Oh God no," I breathe, this time in total dismay. I come down quickly from my high, two thoughts swirling in my brain, fighting for attention. His reputation. I have just been well and truly fucked by none other than the New York Firebirds star quarterback, my brother's new teammate, Lucien Saint. A man slut if ever there was one.

And he has just come inside me.

3

Luc

I COLLAPSE ON TOP of the woman. What the hell did she say her name was? Cherry? Doesn't matter. Probably not her real name.

Since my arms are, just barely, holding my full weight off her, she can probably still breathe. I'm too busy trying to catch my own breath to move at the moment. I can feel her harsh panting against my shoulder. That's a good sign. My heartbeat is still galloping, so I bury my face in her neck, waiting for it to slow down. Or is that the fireworks finale in the distance I'm hearing?

No, it's definitely my heart, I confirm, when silence falls after the last boom outside. Inside the house, my heart is still going way past my maximum target range.

That was fucking amazing. Her tits might feel no bigger than bee stings in my large hands, but I have to say her promotion was well deserved. I'm pretty sure I have never come so hard before. Of course, it could just be that it has been a long while since I last fucked a woman. I'll test that hypothesis with a repeat performance as soon as I can move again.

I lift my mouth to hers and press a kiss of thanks on the corner of her lips. "That was incredible, sugar. Thank you." I kiss her again.

She squirms against me and pushes the heel of her palm against my shoulder, silently telling me to get up. Despite the twitch in my cock caused by her body moving beneath me, I drag myself off her.

Before I can catch another glimpse of the heaven I just found between her thighs, she pulls her legs up and scrambles back from me into the corner of the sofa. Her eyes are wide, and her expression is one of...horror? I return her look with a scowl.

"What's the matter? Did I hurt you?" I may have been lost in my own race toward orgasmic bliss, but I'm pretty sure she'd been right there with me. I remember her clenching me like a vise and milking every last drop out of me.

Every last drop...Fuck! How the hell could I have forgotten to put on a condom?

I take a breath and try to think rationally. She's a professional from an exclusive, high-priced agency, not someone I picked up on a corner. I'd been assured all the women they hired had a clean bill of health and were on birth control. I'd paid a lot of money to make sure it was practically fucking guaranteed.

Standing, I put my hands on my hips and smile at her, trying to let her know it's okay. "Don't worry about it, darling. We'll make sure to use a rubber next time. We were both tested and—"

She pauses in her visual search of the room to scoff in disbelief. "I'm sure you were since you sleep with a different woman every night, but—"

"Hey, now!" I can't help feeling offended at the charge even though I deserved that reputation. "Isn't that the pot calling the kettle black? You're not exactly one to point fingers and start name-calling in your—"

She gasps, her eyes wide before she narrows them in indignation. "I don't sleep around! How dare you, you fucking bastard!"

It's my turn to look at her in disbelief. "You don't sleep around? It's your fucking job!"

"Oh my God! I am not one of those women who collect sports jerseys, you bastard! I'm a fucking professional! And I don't—"

I start laughing. I can't help myself. "Well, that's one way to put it, darling. A fucking professional. That's hilarious!"

"Go to hell, asshole." She unwraps her arms from her knees to push herself onto her knees. She has to hold on to the back of the sofa to keep her balance on the lumpy cushions.

My laughter dies at the venom in her voice and fire in her eyes. I ignore the length of her body and her creamy skin. My frustration helps me keep my focus on her angry face and the issue at hand.

"What the fuck is your problem?" I glare back at her. "You're using birth control and we're both clean, so what the hell are you all fired up about? I paid for an entire night even though I only need you for a couple of hours. And there were supposed to be two of you, so I think you owe me at least one more fuck."

She freezes and stares at me in horror. "You...you paid for an entire night?"

"Of course I did. Didn't your boss tell you?"

"What exactly did you pay for?"

I scowl at her. My irritation mounting, I pick up the beer I'd had the sense to put down earlier. I finish it in two gulps and switch it out with hers, still full. I take a few steps away and catch her reflection in the mirror above the fireplace mantle. Her eyes are glued to my ass—my bare ass. I quirk an eyebrow at her when her gaze travels up and meets mine in the mirror.

Instead of a return smile that matches the bold look, her gaze veers away. She grabs the bedcover to hide her body. And blushes!

What the fuck?

"A little late for that, isn't it, sugar?" I ask.

She raises her chin and gives me a steady look, despite the flush still heating her cheeks. "What exactly did you pay for, Luc?" she asks again.

"What kind of games are you playing?"

"Luc," she says, her voice tight with tension. "Please. Whom did you pay and what exactly did you pay for?"

As I stare at her reflection, the reality of the situation begins to dawn on me. I set down my empty bottle on the old brick mantel with a thunk and face her.

"Fuck me."

"I believe I just did." A giggle escapes her, and she claps a hand over her mouth.

I am not amused at having just realized I not only fucked the wrong woman but also given away the fact that I've hired a hooker—two of them—for the night. The damage this will do to my reputation and my career if the media found out...

"Who the hell are you?" A little late to be asking, but I still need to know.

She has the nerve to huff at me. "As I tried to tell you earlier before you cut me off, my name is Charlotte Hutchinson. Charlie. I'm a producer at *On & Off the Field*, and—"

"Oh shit. A reporter." I reach out to grab the mantel and slump against it, staring down at the old, scratched wooden floor as I wonder how I'm going to escape this debacle. It's a fucking nightmare.

"Nope. Better. A producer."

I open my eyes in time to see her smirk.

"We love to dig to find the juiciest stories."

In the next instant, I'm across the room in front of her, my finger an inch from her face. "No. No, this is not a story. This...this is a misunderstanding. Do you hear me?"

I grab her shoulders in panic and am about to give her a hard shake when I stop in horror. Fuck! I regain control and drop my hands to fist at my side. Sweat breaks out on my forehead as my breath rasps loudly between us.

She puts a hand on my forearm but pulls back as if my skin burned her. Considering how hot I feel, a bead of sweat rolling from my temple, it's a possibility.

"Don't worry," she reassures me. "I won't tell anyone about your penchant for hookers."

She has the fucking nerve to smile at me, as if this is all a big joke.

"I do not have a penchant for hookers," I say between gritted teeth. "I've never been with one before."

"Um, okay," she says, clearly not believing me. "I won't reveal anything about tonight, but I want something in return."

Those words release me from my fear. I sigh and take a step back, disappointed to have this woman live down to my lowest expectations of most people. "Of course you do." Someone always wants something in return. It's the story of my adult life. Why should she be any different?

"I guess I did fuck a prostitute tonight, after all," I say, going back for the beer, unable to look at her for another second. "Instead of cash, you'd like to be paid for your services with a bribe. Or is it blackmail?"

I walk to the window to stare at the darkness outside, taking a long pull from the bottle. "What do you want?" I ask.

She's silent for a long moment, then says quietly, "I'll let you know. For now, can I have my clothes and some privacy?"

I turn to look at her, wondering at her tone. She looks...apologetic. Or is it shame because I called her a prostitute? I take another long, slow sip as I survey her from head to toe. Despite the raggedy throw she holds in front of her, I remember every detail of her slim, creamy body. Is it wrong of me to wish she is exactly what I thought she was so I can lose myself in her again and forget for a few more moments?

Yes, because I don't deserve to forget anything, especially not by losing myself in pleasure.

I face the darkness outside again. It's all the privacy she's going to get. When she moves into my view in the window reflection a few moments later, dressed, I turn back to face her.

"What did you come here for? And how did you find me?" I ask, my voice devoid of all emotion.

Her gaze skitters away from me, but she answers me in a businesslike tone.

"As I said, I've been trying to contact you through your assistant and publicist for a feature segment I'm producing. We'd like to do a series of interviews with you. I'm running out of time, so I decided to start on some background research."

I'd gotten the messages and ignored them because I have no interest in in-depth interviews that want to pick apart my past. It's no one's business except my own. But I don't explain any of that to her. Not her business.

"I was talking to your neighbors and heading back to town when I saw lights on here at your house."

"The house isn't in my name."

She shrugs and looks me in the eye this time. "Like I said, I'm good at digging."

I hold her gaze and she shivers. From fear? Or the attraction that's still buzzing between us?

"Luc," she says, her voice softening. "I'm not going to tell anyone about tonight."

"Yeah, right." Women love to brag about their encounters with me, often exaggerating to make it out to be more than it was. It's how I gained the reputation I have, one I purposely cultivated.

"Really, I promise," she continues. "It's not like I want people to know I was one of thousands, you know?"

I laugh at the irony. When I don't let her in on the joke, she continues, "It wouldn't do my career any good if people thought I slept with pro athletes. That's not a reputation I want, believe me."

Despite her earnestness, I don't know if I can trust her. Only time will tell. I turn to stare out the window again as I finish off the beer. How many bottles have I emptied tonight? Not nearly enough.

I watch her in the reflection as she picks up her bag. She starts to leave but pauses at the door to turn to me and ask, "Are you going to be okay?"

I don't say anything, just raise my empty bottle to her reflection in the window.

She hesitates another moment, before leaving me to my thoughts. Just one more regret to add to my overburdened pile.

4

Charlie

I t's a struggle to keep my focus as I drive along the winding road from Luc's childhood home. My thoughts are in chaos from what had just happened, with *Holy shit!* flashing repeatedly like a neon sign in my mind's eye.

Holy shit! I had sex with Lucien Saint, the highest-paid and top-ranked quarterback in the game.

Holy shit! I had sex with Lucien Saint, who is once again my brother's teammate.

Holy shit! I had sex with Lucien Saint, notorious playboy with a different woman on his arm every time he went out.

Holy shit! I had sex with Lucien Saint who hired sex workers—more than one at a time.

Holy shit! I had *unprotected* sex with Lucien Saint.

I focus on that thought as the road straightens out and I head into town. It had been bustling earlier, especially near the lake where a festival of sorts had kept people busy while they waited for the fireworks. There was almost no one around now. The storefronts were locked and dark, no one on the streets except a lone pickup filled with teenagers heading toward the lake.

I stop at a red light in the center of the small town, one that hadn't been hit by population growth from the looks of it. My thoughts are a jumble again as my plan of going to the pharmacy is thwarted by the big CLOSED sign in the window. Does Louisiana even allow the sale of the morning-after pill?

As my overstimulated brain veers off on a tangent to ponder that heavy question, I absently watch a truck full of rowdy teens drive by until their hollers and the blasting music fades away as they turn onto the road leading to the lakefront.

When I turn my attention back to the traffic signal, it changes from yellow to red. I missed the green light with no one to honk at me to drive. I consider running the red and making the turn toward the motel I'm staying at tonight, but stop when headlights shine at me from my right. The car slows to make a left and I glance at it as it passes me. The passenger's visor light is on, allowing me a glimpse of the two beautiful women inside.

Holy shit! Those must be the two sex workers Luc was expecting. I'm tempted to follow so I can talk to them before they go in to see him, but the thought of them having sex with him not long after I did makes me feel sick. I push the gas a bit too hard as I make my left turn, causing the tires to screech.

The first thing I do when I enter my motel room is jump into the shower. I grab the detachable shower head, needing to wash away all residue of Luc. Unfortunately, the pressure is weak so I do what I can to clean up. I gasp when the touch of my fingers gliding over my nooks and crannies creates a tingle, reminding my body of his touch. Cursing, I rinse off quickly and get out.

I pull on clean underwear and an old San Diego Sailors T-shirt. I've just washed away his touch but it's his number on the shirt. Having worn it so often over the years, it's soft and worn from all the washings. A part of me regrets I can no longer smell him on me.

Sighing with disappointment at how my first—and probably last—interaction with Luc went, I slide into bed with my phone.

I need to talk to someone about what just happened or I'm going to go nuts.

You awake?

I text my best friend, Joey. I'm closer to her than to any of my three sisters, including my twin, Georgie.

The phone vibrates in my hands with an incoming call within seconds.

"Hey, Joey. Did my text wake you?" I ask.

"I just got into bed. Came home a little while ago from Brent's."

My eyebrows jump high. "You were at my brother's this late?"

"Calm down." She laughs. "I was there for a PT session. He asked if I wanted to stay and watch the fireworks after from his terrace. From his penthouse, we could see the Macy's display in the distance and some from the towns in Jersey across the Hudson."

"Okay, what have you done to my brother?" He would normally be partying at a club with a group of people that included beautiful women. Not that Joey wasn't beautiful. I think she blows them all out of the water. She's just not one to party—normally. I still can't believe she went to a club and got wasted for the first time a couple of weeks ago. I'm glad Brent was there to watch out for her.

"Shut up. You know nothing would ever happen between us. He doesn't even like me, especially like that."

I scoff but don't say anything to that, as tempted as I am to boost her confidence. Because he most definitely likes her *like that*. But Brent knows Joey is too good for him, and he would never treat her the way he does other women—fuck 'em and leave 'em. Because he also knows I'd never forgive him if he hurt her. And our mother would rip him a new one.

"Anyway," she continues, "how's your work trip going?"

"It's going. Actually, you won't believe what happened tonight. I just—" I stop, not sure what to say or how much to say. Joey is working closely with Brent as his physical therapist and will soon be working for his team. Which also happens to be Luc's team.

"You just what? Are you okay?"

I decide to keep it vague. "I finally broke my three-year dry spell."

It takes a few seconds for Joey to understand what I'm talking about, then she gasps and squeals with excitement. "Who was it? Do I know him? How was it?"

"You don't know him," I respond. *But you will soon.* Definitely best to not to reveal his identity. "And it was pretty fucking fantastic while it lasted. It happened so fast."

"But it left quite an impression, it seems. Are you going to see him again? Who is it, anyway?"

I dodge the question again. "Someone I met through work."

"So how did it happen?"

"It was actually a case of mistaken identity," I say, laughing. Now that I'm talking about it with Joey, it sounds kind of funny in a farcical way. "It was totally unplanned and unexpected. Though, like I said, it happened so fast I barely had time to think about what was happening."

"Charlie," she says, her voice serious with concern, "did he force you?"

"What? No! It was completely consensual, I promise."

"Okay. Good. Now tell me everything."

I rest my head against the headboard and stare off into space. "It was instant chemistry, like nothing I've ever felt with anyone else. From the second our fingers brushed. Just like in the romance books we used to sneak out of my mom's room."

"Wow," she teases. "By the sound of your voice, I think you're getting turned on just thinking about it. But do you think that maybe since it's been three years since you've had sex, you were primed?" She laughs, but the question makes me wonder.

"And I hope you were being safe."

When I don't say anything in response, she gasps again. "Charlie, please tell me you used protection."

"Like I said, it happened really fast," I say lamely. "I was going to stop at the pharmacy after for Plan B, but it was closed. It just happened tonight and it's called the *morning-after* pill. I'll get it first thing before heading to the airport," I reassure her. "Don't worry, it's fine."

Famous last words.

5

Luc

I WAKE UP ON July fifth as I do every year—disappointed and frustrated because I still do not remember the night my life changed forever. But unlike previous years, this morning, I have a slight hangover. It's nothing like the one I woke up with ten years ago, which makes me wonder just how many beers I'd drunk that night. There had been no other alcohol that I remember.

I groan as I open my eyes and squint at the brightness pouring in from the windows of the bedroom I slept in when I was a boy. I'm fairly certain the dull headache behind my eyes is due as much to a lack of sleep as an excess of alcohol. And the thought of driving several hours to Mississippi while hungover puts a damper on the prospect, though I normally look forward to visiting my only living relatives.

My thoughts drift in the light of day while my brain slowly powers back up. Nothing went as I'd hoped, or expected, last night.

I had gone to bed staring out the window at the sky, sprinkled with twinkling lights. The lights where I live in Manhattan come from an endless stream of planes flying overhead. Here in rural Louisiana, far north of the Big Easy, these shine from actual stars.

I'm still not sure why I bought the abandoned property when I got my first check from the NFL. The house evokes nothing but grief and anger—grief for my mother's death and anger from the hateful memories of the years before that.

No, that's not completely true. There had been happy moments here too. Of my mother singing and grabbing me in impromptu dances. Of the delicious aromas of homemade Creole cooking wafting from the pots on the old stove. Of the delighted babble of baby Daphne whenever she saw me.

I wish I could savor those beautiful memories and feel joy. Instead, I'm filled with frustration because I can't remember what happened. I had hoped the memory would finally reveal itself if I re-enacted my steps from that fateful night.

Of course, I couldn't follow them exactly. I wasn't about to have sex at the lake that now fills up with the townspeople every year and where teenagers still party once everyone else goes home. So I'd paid a pile of cash for a discreet escort agency that I'd been assured provided additional services. Services which I never used because I'd sent the two women away when they arrived at their scheduled time. Hiring them had been a stupid idea. I should have picked up two women in a bar. At least that would have been in line with my reputation. I'm trying hard to remember what demented reasoning had led me to go with an agency instead.

How could I have known Charlotte—Charlie—wasn't from the agency? It's not like I was going to ask a prostitute for ID before letting her in.

Just the thought of her makes my dick twitch, not for the first time since she'd left. What is it about the beautiful blonde that stays with me? It can't be her too slim body. I recall the creamy white skin and slender curves. The twitch becomes a full-on erection as she fills my thoughts. The touch of her soft skin. The scent of her that still lingers on my skin. The vision of our bodies joined together in the most intimate way. The tightness and heat of her clasping my cock. And the image of her, naked and sated, when I'd stood over her for a brief moment before she'd scrambled to hide her nudity. I wish I'd had a chance to have a better, longer look at her.

My mind might think she lacks curves, but my body doesn't seem to mind and is craving her again. Groaning, I slide my hand down my torso, ready to soothe the painful hardness. I can't help the single stroke I allow myself before I let go and force myself out of bed, ignoring the weeping of my painfully hard cock.

I push all thoughts of her out of my head and take an icy-cold shower before heading out for a punishing run on the deserted country road. It might hurt a little more with the hangover, especially since it's so fucking hot and humid, but I am determined to suffer the penance for my brief break from the vows I took ten years ago, especially since it didn't result in regaining my memory.

The plan to recreate the night has backfired in more than one way, thanks to Charlie. I don't know how I'm going to go back to one of those vows after having had a brief taste of her.

Just as importantly—no, more importantly—what will I do if she breaks her promise and does a story about our encounter? Or reveals that I'd hired not one but two prostitutes? And what if she also decides to put her digging skills to use and uncovers more of my secrets?

When I finally round the last bend back to my old house an hour later, my heart nearly bursting from the long run, my cell phone rings. Slowing to a walk, I look at the screen and curse through my ragged panting. It's the last person on earth I want to talk to, but I answer anyway, knowing the man who fathered me will not give up until he makes contact.

"Yeah." Even if I have the breath for more words, I wouldn't have bothered wasting them with a more polite greeting.

"Well, hello to you too, sunshine. What's the matter? Hungover from drowning your sorrows last night?" Victor Miller, the devil who spawned me, chortles in glee at the possibility of my pain. As much as he enjoys the benefits he reaps from having a multimillionaire football star for a son, jealousy eats away at him. Of course he'd never admit that he hates seeing his son have an NFL career ten times more successful than his own. He tries to hide his true feelings with deference and charm, neither of which affect me because I found out the hard way that it's just a shiny veneer he uses to distract from his real purpose.

"What do you want?" I ask, as if I don't know. Victor only calls me for one reason, especially on this date. To make sure the guilt is still there and to demand cold, hard cash.

"To see how you're doing, son. Can't a father call to make sure his son is happy and healthy and free to live his life in peace?" The Texas drawl he intentionally picked up while in college in Houston grows more exaggerated. "You haven't forgotten that it's because of your good ol' daddy that you're living the gilded life you got now, right?"

"Yeah, right. Now tell me what you really want."

"I need a million."

"What the fuck? I just gave you a quarter mil when the season ended." And he's been living rent-free on one of my properties in Las Vegas for the last several years.

"That was then. This is now. With your new contract, you are now the highest paid QB in league history. I deserve a little bigger piece of the pie, don't you think? Especially seeing as it's the tenth anniversary of your freedom to keep playing football and making the big bucks. It's a momentous occasion and deserves an equally momentous form of gratitude, don't you think?"

"This is bullshit and you know it. How long are you going to keep doing this?" I already know the answer. Forever. Or until he's bled me dry if the amount and frequency keep increasing.

"Look, I got myself in a little bind with some debts and I need to pay them off."

"I'm pretty sure I've heard this story before." Just a few months ago, in fact.

The pounding in my head intensifies with a vengeance. I'm never going to win this battle. Besides, what's a million to me, especially if it gets him off my back? Like he said, I signed a new contract. A million is a drop in the bucket. A big drop, but my bucket is pretty big too.

Maybe I'll be lucky and this really is the last time. I shake my head at my own naivete and tell him, "I'll wire it as usual."

"Today. I'll be waiting for it."

My phone beeps, indicating Victor has hung up, having gotten what he wanted. I sigh deeply, suddenly exhausted, and hang my head in desolation.

6

Charlie

"**M**a'am, please put your seat up for landing."

The flight attendant's annoyed voice wakes me with a start. Thanks to a restless night after my encounter with Luc, I fell asleep near dawn. When my phone alarm beeped, I groggily turned it off instead of snoozing it. I woke up in a panic almost two hours later with barely enough time to dress and drive to the airport—and none at all for a trip to the pharmacy.

Looking out the window of the plane as it descends over the rooftops of Queens toward LaGuardia, my thoughts inexorably turn back to Luc and the possible consequences of last night. I'm not sure what I am more worried about.

Acquiring an STD? Definitely a possibility with as many women as Luc is rumored to have slept with, especially if he frequently skips the condom. Though that one's on me too. How could I have been so irresponsible? I'm definitely making an appointment to be tested.

My professional reputation? It feels like I've just started earning the respect of my colleagues, most of whom are older and more experienced. I've had to work twice as hard to prove it was more than my connection to Brent that got me the job, and more recently, the promotion as the youngest segment producer. I proved something all right—that I'm an idiot and had done the worst thing possible as a woman in this field. I behaved like a jersey chaser—an irresponsible one, at that.

Being pregnant? The chances of this are probably less than the other two, but it's way more life-changing. The ramifications of being pregnant...My stomach clenches just thinking about it. Pregnant without a husband, or even a boyfriend. Pregnant with a superstar athlete's baby while working as a producer in sports media, a demanding career that requires long hours and endless travel. As much as I want a family one day, this is not how I had expected it to happen.

I take a deep breath and let it out slowly. I'm getting ahead of myself. I might not be pregnant. The morning-after pill, once I can get my hands on it, might help prevent it.

I shake my head in despair. That's two too many *mights* for my peace of mind. Okay, the pregnancy concern wins, hands down. I need to go to the pharmacy ASAP.

I can't believe my one small decision to do background research on Luc for the segment might result in any or all of these serious consequences. I should have waited for his people to call me back or continued trying to contact them. But no, I had to "take initiative" and book a trip to his hometown.

I wasn't lying to Luc about being good at digging out information. When I discovered that he still owned his childhood home, I decided that was a good place to start. But I drove out there only to find it looking as if no one lived in the place. I took some photos and tried talking to his neighbors. Can they be considered neighbors if they live a half mile or more away?

All I learned from them was that they were proud of Luc and he didn't come around much, but he still donated to the town in various ways. I got the feeling there was more to the story, but when I pressed, they wouldn't say more than it was a shame his mother died too soon and wasn't around to see Luc's success.

Exhausted and dejected after learning nothing more than what I already knew from other sources, I was heading back to the motel in town when I noticed lights on his house. There was no car there, so I decided to check it out, maybe catch a glimpse of the interior.

Through the half-opened curtains of the front window, I was shocked to see Luc standing at the opposite window, facing away from me. As I watched him, all broody and contemplative, I took a minute to devise a strategy to persuade him to say yes to the interview.

Having sex with him had not been one of the strategic options I'd come up with. But ambushing a high-profile QB, the biggest star in the NFL, should not have been one either.

My calm dissipates when the plane lands and I turn on my phone to find a voicemail from my boss. "I talked to Lucien Saint. Come to the studio right away."

Oh shit. I'm about to be fired.

But when I arrive, it's to find a frantic Mark ready to pounce on me.

"You could have warned me that you secured an interview with Lucien Saint." He's practically dancing, with double his usual manic energy.

"What?" I stare at my boss in confusion.

"I just got off the phone with Saint. He's agreed to be interviewed. Can you believe the guy called personally? He's coming in tomorrow afternoon. It's going to be tight to set things up, but I didn't want to give him time to change his mind. Tom's going to do the interview. I need you to..."

I would normally interrupt Mark's monologue just to give him a chance to take a breath, but I'm too busy trying to catch my own breath. I listen with one ear while my thoughts whirl.

Luc agreed to be interviewed. Why? Would he say anything about our encounter to anyone? To my boss? No, he wouldn't.

Right? Because it would expose him as well. He won't say anything.

I hope.

I hold on to that thought for the next twenty-four hours, as I work almost nonstop to organize the interview. My eyes are gritty from sitting with the editor half the night pulling articles and video clips of his football career and past interviews to go with the questions Tom and I put together.

By the time Luc's arrival is announced, I'm a flustered mess. Rather than proving to everyone that I'm competent and deserving of the promotion, I've made one error after another during the preproduction work. It's taken me longer than it should have to do what I need to since I'm constantly backtracking to fix my mistakes before anyone discovers them.

While Mark goes to reception to greet Luc, I run to the restroom to fix my face and finger comb my hair, the best I can do before I go to the greenroom. I enter the brightly lit room but stop just inside the door when I realize Luc is alone, sitting in the chair with his back to me, typing on his phone. Our eyes meet in the mirror he's facing, and we stare at each other, neither saying a word. My only thought is of that moment when I'd looked into his eyes as he'd entered me, of how he'd filled me. Heat suffuses my cheeks and between my legs as my thighs clench at the memory. I'm not a blusher like Joey, but for some reason, Luc has me doing it again.

The ding of his phone jolts us, breaking our connection. I hope he can't read my thoughts, but I wonder what he's thinking, because all I can think is that the man I'd had fast, sweaty, best-ever sex with is sitting a few feet away from me.

And I want to do it with him again.

Before either of us can break the tense silence, Paula, the makeup artist, bustles past me into the room.

"Hey, hon."

I'm not sure who she's talking to. Paula calls everyone hon, and her eyes are focused on the powders and brushes laid out on the counter in front of the mirror. She looks briefly at Luc, then back again, putting away several items and choosing different ones. "Okay, let's start. Not much to do with this handsome face, but let's make sure you don't have a shiny nose or forehead, all righty? Nothing worse than not listening to a word someone's saying because you just can't get your mind off the hot spot on their nose or cheeks. And I'm sure you've got something to say that people want to hear, am I right? Or am I right? Though these cheekbones are something to look at, I tell ya."

Like many makeup artists I've met, Paula likes to talk. It's probably partly to make the person feel comfortable about getting in front of the camera, and partly because the person being made up can't talk while someone is whisking a brush or sponge of some kind across their face. Celebrity status doesn't faze an experienced makeup artist. She knows her worth in making someone look good, and everyone is friendly to the person who is responsible for making them look that way.

I have my own responsibilities, which means facing Luc to go over the interview details with him. I take a deep breath and interrupt Paula's monologue.

"Mr. Saint. Thank you so much for agreeing to the interview. We're doing in-depth segments that will be released before the first game and..."

As I speak, I keep my gaze on his chin and avoid his penetrating gaze. I can feel him staring at me, and it's unnerving as hell. Is he afraid I'll reveal what happened in Louisiana? No chance of that! I lift my gaze to try to assure him with my own look but am so caught by the intensity of his gaze, I stop in mid-sentence.

Fortunately, Mark walks into the room before the silence can give away too much to the observant makeup artist who for once doesn't fill the quiet with her chatter. But a quick glance at Paula tells me it's too late. Ignoring her curious look, I turn to Mark.

"Saint, we're all set for you as soon as you're done here. Tom Wooster will be conducting the interview. We'll do a formal sit-down first, and then we'll loosen up a little and do some fun stuff. I'm sure our little superstar has gone over all that with you. But you probably already know how great Charlie is, right, being friends with her brother?"

I give him a tight smile, even as I cringe at the "little super-star" comment and steam in silence at the inference that it was the connection to my brother that got me this interview. It's shit like this that has me constantly striving to prove myself.

"Okay, unless you have any questions, I'm going to make sure Tom's ready. See you in a few."

And, before anyone has a chance to say a word, Mark leaves as quickly as he came in.

"Well, I guess you didn't have any questions. And too bad if you did, huh?" Paula laughs.

I look back at Luc to see that his eyes are closed as Paula swipes a lightly powdered brush over his eyelids.

"Five more minutes, Paula?" I ask. When she nods, I continue, "Okay, I'll come back for Mr. Saint."

Luc opens his eyes, and Paula makes a small sound of alarm as she almost pokes him in the eye. Before he can say anything, I escape as quickly as my boss had. I'm not ready to interact with him and need the few minutes to pull myself together again. I don't want to say or do something stupid in front of everyone, a very real possibility with the way I'm reacting at the moment.

My heart is racing, my palms are sweaty, and my mind is scattered. I am never like this with anyone, and I've met lots of high-profile athletes. Lots of gorgeous, sexy ones too, so I don't know what it is about Luc that makes me behave like a star-struck fangirl. Or a flustered virgin.

That is not the image I want to project during my first major interview, either in front of my co-workers or Luc. I stop in the hall to collect my thoughts and take several deep breaths, pretending to look at my clipboard in case anyone happens to pass by.

Too soon, I hear Paula say, "You are all set, hon!"

I take one last deep breath and head back into the room to take Luc to the set.

"Mr. Saint, I'll take you over to Studio B. Can I get anything for you first? Water?"

I avoid looking at him as I lead him down the hall to the studio, not even looking back to see if he's following. I don't have to. My senses are on high alert, letting me know he's close behind. His heat, the weight of his gaze on my back, the warmth of his hand on my shoulder...

I jump as if scalded and turn to face him, the clipboard against my chest like a shield.

"We need to talk," he says, his voice low.

"No, we don't. I told you, you have nothing to worry about from me."

"We need to talk," he repeats, a demand this time, not a request. "After the—"

"There you are!" Mark's booming voice interrupts Luc. Relief courses through me, as if the band of tension around us has snapped. I turn into the studio and let my boss handle Luc while I check in with the crew.

7

ℒuc

INWARDLY CURSING, I WONDER what in the hell made me give in to the impulse to do the interview. As I watch Charlie flit around the set, I remember why. I felt the need to see her again. Our encounter had been so brief, and if I'd been more drunk, I'd have wondered if it was a dream. But the sight of her silky, thin bra on the floor by the sofa gave proof that it had really happened. And that there might be consequences—more than one—from it.

So I called the studio to track her down. Good thing she was the only Charlotte that worked there, because I couldn't remember her last name. Instead of letting me leave a message, I was transferred to the executive producer, Mark. I kicked myself for making the call instead of telling my assistant to do it, but I wanted to keep this between us. Since I couldn't exactly tell Charlotte's employer the real reason I wanted to talk to her, I ended up agreeing to do the interview, with the caveat "ASAP or never." Unfortunately, the answer was a resounding yes.

Keeping my public face firmly in place, I'm brought to the set and miked up. I smile and joke around with Mark and the rest of the crew as they work around us, adjusting the lights and cameras and doing sound checks.

"Hey, Tom," I greet the reporter who will be interviewing me when he sits across from me. The set has gone quiet, telling me the cameras are recording. I turn up the wattage and the charm. "Great to see you again. Congratulations on getting your own show. I hear it's doing really well." I chat with him as if we're great buddies and ask about his wife and kid. I've learned over the years that it's important to remember details about the members of the media and keep a friendly relationship, no matter how superficial. It makes it a hell of a lot easier to keep up appearances when the reporters love me and are on my side.

I understand how to play the game and give the media just enough to make their job interesting, so they won't become bored and go looking for more. I have too many skeletons in my closet, and I need to make sure they stay there.

I prepare to do that now when Tom gets serious and says, "Let's jump right into it, Luc. You ended last season with a tough loss in the Conference..."

I smile, laugh, and give non-answers to questions that would cause controversy if I said what I really wanted to say. I give pat bullshit answers to the usual vapid, unoriginal questions.

You were so close last year. You think you'll make it to the Super Bowl this year?

How do you feel about being back together with your former team-mate, Brent Hutchinson?

Have you seen him since your rookie year?

Are you going to revive your end zone dance or have you two come up with a new one?

Then Tom throws me a curveball. "How is your father doing?"

I freeze for the briefest of moments. "My father?" Forcing an easy smile, I respond, "He's doing great. I just talked to him yesterday, in fact. Yeah, thanks for asking. I'll be sure to let him know you asked about him. He's a big fan of yours."

Tom preens with the compliment, and we continue with the "fun" portion of the interview—looking at social media posts from haters, followed by slightly more personal questions about my off-season activities as well as tabloid photos and rumors. Glancing at Charlie, who is standing next to one of the cameras, I wonder if these questions are ones she suggested to the reporter.

When it's finally over and I'm freed from the mic, I stand, shake hands with Tom and Mark, and have my picture taken with various crew members. I dole out autographs and shake more hands. I've been on enough sets to know the crew is discouraged from engaging with me, but I take a few minutes to acknowledge them.

Throughout it all, I keep my eye on Charlie as she talks to Tom and a few other co-workers. After the final photo is taken, Mark beckons her over to us.

"Saint, Charlie will go over the details of the other interviews. I gotta run, but thanks again for coming in." Once again, he leaves without letting anyone else say a word.

I shake my head at Mark's departing back. "Does that man breathe when he talks?"

Charlie also looks at her boss as he hurries away. "He is a bit hyper, I guess, but he's really good at his job."

"Like the people on his staff who'll do anything to get the job done?"

She doesn't respond to the jab or even look in my direction. Instead, she motions for me to follow and takes me back to the greenroom. "Why aren't any of your people with you today? I'd normally go over the schedule with them."

"I'm capable of putting things into my schedule. They'll see it when I do. I let people do it before, and they scheduled me for something every minute of the day, so now no one but me can add anything without my permission. And my agent, after he's cleared it with me."

"Okay, well, as Mark said, we'd like to do additional interviews. One at the stadium, preferably during training camp. We'll coordinate with Brent's segment and, of course, I'll clear it with the powers that be at the Firebirds. But also one in your hometown, so if—"

"No."

Charlie looks up from her clipboard, eyes wide. "Um, no?"

"No interview in my hometown. Not happening."

She narrows her eyes and stares at me, but I can't make my tense features relax.

"I'll let Mark know, but he's going to want to know why. He—"

"Because I fucking said no, that's why!" I spit out savagely. "I give you guys the interview you were hounding me for, and now you want more. Fuck, you want my blood, too?"

Charlie closes the door to give us privacy and looks at me with the same expression she had the other night. Seeing it again, I'm inclined to believe it's a mix of both shame and apology.

"Okay, I'll tell him your schedule doesn't allow for a hometown interview. But, Luc, he's still going to want me to send a crew to film visuals and talk to people who knew you when you were younger. We'd like to talk to your high school teammates, shoot footage of the house you grew up in, talk about your memories of your mother and how the accident—"

"God, no! Why do they have to dredge all that up again? It's been ten fucking years, and they picked it apart to death when I got drafted. Why can't you all just fucking leave it alone?"

I whirl away from her and link my hands at the back of my neck, pulling my elbows forward so she can't see my pain and fear. Let her think it's anger at the invasion of my privacy.

"I'm sorry, Luc," she says, her voice full of apology. "But this is still a relatively young streaming channel, and we're trying to compete with the giants. Mark wants to do these extended segments on the biggest athletes, go deeper than most interviews so that we can attract—"

She breaks off when I lower my arms and turn, narrowing my eyes at her. What the fuck do I care about market share when it's my life that will be picked apart for entertainment purposes?

"I'm sorry," she repeats, her voice soft with compassion despite the business logic she was just spouting.

"Are you? Are you sorry enough to stick to just football? My personal life isn't anyone's goddamned business. It has nothing to do with football. Fucking vultures!"

She flinches and bites her lip. Fuck. I'm scaring her. It's not her I'm pissed at and frustrated with. She's just doing her job, and it's what the fans probably want, but why can't it just be about the sport?

Her gray eyes are wary as she approaches me like I'm a wounded animal. She moves close enough to put a hand on my arm, causing a tingle to run through my body.

Read the room, I scold my dick that's perking up at her innocent touch. *This is not the time.* Normally, I have no problem restraining my desire, no matter how attractive or willing a woman is. I don't understand why this woman tempts me to lose control.

I take a step away from her. What took place the other night can never happen again.

She drops her hand and becomes all business again, her voice losing the earlier softness. "Look, let me see what I can do about your piece. I'm the one in charge of putting together, although Mark has final say. But I won't be able to keep everything personal out of the segment. A lot of it was already dug up when you were drafted, as you said, so I'll have to use what's already there. If there's anything else—"

"There's nothing else, so don't bother looking. I have to go. Send my assistant the possible dates for the stadium interview. But I warn you, if there are any questions about my past that are not about football, I'll walk out."

I wrench open the door and stalk out, angry at myself for giving in to the need to call her at the studio. I should have practiced that self-restraint I'm normally so proud of. But then, there are a lot of things I should—and shouldn't—have done.

8

Charlie

I GO DOWN THE packing list for my trip for an out-of-town player interview. Unlike Luc, this player—a wide receiver for the Patriots—is looking forward to having a segment that includes his childhood and family life.

I quickly scroll through the checklist on my phone. Though I've become adept at packing, with all the travel I do, it gives me peace of mind to double-check.

That peace of mind goes flying out the window when the word *tampons* jumps out at me.

Shit. Shit, shit! No, it isn't possible, is it?

I switch over to the period app on my phone. My cycle has no rhyme or rhythm, so I don't know why I bother checking. But it confirms I'm more overdue than normal. It also indicates that my encounter with Luc fell just after my estimated fertile days. But does that even mean anything if I'm not regular?

This is my first time having sex in about three years. Am I really so unlucky as to end up pregnant from one fast fuck? Ugh. Am I so dumb as to think it isn't possible?

Don't panic. Maybe it's just stress hormones from the long hours at work. A quick internet search shows that the timing of my period could be impacted by the morning-after pill, which I'd finally taken the night of Luc's studio interview. It had been about forty-eight hours after sex, but the chance of pregnancy is still supposed to be low.

More frantic internet searches indicate pregnancy is possible, though rare, but the anecdotal evidence on various forums isn't reassuring. I cling to the assurance from another site that says a period could be late by up to a week after taking the pill.

So I'll wait another few days. It will come.

When my period still hasn't made an appearance several days later, I finally bite the bullet and buy a pregnancy test. Since I'm still in Arizona for background interviews, I don't have to sneak it by my eagle-eyed mother or nosy little sister, with whom I live.

Sitting on my hotel room bed, staring at the stick, I can't believe I fooled myself into thinking my bout of nausea when helping Joey move to her new apartment last weekend was from something I ate.

Not when I've been feeling slightly sick this entire trip, which I've put down to the heat, the change in time zones, the erratic eating due to a hectic schedule...

I stare at the stick until it blurs, but still, the pink plus sign won't change or disappear. There's no avoiding the evidence.

Pregnant. Single and pregnant and barely earning enough to live on my own, never mind supporting a child. Everything the complete opposite of what I'd always dreamed about.

I pick up the phone to call Joey but hesitate. She's not only working with the team but she's now in a relationship with Brent. I trust Joey to keep it a secret from him, but I don't want to put her in that position, not when what they have is so new. And I can't be sure if Brent will react the way he did when we were younger and his teammates looked at his sisters the wrong way.

No, better to not say anything to anyone until I figure out what to say to Luc whom I haven't seen since he came to the studio almost three weeks ago. The interview at the stadium, set up through his assistant, is coming up in a few days. Should I tell him? Would he care? Maybe he's already a baby daddy and that's why he doesn't want anyone poking into his past.

Maybe one of his secrets is that he already has a child stashed away. Maybe even a wife. After all, he'd been adamant that I not include his past or personal life as part of the segment. I haven't found anything in my research that indicates he's already a father, but it's something to look into when I go back to his hometown. Mark insists we need background on his childhood, though I'll try to keep it on the subject of football. Anything else I look into will be for my own sake.

Whatever secrets he's hiding, I'm about to present him with a situation that will likely add to his burden. Perhaps it's best to wait until I've confirmed with a doctor first. Until then, I need to get through my next meeting with him.

I can't take my eyes off Luc as he executes drills with the offense when I see him at practice several days later. Training camp has started, and the cameramen and I are getting footage of Luc on the field. The late July weather is blistering hot and suffocatingly humid. His jersey, cut off at the sleeves, is soaked through, and a sheen of sweat glistens on skin that has darkened to a rich caramel color.

Mm, I love caramel. Sticky, sweet, and just a tiny bit salty. When I catch myself licking my lips, I look around, hoping no one else has noticed. I tell myself I'm drooling because the thought of caramel makes me realize how hungry I am, having missed breakfast that morning due to a queasy stomach.

Yeah, right.

My eyes gravitate back to him as he grips the ball with long fingers and his calves flex as he dances on light feet, backward and forward, waiting for a receiver to open up. Finally, he throws it, and I reluctantly take my eyes off Luc to follow the ball as it flies in a perfect spiral straight into my brother's hands. My attention goes right back to Luc, who points a finger at my brother then pumps a fist in the air.

"Those two are like poetry in motion," comments Allen, one of the cameramen.

I blink and drag my gaze away from Luc. "What?"

"Those two have some serious chemistry. Your brother must be happy to be with his teammate again, huh?"

"Oh, yeah," I say lamely, looking back at Luc, rather than Brent.

Allen gives me a knowing smirk before moving upfield to shoot from a different angle on the next play.

The crew and I have been at the Firebirds practice field most of the day, getting footage of the open practice, a meeting, a workout in the weight room, and sound bites from Luc's coaches and teammates. The hours of footage will be condensed into just a few minutes during the edit, which I will oversee.

For now, I force myself to keep my eyes off the field. I am not here to ogle the QB. I look for Joey and, spotting her on the sidelines finally alone, head toward her. We've only had a chance to wave at each other a couple of times, both of us here to do a job. I desperately want to talk to her, to ask her to come to the upcoming doctor's appointment with me. Instead, I give her a forced smile and a tight hug.

"Hi, Charlie! I've missed you," she says. We've both been too busy to even talk much on the phone lately. "Hey, you okay?" she asks in concern when the hug goes on longer than it should have in a workplace.

"Yeah, I'm fine." I release her and take a step back. "Just glad to see you."

"Aw, me too. It's been crazy, but it's only for a few more weeks. Then I'll be unemployed and have plenty of time." She looks to the field when her name is called, then turns back to me apologetically.

"Go," I tell her, waving her off. "We'll catch up soon." I watch her run to a player clutching his leg, noticing how she looks more self-assured than I've ever seen her. This job—or her relationship with Brent—seems to be doing wonders for her self-confidence. I hope the eventual end of either of those doesn't make her lose it again.

Hearing a whistle that signals the end of practice, I go back to work. Luc's interview will begin soon.

A short while later, I stand just outside the range of the cameras set up around Luc and Tom. The two are sitting on high stools under a canopy at the edge of the practice field. The overhang not only keeps them in the shade, it also prevents glares and overexposure on camera. I keep my eyes on the monitor that shows the three camera angles we've set up.

It took effort to talk to him casually when he came back to the field, fresh from his shower, his long, lean body dressed in jeans and a light blue T-shirt that make the blue swirls in his hazel eyes stand out. Like the ocean in the tropics, I think, one I could happily drown in.

I was thankful for Paula's endless chatter as she applied shine-reducing powder to Luc's face. Her presence helped to prevent any awkwardness that might have otherwise fallen between us.

I snap out of my thoughts when Tom says, "Okay, Luc. Enough about football. Let's discuss what the ladies really want to know." He winks as if to say he has to indulge that demographic.

Ugh. I'm going to have to edit out that sexist bullshit, though in reality, there are likely some women who watch for the hot guys in tight pants.

Admittedly, I added this last part to the list of topics to talk about for my own reasons. It was my way of getting an idea of what Luc's reaction might be if I told him I could be pregnant.

"You're approaching thirty. Have you thought about settling down, starting a family? Maybe a third generation of football players to follow in your and your father's footsteps?"

I hold my breath, not sure what I'm hoping to hear.

Luc laughs, his demeanor still easy and relaxed though I think his eyes flicker to me for a quick second. "You're making me feel old, Tom. I still have a couple of years to go before I'm thirty. Ask me again in a few years. For now, I have no plans to settle down or start a family anytime soon. I'm having too much fun playing." His tone indicates it's more than just football he's referring to.

My stomach decides to roil in that moment. I'm not sure if it's due to dismay at his answer or the unpredictable nausea that plagues me throughout the day. Without thinking, I place my hand over it in a useless effort to calm the queasiness just as my gaze meets Luc's. His eyes flicker down to my stomach and back up again, widening in shock for a brief second before he remembers the cameras. He glances away from me and laughs at something Tom said, which I don't hear because my ears are filled with a rushing sound.

I've given myself away before I've come to grips with it myself, before I've formulated a plan—or the words—to tell him. *Breathe. Don't panic.* He might not have drawn the conclusion that I'm pregnant. *Might* be pregnant. There's that word again, but until the doctor confirms it, there's still the chance the test was wrong.

Focusing on work, I tell my crew to pack up the equipment while I collect the memory cards from the cameras and carefully label and store them. I should go to Luc and thank him for his time, but I can't make myself face him.

It doesn't matter, because he's heading toward me. Straightening my spine and taking a deep breath, I put a smile on my face and hold out my hand.

"Thank you so much, Luc, for your time. That—"

"We need to talk."

He ignores my hand. I put it down and look around to see if anyone is watching us. Luckily, my co-workers want to go home after a long day and are focused on their tasks. Tom is already heading off the field, his job done.

Deciding ignorance is my best defense at the moment, I ask, "Oh? About what? I thought the interview was—"

"Cut the crap. Are you—"

I hiss, "Not now," when Allen comes near us. I smile, hoping it doesn't look as fake and forced as it feels, and say brightly, "The interview went really well. Thank you for taking the time to sit down for it."

"Sorry to interrupt, Charlie, but we're going to load up and head out. Are you grabbing a ride back with us in the van or with Tom?" Allen asks.

Before I can answer, Luc asks me, "Didn't you want to ask me some background questions?" He turns to the cameraman and gives him his trademark megawatt smile. He must have a lot of practice using it, because it doesn't look fake or forced, though it has to be. "I'll make sure she gets a ride back if Tom has already left."

"Okie dokie." Allen waves and leaves us before I can protest.

I make a move to follow, but Luc puts a firm hand on my arm.

"We need to talk," Luc repeats, no longer smiling.

9

Luc

"**A**RE YOU PREGNANT?" I get right to the point, hoping like hell my suspicion is wrong. Maybe she'd just been smoothing a wrinkle out of her shirt.

Charlie turns away, but I hold on to her, careful not to dig into her flesh despite my anxiety and anger. I'm not angry at her. I'm angry at myself and my idiocy. Having sex without a condom, especially with someone I thought was a prostitute, might be the most reckless thing I've ever done. Okay, the second most, I correct myself. If it wasn't for what I did ten years ago, I wouldn't have been at the house this year when Charlie showed up.

Since the moment she arrived with her crew this morning, I began sneaking glances at her, watching her work and joke around with my teammates on the sidelines. I'd wanted to rip Hutch's arms off when I saw him hug her, lifting her off her feet, making her laugh.

She tries to pull her arm out of my grasp, and I let go, not wanting to hurt her. She crosses her arms in front of her and looks away from me. "Um, maybe. I don't know for sure yet."

"Shouldn't you know by now? Look at me!"

Her eyes narrow as she faces me. "I'm not sure, okay? I took the morning-after pill..."

Unlike my recklessness with the lack of condom before the fact, she had been responsible after the fact. I never even considered that option.

"...But not exactly the morning after," she continues. "I took a home test and it came out positive, but I'm hoping it's messed up because of the pill."

A home test? Positive?

A mix of emotions churn inside me, and I don't know what to feel. Trying to get a grip, I take a breath and focus. First things first.

"How soon until you know for sure?"

"I have a doctor's appointment in a few days. That should be enough time to get a positive result. I mean, a conclusive one. Not positive—"

At Charlie's fumbled words, I realize a possible pregnancy would impact her as much as me—if not more. While I'm worried about my father, my guilt, my reputation, her entire life could change.

"I understand," I reassure her, my voice softer. "You think the home test was off because you took the pill?"

"It could be."

My thoughts racing too much for me to think clearly, I don't know what to say to her.

"I really need to go before my ride leaves. I'll call you after my appointment, if there's anything to discuss. Let's just hope it's a false alarm." She smiles briefly, her expression not as hopeful as her words.

"And if it's not?"

She looks away and shrugs. "I don't know. I guess I'll look at my options and figure it out."

Before I can even process those words, she sways slightly. I hold out a hand, ready to catch her.

"Are you okay?" I peer at her closely, noting her already pale skin is almost ghost white.

She places a hand on her stomach and closes her eyes, exhaling slowly before answering. "Just feel a little sick. Probably the heat and hardly eating anything all day."

And here I am, keeping her outside even longer.

Opening her eyes, she smiles wanly at me. "Or morning sickness."

And just like that, I gasp out a breath, feeling like I took a punch to the gut. Morning sickness?

Taking her arm, gently this time, I lead her to the athletic center. "Have you felt sick before today?"

Charlie hesitates before answering. "For a little bit in the mornings. But not this late in the day, so I really do think it's just the heat and lack of food."

She shivers as the cold blast of the air-conditioning hits us when we enter the building.

She looks slightly green now and is doing the slow, deep breathing thing again.

"Can I do anything for you? Get you anything?"

"I just need a second," she says, closing her eyes.

"Sit here for a minute. I need to make a call." I guide her to the seating area and nudge her into a chair. Walking a few steps away, I pull out my phone and call Reggie. "Hey, Reg, can you grab some water, a ginger ale, and some food—snacks or something—and come over to the entrance by the practice field? I need you to drive someone for me." I pause to listen. "Thanks, man."

I hang up and come back to Charlie, whose color is coming back a little. "I think Tom is long gone. Since I made you miss your ride, my driver will take you back." When she looks at me, ready to protest, I say, "I'd take you myself, but we're not allowed to leave the facilities except to go to the hotel. And I have to be here for the meetings right after dinner."

The first couple of weeks of training camp are like boot camp, and the rules are enforced strictly. Not many players risk breaking them since it could mean getting cut from the team. I wouldn't be cut of course, but a serious infraction like disappearing for a few hours would have significant consequences. Besides, as a team captain, I like to set a good example for the others to follow.

I sit across from her. "How are you feeling now?"

She gives me a pitiful smile. "Better."

We sit in silence for several minutes. I am at a loss as to what to say to her. I barely know this woman, yet my entire life might change because of the brief moment of bliss and forgetfulness I found in her body. I don't blame her for the consequences. I take full responsibility. I can only guess what this will mean to her.

But I have an idea what it will mean for me. If Victor learns of the pregnancy, I'm sure the bastard will find a way to use it as leverage against me. That thought propels my next words.

"Charlie, I need you to keep all of this between us for the time being."

"This?"

"Our meeting in Fontaine, the possibility you might be…" I can't say the word aloud again. "In fact, it might be a good idea for you to sign a nondisclosure agreement. I can't have anyone—"

Charlie stands up suddenly, her face now flushed. "An NDA? Good idea for whom? You think I want anyone to know about this? My job, my career is on the line here. So if there's going to be an NDA, I think it would be a good idea for you to sign one as well."

I feel my mouth curve into a smile before I can stop it. Her eyes are like thunderclouds, and they narrow as if getting ready to shoot lightning bolts at me.

"You're right, of course. I'll have my attorney draw up something, I'll sign it, then send it over for your signature."

And just like that, the storm clouds clear. "Really?"

"Really. And just so you know, I agreed to do these interviews for *you*. Not as a quid pro quo," I quickly add when her eyes narrow again. "Because I understand you're just trying to do your job. But I'm taking the precaution of having my lawyers send the studio a letter to request that the episode not include anything about my personal life that I don't answer directly in the interviews or that doesn't pertain to playing football. They're free to refuse my request, but then I have the right to refuse any further interviews with the company in the future. Understood?"

Before she can answer me, we are interrupted by Reggie striding toward us. Although lumbering might be a better word due to his size. He was my offensive lineman in college, guarding me from potential sacks. He now guards me from any potential threat—fans, paparazzi, aggressive women...Fortunately, his size alone keeps most people at bay when he's nearby.

"Charlie, this is Reggie Wilson. He'll drive you back to the studio."

Reggie smiles at Charlie, showing several gold-capped teeth. I'm not sure the smile does anything to make Reggie appear friendlier, but I'm not surprised when Charlie holds out her hand to shake Reggie's. I don't know much about her, but I'm quickly learning she is gutsy. A big black man almost three times her size isn't going to intimidate her.

"Nice to meet you, Reggie."

"You too. Looks like you could use the cold drinks I got waiting in the car. Traffic's a bitch right now, so you're gonna need them. You got any bags or anything?" Reggie looks around, then back at Charlie, who is shaking her head.

"No, just this." She pats the messenger bag that is slung over one shoulder and resting against the opposite hip.

"Alrighty. Ready when you are." Reggie gestures toward the door.

When Charlie takes a step toward the exit, I stop her and lean in close to demand softly, "Call me after your appointment, Charlotte."

The next day before practice, I tune out the noise around me in the training room while waiting for Randy to work on my shoulder, a heating pad warming it up. Lying facedown on the padded therapy table, I keep my eyes closed, trying not to think about Charlie and what I'll do if she is pregnant.

"Hey, Joey. When are you going to see Charlie again?" Horndog CJ, my go-to wide receiver, booms the question from across the room. My ears perk up at the mention of Charlie, and I tune back into my surroundings.

"I'm not sure," answers Joey, a trainer who was hired to fill in for a few weeks. She's only a few years younger than me but light-years apart when it comes to how sweet and innocent she appears. Yet she has somehow managed to not only survive the male-dominated, testosterone-filled environment so far, but also win the respect of many of the players who'd been hesitant to let a woman treat them. Not that they didn't first try to hit on her since she is quite pretty. Some backed off when they realized she wasn't interested. Others received glares and harsh words from several players on the team.

"How about you, Hutch?" CJ yells to the other side of the room where Brent Hutchinson, my new tight end, is being treated. Hutch is one of those players who shoots daggers at anyone who even looks a little long at Joey. "When is your sister coming over to visit you again? Remind her I'm just a few floors down and to visit me too."

What the fuck?

"Why are you asking about my sister, asshole?" Hutch asks.

Oh shit. Charlotte is Hutch's sister? I hadn't even thought to make the connection when she told me her name that night. I vaguely recall her boss mentioning her brother, but my mind had been on other things at the time.

"Who the fuck are you guys jabbering about?" asks one of the newbies. Kid isn't going to last long, the way he swaggers and tries to talk like he belongs before he's even secured a position on the team.

Most veteran players ignore tools like him, but I can tell CJ wants to needle Hutch when he responds, "I'm talking 'bout that hot blonde who was interviewing pretty-boy Luc yesterday. Hutch's little sister and Joey's BFF."

"Oh yeah, dude. She was really hot," Tool enthusiastically agrees.

"Watch it, asswipe. That's my sister you're talking about."

"She's not your sister." I decide to join the fray. I open my eyes and lean up on an elbow. "There's no way someone as ugly as you is related to her."

Hutch ignores me, too busy giving Joey a possessive look as she passes him, one that causes Joey's cheeks to heat. Hmm. Something there.

If Joey, who is Charlie's friend and has a thing with Hutch, who is Charlie's brother and my teammate...this could be tricky.

Since I'm the franchise quarterback, Randy is the only trainer who I allow to treat me, but I might have to make an exception to get closer to Joey.

With that in mind, I sit up and call Joey over, since Randy is still busy with Hutch. "Hey, Joey, darling." I lay on my Southern charm, complete with lazy drawl, and smile at her. "Think you could help me out here?"

Hutch frowns in my direction. Yep, definitely something going on there.

Joey looks at me in surprise but comes over and takes the kinesiology tape I'm holding. "Shoulder?"

I nod, figuring I'll be good with just the tape for the light practice this morning and get treatment later. But instead of cutting off a piece, she puts it down and moves to stand beside me so she can reach my right shoulder, always tight in the mornings.

"Okay if I work on it first? You don't want to tape it up if the muscles are still tight."

She waits for my response, her teeth worrying her bottom lip. This is the first time I've asked her to help me, but I've heard no complaints from any of the guys she's treated so far, so I nod.

She starts with gentle strokes that deepen, and I almost groan at the relief. From my lowered lids, I confirm Hutch is staring daggers at us, so I close my eyes in bliss and let the groan out this time, purposely making it sound sexual. "That feels good, darling."

I gaze up at her with a practiced look that usually makes women fall into my arms. Joey's face goes pink under her honeyed skin tone, and her teeth pull on her lower lip again. How did a sweet, shy thing like her end up with a womanizer like Hutch?

Okay, that might be the pot calling the kettle black, considering my own reputation, but Hutch actually lives up to his. At least according to the tabloids. But then again, I know better than anyone what's written in those rags can be so easily manipulated.

She surprises me when she says in a firm tone, "My name is Joey."

I give her another smile. "Okay, *Joey* darling." I flick a glance at Hutch, then back at her, and wink to let her in on my little game to push his buttons. I take one of her hands and study it, caressing a thumb over the palm. "Your hands feel so good."

Joey's blush deepens. She pulls her hand out of mine and shakes her head at me in exasperation, but she smiles, making her already pretty face beautiful.

I can't help laughing when Hutch takes the bait and makes a move to stand. Randy keeps a firm grip on the leg he'd been taping up so Hutch can't swing it off the table. The trainer says something and pats him on the shoulder. Hutch leans back against the table, but continues to stare at me with narrowed eyes, his mouth tight and body tense, like he's ready to pounce.

Done with yanking his chain, I turn my attention to Joey who has resumed kneading the tight muscles on my right shoulder. "So," I say, lowering my voice so only she can hear me, "looks like you're pretty close to the Hutchinsons." What I really want to know is whether Charlie might have confided in Joey.

"Yes, I've known the family for years," she says, her voice overly casual.

"You were neighbors or something?"

"I met them while on vacation. We were staying at the same campground."

"Oh yeah? Where? You like camping?"

"Lake George. That was my first and last time. And it wasn't real camping. My father and I stayed in a cabin."

Her eyes glaze over with memories and her mouth turns down. I can practically feel Hutch's glower burning a hole in my chest. With our heads next to each other while she leans into my shoulder, it probably looks like we are having an intimate conversation.

Not wanting him to come over and knock out my teeth, and feeling guilty for making her sad, I tease, "I can't imagine Hutch glamping. I bet he brought a feather pillow and his favorite blankie. Tell me I'm right."

She laughs. "I can't imagine him glamping either. No, the Hutchinsons stayed in tents. I went into the one Charlie shared with her two sisters, and it was like being in a cozy fairy hut in the woods. A purple one with pink sleeping bags and strings of lights inside."

Her eyes are shining now, her lips turned up in a soft smile.

"Let me guess. You discovered you lived in the same town?"

"I wish," she laughs. "No, we lived a couple of hours apart. But we kept in touch by snail mail at first and then email and messaging when we were a bit older."

"Snail mail?"

"Neither of us could afford cell phones back then, even if our moms allowed us to have them. So we wrote letters to each other, sometimes pages long and sometimes a quick paragraph if we needed to get something off our chest."

"Sounds like you two were very close, despite the distance."

"There was so much going on at the time in both our lives, I think being forced to communicate that way definitely made us closer. It was like writing in our diaries. We told each other everything."

That's what worries me. But so far, Joey has given no indication that she knows about me and Charlie. From what I've observed of Joey, I don't think she'd be able to hide it if she knew. I'm safe for now.

While she was talking, she'd moved behind me to apply the tape. She's silent, and I glance over my shoulder to see her biting her lip.

"What's wrong?"

She shakes her head. "Sorry, I'm not normally so talkative while working."

I bet she's not very talkative even when not working, based on what I've observed of her. While she's friendly, there's a quiet reserve about her.

"Don't be sorry, dar—Joey. I think it means we're already becoming friends," I say with complete honesty, despite calling her over under the ruse of learning more about Charlie. I don't have a lot of real friends, but I like Joey, and I'd be lucky to have her as one. Not that I'll spill any of my secrets to her. Underneath the public persona I've created, I'm as reserved as she is. I'm just more experienced at hiding that part of myself.

She looks as if she doesn't believe me, and it makes me wonder why. Perhaps she has secrets too. Still waters?

"How does that feel now?" she, asks, smoothing her hand over my shoulder one last time.

I move my arm around in small circles, then bigger ones. It feels a hell of a lot looser.

"You've got magic hands, Joey darling. Thank you."

"Thank you for letting me work on you."

As Joey inputs notes into her tablet, I try to think of a way to bring the conversation back to Charlie. There's no good segue so I bluntly ask, "Is Charlie seeing anyone?" I force a grin when she looks at me in surprise. "What? As CJ noted, she's hot."

She smiles back at me. "Yes, she is."

Yes, she's hot? Or yes, she's seeing someone?

10

Charlie

I SIT AT MY desk, updating my notes for the various segments I'm overseeing, so engrossed I don't even notice that it is long past quitting time.

Mark pops his head into my cubicle. "How's it going?"

I look up, not letting my annoyance at being startled show. "We're on track on all the episodes." I hesitate before reluctantly adding, "Except Saint's. Since we won't be doing the in-depth look from his hometown, we'll have to fill that time with something else."

"Shit. You think he's serious about never doing an interview with us again if we—"

"Yes, Mark," I interrupt. He'd asked me that ten times already.

"He is obligated to talk to the media..."

"But not to us specifically. Or he could do what some players do and give bullshit answers if any of us ask him a question. Technically, he'd still be talking to us."

"You ever find out why he doesn't want us to go back earlier than college?"

"I think it's just that he doesn't want to relive the pain of losing his mother," I reply. I don't think that's the entire reason, but remembering Luc's anguish, I need Mark to back off. I don't tell him I'm still digging, although not for the segment. I'm trying to find out everything I can about the man who might be the father of my baby—if I am indeed pregnant. "That's a devastating thing to have gone through. I'm sure he wants everyone to focus on the present, just like he's trying to do."

"That's great, kid. You think you can get him to say that on camera?" he asks, always thinking of the viewership numbers.

"Sorry, I don't think he wants any reference to it at all."

I know some of Luc's past through reading every tidbit about him I could find when I had my obsessive crush on him. Since starting on his segment, I've dug up more, and read and watched everything I could find about the death of his mother, Angeline, and about Victor Miller's involvement in Luc's life. Angeline was killed when the car she was driving lost control, flipping over and catching on fire. Luc was thrown from the vehicle and sustained no major injuries.

What I hadn't known before my recent research was that a young child had been in the vehicle, one who had suffered life-threatening injuries. I wonder why Luc never mentioned her and what happened to her. No further articles, no follow ups, were written about her. If there was no media interest in her at the time, I assume the girl was not related to Victor or Luc.

There was conjecture in some articles that Angeline might have been trying to commit suicide. Luc flatly denied in early interviews that she would ever do such a thing.

Soon after the crash, Victor was quoted as saying, "I did what I could for her and my boy over the years, but she was a troubled woman. That's all I'm going to say, because I'm not going to disrespect the dead. She'll always have a special place in my heart because she gave me my son." He'd gone on to talk about Luc and his football prowess and how his son was going to be almost as good as his daddy.

I'd snorted in disgust at that comment. *Almost* as good? Victor hadn't even played the same position. There was no comparison. And if there was, Luc surpassed his father's entire career within the first three years in the NFL.

I've never met the man, but what many people describe as charm comes off as insincere and narcissistic to me, like a slick veneer that hid something rotten inside. I'll find out if my perception of him matches reality when I interview him in a few days. I'll respect Luc's wishes and not include his past in the segment, but I still plan on asking Victor a few questions about the accident.

Since there is already a plethora of mentions about the death of Luc's mother in older articles, I can't figure out why Luc would be bothered by it being covered now. Everything else in his childhood seems relatively normal despite being the son of a high-profile football player, albeit illegitimate. But no one cares about that kind of thing anymore. It's a fact of life, whether it's athletes or everyday people.

Like me, Mark had been lost in thought, staring off into space with narrowed eyes. I shift uncomfortably. It's never a good sign when he stops talking to think this hard. His next words prove me right.

"Okay, here's what we're going to do. We'll use whatever is already public knowledge from other sources. But I want you to find out what he's trying to hide. Go to his hometown, do the interviews, and let's see what comes out of it. If it turns into a really big story, I think the higher-ups will take the chance."

My stress level immediately goes up by several notches. "Why? It's not like we're a hard-hitting news show. And what about his boycotting us? The legal document?"

"I don't think he has a leg to stand on with that. He's just trying to scare us off. And that's what makes me more curious."

Despite Mark's chauvinism, he has been a role model for me as a producer, with his experience and doggedness. I'm not appreciating the latter quality at the moment. However, Luc's insistence has made me more curious too. If he hadn't said anything and let me do my job, I would have likely kept to the usual topics and not looked too deep. But it's one thing to satisfy my curiosity for personal reasons and another to do it for the purpose of exposing his secrets to the world.

"I don't know if we sh—"

"Charlie, you're a producer now. I promoted you because I thought you were ready." He shakes his head as if disappointed. "You can go back to being an—"

"No, I am, but—"

"Good. Let me know what you find." He leaves as abruptly as he'd arrived, leaving me in a puddle of resentment from his threat to demote me and anxiety from what he's asked me to do.

The thought of going behind Luc's back doesn't sit right with me. I'm caught in the middle of doing as my boss wants and what Luc has begged me not to do.

Begged in that tortured voice.

I haven't talked to him since the stadium interview a few days ago. When I texted him earlier with the date and time of my doctor's appointment, he replied with a simple "keep me posted." I tried not to let it bother me that he hadn't offered to come with me. He probably can't anyway since he has to stay at the hotel near the Firebirds complex during training camp. Between practices, meetings, watching hours of film, and learning new plays, he's likely as exhausted as I am each night. More so since his job is much more physical. I wonder if Joey works on him, on that magnificent, lean, muscled body.

I stir restlessly in my office chair as I think of Luc's form and how he felt on top of me, inside me. It's so unfair to have really great sex and have it be over after just the one much-too-quick time. I wish

Luc had gone more slowly so I had more time to see him, touch him, feel him.

I bite my lip to hold in a moan and hurriedly glance around. No one is looking at me over the low cubicle walls.

As I cross my legs to stem the desire from my brief encounter with Luc, a question pops into my head: *Why does it have to be just the one time?* Since I'm already pregnant, why couldn't we continue to have sex?

I shake my head. What am I thinking? It's not as if we're dating. He has given no indication he's interested in having anything more to do with me. I'm certainly not his usual type, as evidenced by the tabloid photos in my research files of women whose breasts are always on the verge of falling out of their necklines.

So what if I don't look like his usual women? He didn't seem to mind. We had great chemistry. And I like what I've learned of him so far after talking to some of his current teammates. I've discovered that he's hard-working, well-respected, and takes his responsibilities as a leader on the team seriously. Only his reticence about his past bothers me. If there is something he's hiding, I'll find out. Not for the segment. And not only for the sake of the baby, if there is one. But also because I want to see what might stand in the way of turning our chemistry into something more.

11

Luc

"**M**IND IF I JOIN you?"

Joey looks up from the tablet she's typing on with one hand while she eats with the other. She smiles and nods, pushing papers aside to make room for me at the small table in the team cafeteria. I notice again how her face lights up when she smiles. She and Charlie must make quite a pair when they are out together, one dark-haired and curvy, the other fair and slender. Both tall and gorgeous.

Hutch glares at me as he walks by to sit at a bigger table with some other players. He's already warned me to behave with Joey, claiming he's looking out for his sister's best friend.

What utter bullshit. I was able to stop myself from laughing in his face, but I couldn't prevent the smile that I had to hide by turning away. There's more than just a family friendship between him and Joey. If they're trying to keep it a secret, they're not doing a very good job of it. The way they look at each other gives them away. Randy is likely turning a blind eye to it since Joey is a temporary employee, only here until the injured trainer returns in a couple of weeks. And at least they're trying to pretend for the sake of appearances.

"You know, you guys aren't fooling anyone," I tell Joey.

She looks at me innocently—not that hard to do considering her big brown eyes and shy smile. During our frequent conversations while she treats me or on the sidelines during practice, she's become more comfortable around me. With some prodding, I've learned more about her friendship with Charlie. But about Hutch, all she'd admit is she had a crush on him when she was younger.

She doesn't say anything as she takes another bite of her chicken Caesar salad. Starving, I down half of my minestrone soup before continuing the conversation.

"Okay," I say, pointing my soup spoon at her. "Let's assume he's only looking out for you because you're his sister's friend. Then what's he like with his sisters?"

"According to Charlie, he was a nightmare, especially for Stevie since they were in high school at the same time. Worse than their dad would have been."

She laughs suddenly and looks down, biting her lip.

"What?" I ask.

She grins and shakes her head, not saying anything.

"Tell me, or I'm going to plant a kiss on you right in front of Hutch just to see what happens."

Her eyes widen. "Just to see—? If you do that, you probably won't be able to throw the ball this season."

I just raise my eyebrows and wait.

She sighs. "I was thinking I'm surprised he didn't already threaten you when you were playing in San Diego."

"In San Diego? Why would he do that? I didn't know you then."

"Not me. One of his sisters."

"What? I never even met any of them."

She grins again. "He's the reason you never did. He found out one of them had a crush on you, and she wanted him to introduce you to her."

Her slight hesitation tells me which sister it was. I grin. "Oh yeah? Which sister?"

As expected, she doesn't tell me, but I think I know. Having gotten that little tidbit, I change the topic.

"What about your crush? Did he know about that?"

She blushes. "Yes. Apparently, he warned *himself* away from me, and ignored me so I'd think he was a jerk."

"Did you?"

"No, because I knew he was still a good guy."

"How did you know that?"

While I ask out of genuine curiosity about Joey and Hutch, I'd be lying if I wasn't also hoping to get a glimpse into Charlie's life. I've avoided calling her, not ready to have her embroiled in my complicated life. Not until I've figured out what to do about Victor.

Joey's eyes shine as she starts talking about Hutch. "When I first met him, I thought he was a jerk, always teasing and annoying his sisters. I liked his older brother who was much nicer to them and so kind to me. They were both tall, but Brent was still a bit skinny, all arms and legs. But by the end of the week, I saw that he really loved his sisters and was protective of them. No one outside of the family was allowed to tease them. And God forbid anyone was mean."

"They sound like a close-knit family. It was just me and my mama for the longest time."

Joey nodded. "I was the only child of divorced parents. That week at the campground was the most carefree one I'd had as a kid. I ended up spending all my time with the Hutchinsons. I was drawn to what they had—the noise and chaos, the teasing, even the squabbling, because under it all, there was so much love. Being around the Hutchinsons was like...like being part of a TV family where every conflict is worked out by the end of the episode." Despite her self-deprecating smile, her tone is wistful.

Her smile dims. "Except it doesn't happen like that in real life, not even for a family as perfect as theirs was. I think those might have been the last carefree days we all had before everything changed."

"What do you mean?"

She focuses her eyes back on me and hesitates before answering. "We all went through so much after that vacation."

I don't want to push, but I wonder what all the "stuff" was that they had gone through.

The hell with it. I need to know. "What kind of stuff?"

Joey looks uncomfortable at my invasive question. To make up for it, I confess, "I went through a little bit of stuff, too, and I'm wondering how you guys got past it. You and Hutch seem pretty happy and well-adjusted."

Joey gives a little laugh. "Well, I don't know how well-adjusted I am, but I'm glad I seem that way." She becomes serious when she sees I'm actually interested in her response. "The Hutchinsons took me in when my mother died, and I lived with them for a couple of years. Brent and Charlie's mother, Sandra, suggested I see a therapist to help me process."

"I'm sorry about your mother. I lost mine when I was eighteen." I never talk about it voluntarily, and I'm not sure why I'm doing so now. It must be something about Joey's sweet, nonjudgmental, and compassionate nature.

She reaches for my hand but doesn't quite touch it before pulling away. "I'm sorry. Was she ill?" she asks, then gasps. "I'm sorry. That was so rude. Especially since I don't like talking about my mom's death."

"It's okay." Though I don't really want to talk about how she died. "She wasn't ill. She died in a car accident."

She looks at me, her eyes soft with sympathy. As if to make up for her bold question, she admits quietly, "Mine too."

"Yeah, but were you driving?"

I don't even realize I've said it out loud until Joey jerks in surprise, her eyes wide. I shake my head at my reckless words and backtrack. "I meant, were you driving with her and know how it happened?"

"No, I wasn't with her. She was alone."

"Apparently, I was with my mom, but I don't remember what happened," I admit.

Brows furrowed, she asks, "Post-traumatic amnesia?"

I shrug. "The doctors said I might remember, but ten years later, still nothing."

I can't believe I'm pouring all this out to Joey when I've never talked to anyone about this besides Reggie. And he doesn't even know all of it.

"How awful." This time, Joey's hand touches mine briefly in comfort before going back to her lap. I realize she only touches me during treatment, never casually during our conversations. Of course I touch her casually all the time. Partly because it's in my nature and partly to piss off Brent. I glance over at him to see he's itching to come over and break my hand, or at least a finger or two.

After a brief moment when she seems to struggle with how to respond, she says, "I don't want to pry, Luc, and I don't mean to presume, but if you want to try to remember...I had a really great professor who has a private practice in the city. Her specialty is hypnotherapy to help people recall traumatic events in their past. It might—"

I pull away abruptly. "A hypnotist? I don't think so." Why the fuck did I open up? I stand up with my tray.

Joey slowly stands as well. "Not a hypnotist," she clarifies, her voice gentle and her eyes compassionate. "A psychologist who uses hypnotherapy to treat patients. But I understand. It's scary to think about what you might remember. And when you hear 'hypnosis,' you automatically think of someone squawking like a chicken." She shakes her head. "But it's not like that, I promise. Think about it and let me know if you want her number. And it'll stay just between us."

"Thanks, but I don't think so."

"Well, if you change your mind, I'm here." She gives me a sweet smile. "And I'm also here if you ever want to talk about it."

I walk away without responding and catch Brent's glare. I manage to smile and salute my teammate, insinuating there had been something intimate in my conversation with Joey. I wonder what Hutch would do if he knew it was his sister that I'd already been intimate with.

Jesus. It hits me for the first time that Hutch and I would be related through the baby, if there is one. While he and I had been friends in San Diego, distance and busy lives forced us to drift apart. We get along fine and we work together well on the field, but I consider him a teammate, not a friend. Besides Reggie and my agent, I'd probably consider a couple of veteran players from the Firebirds as friends. It's hard to have close friends when you have secrets.

I've intentionally kept myself closed off from more personal relationships. I'm not sure how I feel about the sudden connection to not only Charlie but her entire family.

12

Charlie

"**C**ONGRATULATIONS, Ms. HUTCHINSON. YOU'RE pregnant." The doctor smiles at me, and I promptly burst into tears.

It wasn't supposed to happen like this. I wasn't supposed to become pregnant after a one-night stand with a man I only know by reputation, and not a very good one at that.

"Ms. Hutchinson? Charlotte." The doctor hands me a tissue. She is a kind-looking older woman, a complete stranger since I went to a clinic far from home instead of my regular doctor to ensure complete privacy.

"I don't know your situation, but I do need to know that you are safe and have a support system."

I can respond to that without hesitation. "Yes, I have a great support system and I'm...safe."

"That wasn't a very reassuring answer," the doctor chides. "Is the baby's father a problem?"

"No." He isn't as far I know, but his secrets might be. To the doctor, I only say, "We're not a couple or anything. But it's fine. Really," I add when the doctor doesn't appear convinced.

There's a waiting room full of patients, and I'm thankful she doesn't have the time to pursue her questioning. "I'm sorry if this was not the news you were hoping to hear. Make an appointment with your gynecologist to go over your options. It's not something you have to decide right away, but the sooner the better."

My hand automatically goes to my stomach protectively. Options? Not for me. Whatever happens, this baby is mine, and I am keeping it. This may not be the way I wanted it to happen, but I've always wanted children. It was my dream to be a stay-at-home mom like my mother until the death of my father made me realize I better have a career of my own in case my own circumstances ever changed. I don't know how I'm going to manage as a single mother with a job that requires long hours and extensive travel, but I'll figure it out.

I wipe away my tears and assure the concerned doctor that I'm fine.

"Okay. Just know that you have alternatives available if you need them. Check the online portal in about three days for results of your STI labs. Start taking your prenatal vitamins and make an appointment with your regular ob-gyn," she tells me before leaving me to dress.

On the long drive home, I think about the abrupt turn my life has taken. The last time everything changed in an instant was when my father and oldest brother died. My father was a firefighter and RJ was in training to be one. On one call, RJ ran after my father into a burning warehouse. Neither made it out alive.

The tragedy changed everything for all of us, most of all my mother. She'd been lost, financially and emotionally, having been completely dependent on my father for all her needs. I had to watch Brent, only fourteen at the time, take on the mantle as man of the house. My oldest sister, Stevie, was forced to take up a lot of Mom's responsibilities at such a young age. And the financial struggle we'd faced meant Georgie had to give up the one thing she loved most—her dance classes. And I'd given up my idealistic dream of being a stay-at-home mother like Mom. I swore I'd never put myself or my children in that type of situation, not that I blamed anyone. I just wanted to be better prepared if anything like that happened to me.

But I thought I'd have time to build a career before I had kids. Despite my promotion, my salary is ridiculously low, barely enough to support me if I lived on my own. It's why I'm still living at home with my mother and Bobbie, my baby sister.

The more immediate worry is how Luc will react when I confirm the pregnancy to him.

Not knowing what he'll do with the news underscores just how little I know him. His reaction could range anywhere from expecting me to terminate the pregnancy to offering marriage.

My brooding screeches to a halt at that thought. Marriage? Does anyone still do that anymore just because of pregnancy? I scoff. He's not going to offer to marry me after a one-night stand. Nor would I accept.

I hardly know him, and what I do know comes from media reports, tabloids, and his interviews. What I don't know and what he wants to keep hidden is concerning.

Maybe I can ask Brent about him. They were close when they played together briefly in Luc's first season. But I don't know how close they remained once Luc was traded to the Firebirds while Brent remained in San Diego.

No, it's best to keep Brent out of it. I don't want him going into big brother mode and putting their professional relationship in jeopardy. Besides, a lot has changed for Luc since Brent played with him, especially money and fame, two things that can change a person entirely.

I'm determined to unearth whatever there is to know about him. I'm going to have this man's baby, and I damn well intend to find out what makes up half of it.

But first, I have to break the news to him. His reaction will tell me a great deal about the type of man he is. I text him to call me when he's done with practice.

When the phone rings a few hours later, I brace myself before answering.

"Hello."

"What did the doctor say?" He barks the question without a greeting, immediately raising my hackles.

"Hi, Luc. I'm fine, thanks. How are you?"

"Charlotte," he growls.

"You know, only my mother and strangers call me Charlotte. And my mother only does it when—"

"Fucking Christ, Charlie!"

"Okay, fine. No small talk first. Congratulations. You'll be a daddy around the end of March, so don't plan any celebrity spring break cruises next year."

He doesn't say anything for long moments. If it wasn't for his harsh breathing, I would have thought he'd hung up.

Recalling how I reacted this morning when the doctor congratulated me, empathy belatedly fills me.

"Yeah, it's a shock," I say, all snark gone. "And as the doctor said to me after I burst into tears, I'm sorry this is not the news you were hoping for. We can talk about what you want to do, but you don't have to decide anything right now."

I pause, but Luc doesn't reply.

"Hello? Luc, are you still there?"

"Give me a minute," he rasps out.

"Are you okay?" I ask gently.

"Give me a fucking minute!"

I pull the phone away from my ear and stare at it in shock. Well, I guess that's a clue as to what kind of person he is—at least when he's not with his teammates or in public.

"You know what, asshole? Take all the minutes you want."

I hang up and burst into tears as I did this morning.

My crying jag ebbs as my empathy for him returns. This is as much a shock to him as it was to me. I can't be mad at him for his initial reaction. He'd sounded shell-shocked even though he knew it was a possibility. But possibility and confirmation are two very different things.

His life—our lives—are about to change forever.

When Luc calls back, he speaks as soon as I pick up, before I can say anything.

"I'm sorry. I *am* an asshole."

Any remaining hurt and anger I have fade at Luc's apologetic tone.

"I understand. Are you okay?" I ask.

"I should be asking you that."

I shiver suddenly. His voice is low and sexy and right in my ear, as if he's there next to me. I hadn't noticed it before, probably because I had been anxious and he'd been impatient. But now, goose bumps cover me as if he's stroked my body with his voice. Is that even possible? I want to hear him speak again to find out.

"I'm fine. But really, how are you with all this?" I hear him sigh.

"It's a game changer, that's for sure. I feel like I got sacked by a four-hundred-pound linebacker. Three of them, all piled on top of me. I'm sorry for yelling and swearing before. It took a few minutes to catch my breath again."

I half-listen to his words. The other half of me confirms it's possible to feel his voice whispering over my skin. I'm getting turned on just listening to him.

"Mm-hm. No problem." I catch myself and hear what I'm actually saying. I straighten up and make my voice stern. "Just don't do it again."

"No, I won't. I'm sorry."

"You already said that. Several times. So let's move on. About what I said earlier...talking about what you want to do..." I trail off, hoping he'll pick up the thought and finish it with his own.

"What I want to do? You mean, I have a say?"

"Of course. It's your baby too."

"But you're the one who has to—"

My heart sinks at his words, and I don't let him finish. "Listen, if you don't want to be involved, that's fine. I can—"

"That's not what I'm saying. I was...I thought you might be considering...abortion—"

"Abortion? You think I should get one?!" I feel more than just disappointment now.

"No! That's not what I said, Charlie. That's not what I want."

My breath catches at the intensity in Luc's quiet words. I wish I could see him, his expression, for a hint of what he's feeling, because his words hold deep emotion.

I sigh, my anger going up in smoke. "I don't either. I was talking about how involved you want to be. Since the baby is also yours, I want to let you decide that for yourself. And it can start as soon as the doctor appointments, if you want to. Though, of course, you don't have to."

I trail off, embarrassed. As soon as I make the offer, I realize how dumb it sounds. The barely there fetus isn't going to know whether its father is around or not. And we're not a couple in any way that would obligate him to go with me to the doctor's appointments.

"That's not a good idea."

"Right. Of course not. You've got cameras following you around all the time." I laugh lightly to hide my disappointment. It's not a good idea for me and my career if people find out Luc is my baby daddy, but what's his reason?

"Yes, I do. The media cannot find out about us. In fact—and I'm going to be an asshole again, but I need you to trust me on this—I don't want anyone knowing this baby is mine. I can't even be seen with you anymore now that the interviews are done."

"Oookay." My chest tightens with unexpected hurt. "Well, then. I guess I'll—"

"Charlie," Luc interrupts, his voice soft, "please understand. This has nothing to do with you. There is some shit going on in my life that I don't want you—and the baby—involved in, and I need time to figure it out. Okay? Can you give me some time and just keep this between us for now?"

His words reinforce my determination to find out what he's hiding. I don't know if he and I will ever have the kind of relationship I was hoping for, but he will always be my child's father.

"How much time?" I need to know when I'll be able to answer the questions my family will have when I tell them about my pregnancy, something I want to do sooner rather than later.

"I'm not sure yet. This is all happening really fast, and I need a chance to think about it."

"Okay, but I'll need to tell my family before too long. They'll be hurt if I keep it from them."

"It's up to you if you want to tell them about the baby. Just wait to tell them it's mine, okay? Let me see how things stand."

His request reminds me of how he's reacted when he thought I would reveal his secrets to the public. Panic when he thought I was a reporter...anguish when I asked for hometown interviews...earnest when he wanted me to sign an NDA...

"Luc, does this have anything to do with why you don't want me to include any stories about your past, your hometown?"

"Jesus, Charlie. Let that go. Please. Just trust me. I'm...I'm begging you."

I suck in my breath at the sudden change in tone. He sounds...afraid.

13

Luc

Exhausted and sore from the morning's weight lifting session and padded practice, I sprawl on the sofa with my laptop during the afternoon break. I'm trying to catch up on emails and texts from my agent and assistant, but my mind keeps wandering to Charlie, the pregnancy, and the future, as it has since her call last night.

You'll be a daddy.

Congratulations. You'll be a daddy.

Holy fuck, I'm going to be a father. An unfamiliar feeling starts to build inside me. It takes me a moment to realize it's joy.

I'm going to be a father!

When I rushed to an empty meeting room to call Charlie as soon as I saw the text during the dinner break, I wasn't sure what I'd wanted her to say. Despite the complications it would bring into my life, I think deep down, a part of me was hoping she'd be pregnant. Since I've sworn off relationships and any chance of happiness, this might be my only chance to have a child. I haven't technically broken my vow if I didn't intentionally set out to make this happen, right? And being a part of the child's life would be the right thing to do. Unlike my father, I won't deny attention to my offspring because of my own issues.

And having a baby with Charlie means I get to maintain a connection with her. I don't know much about her, but I know she's feisty and smart and has depth, not like the one-dimensional women I intentionally surround myself with. Women who just want to be seen with me for their social media popularity and don't care about getting to know me on a deeper level.

A few women have tried to break through my walls without success, but Charlie did it within minutes of our meeting. And finding out that she hasn't even told her best friend about our encounter proves she's also a woman with integrity, making a confidentiality agreement unnecessary. I couldn't have found a more perfect woman if I'd tried.

Since I can't be with her in all the ways I wish I could be, a baby with her would keep her in my life. I feel something for her—I have from the moment I saw her—something so deep that I lost control. And I never lose control. Ever.

And it's not just a physical attraction...though, fuck, she's sexy! I can still feel her silky blonde hair as I gripped her head while pushing into her...her soft skin when I dug my fingers into her ass when I let go and poured myself inside her...her long, slim legs wrapped around me...her small, firm breasts with the perfect pink nipples...

My body reacts with the memory, and I shake off the thoughts of her soft skin sliding against mine.

What the fuck am I thinking? I have no right to have such dreams.

No, I can't have her. Not only would it violate my self-imposed rule about being happy, of having a normal life, it would be too dangerous because of Victor. But unlike him, I will financially support my child and his or her mother. And when the day comes that Victor is no longer a threat, I'll acknowledge them to the world.

The intrusive thought of my father shatters the last of my growing bubble of euphoria. How will he react when he finds out?

No, Victor can't know. I have to keep this from him at all costs or he will do everything possible to cash in on the story. Against my better judgement, I already sent the million he asked for, hoping it will be months before I hear from him again.

As if my thoughts conjured him, the phone rings in my hand and it's the devil himself calling me.

"What?"

"Now is that any way to answer the phone? Didn't my Angie teach you any manners?"

My blood begins to boil. "I save my manners for people who deserve them. And you keep my mother's name off your tongue. I don't want you even thinking of her."

"Trust me, I don't," he responds callously. "Listen, I got the money you wired, but I'm going to need a bit more."

"How do you already need more? It's only been a month since I gave you a million. You paid off the debt, right?"

"Yeah, I made a down payment. But I didn't want to ask you for more so I figured I'd use the rest to make back what I owed and a little more. You know? I was trying to do you a favor."

The nerve of this fucking man.

"Why don't you do me a favor now and stop calling me every time you need money?"

"No, you don't get it. These are some bad hombres."

"And how do I know you're not just going to land in trouble again?"

"I swear I've learned my lesson this time, son. Trust me, I do not want to tangle with these dudes again. This will be the last time. I swear it."

Yeah, right. Maybe it won't be with these loan sharks, but I know it'll happen again like I know he's a piece of shit. Always has been and always will be.

Despite knowing better, I ask, "How much?"

"Two mil."

What the fuck?

"Yeah, I don't think so."

"Listen up, boy."

Ah yes, there it is. That tone, that condescension, that...flat out racism. From my own father. It doesn't surprise me, considering he pretends his Mexican ancestry is wiped away by a more recent European bloodline.

"Have you forgotten what I've done for you so that you could have the life you have now? You best remember that you wouldn't have any of this if it weren't for me. I've kept your secret for ten years. I think that's worth a measly two million."

He's already bilked me for several million over the years, not including the most recent payment.

"Wire it to me by the end of the week unless you want the world to know how your mother really died."

Before I can tell him the timing is impossible, he hangs up, expecting me to comply as I have since my first contract was signed. He's preyed on my guilt for long enough. I'm not wiring anything this time. He can fuck off.

No, he can't. Because it's not just me. I have Daphne to think about. And now Charlie and our baby.

I need to think about this carefully and come up with an exit strategy. Victor's exit from my life.

I'd have been willing to support him, give him a life of luxury, if he'd been any kind of father, but I don't want to continue to be extorted and threatened. I can't keep making those payments now, especially since the amount keeps increasing. I'm going to have a kid to support soon, to provide a future for. I need to preserve what I make while I play because one bad injury could mean the end of my NFL career and the millions I earn from playing and the resulting endorsements.

I need to find a way to shut Victor down.

My phone dings, bringing me out of my thoughts. I shoot straight up when I read the text from the offensive coordinator.

Where the fuck are you?

Another ding.

Coach is threatening to bench you if you don't get your ass here now!

I check the time. Afternoon break is over and the second practice started ten minutes ago.

Shit. I run out of my hotel room.

"Yo, what's up, boss?" Reggie answers as he always does when I call.

I've long given up telling him to stop calling me boss. It feels weird since we were teammates and roommates who quickly became friends. It hasn't gotten any less weird over the years, because we're still friends even though I *am* technically his boss. Just one of the many people I pay—for actual work they do—from the money I make.

"Shouldn't you be getting your beauty sleep now?" he asks.

"Ha. I don't need anything to make me this pretty," I retort.

"True dat, man. But you gotta be tired. Training camp is the biggest reason I'm glad I don't play no more."

I am exhausted but my mind hasn't stopped racing since the two bombshell phone calls in the last twenty-four hours.

"I need you to do something for me."

Reggie knows some of my past, having coaxed it out of me after being woken by my tortured nightmares almost every night since the first day of football camp at LSU, barely a month after the car crash.

"Anything you need, boss."

"Victor asked me for money again. Two million this time."

Reggie knows about Victor's frequent requests for money, but not why I keep giving it.

"Is he outta his damn mind? You need to stop this shit, man! He may be your old man, but you don't gotta keep sending so much money all the damn time."

"I know, but I need to find a way to stop him without him getting a whiff of what I'm up to, or who knows what he'll do."

"I can take care of him for you. No one will ever know."

I can practically hear Reggie cracking his knuckles at the prospect of dealing with Victor and can't help but smile. I love the guy. There is no one more loyal than Reggie.

"Hell," he continues, "I'll even make sure you never know how or when—"

"Easy, big guy. Trust me, I'd love to *take care* of him myself if I was sure I could get away with it."

Reggie sighs in resignation. "Okay, then. What you want me to do?"

"I need you to go see Gabe for me tomorrow."

Gabriel D'Angelo and his brother, Raphael, own a full-service personal security firm catering to wealthy clients who are at high risk from all kinds of threats. Reggie is my driver and acts as my bodyguard when needed, but I've hired Guardian Angels to install state-of-the-art physical and cyber security measures in all my properties.

"Ask him to dig up everything he can on Victor, especially where the money I give him is going and who he hangs out with." I figure following the money trail and finding out if he's associating with criminals might give me just what I need.

"Hallelujah, brother. It's about damn time. I been telling you to shut him down for years. I don't know why you ain't done it before. So why now? What's changed, boss?"

"I'm sick of his shit. The only way to stop him is to find some dirt on him so I can turn the tables." I hesitate before adding, "And I'm going to have a kid, Reg."

It feels surreal to say it out loud, but I can trust Reggie with the news. He's earned it with his discretion and loyalty over the years.

"Whoa. Back up. Who with? And do we need to worry about her trying to take money from you now too?"

"No," I say without having to think about it. I don't know Charlie well, but somehow I'm confident she's not the type to do something like that. "It's Charlotte. Charlie."

"The blonde I drove the other day? Didn't you just meet her like a couple of weeks ago? You sure it's yours?"

"Yes, I'm sure." No hesitation again, though I'd question it with any other woman. "And I met her in Fontaine. On the Fourth."

"Yeah, alright. Now it all makes sense. I see why you wanted me to disappear after I drove you to the house."

I don't bother to tell him Charlie's appearance had been completely unexpected, nor that I'd in fact been waiting for two women I'd hired to try to replicate the night of the accident. Since the last place I remember being that night was at the lake with my friends, I'd had Reggie drive me there earlier in the evening before dropping me off at the house where Charlie had tracked me down.

Ten years ago, I'd gone into the woods a couple of times, with a different girl each time. I had shrugged when the second girl had offered, right in front of the first one who just laughed in encouragement. I remember thinking, *Hey, if they don't mind sharing, who am I to complain?*

I couldn't replicate the night exactly since I didn't want to risk being discovered having sex at the lake. But I also didn't want Reggie around while I had sex with two hookers, so I had told him I needed to be alone as I tried to remember what happened.

Instead of correcting his mistaken assumption about that night, I tell him, "And she's Hutch's sister."

"Yo, what the fuck!"

I've blown his mind so I wait for him to process the bombshell.

"What were you thinking, man? Your teammate's sister?" he asks.

"I didn't know when I...met her. She and the baby are why I need to stop Victor."

"Right. Well, I'm telling you, brother, let me have someone take care of him for you," he offers again. "Hutch can be your alibi. By the way, how did he react when you told him the news?"

"He doesn't know." I don't give him time to process my words this time. "Reg, listen to me carefully. He can't know. Not about me and Charlie. Not about the baby. No one can. I don't want Victor to find out. Got it?"

"Yeah, boss. I got it." His forceful sigh lets me know he's not happy about it.

"Please, just talk to Gabe about Victor and make sure he knows to keep my name out of it."

"A'ight." Another loud sigh. "I'm on it. But I think you let that mofo get away with this shit for way too long. It shouldn't even have started in the first place."

Hanging up, I drop into bed, knowing another long, grueling day lies ahead tomorrow. But sleep won't come. I put one arm under my head and lay staring up at the ceiling, my thoughts unavoidably wandering back to the night of my mother's death.

I must have fallen asleep, because I wake up just before dawn, bathed in sweat and gasping for air, my heart galloping. After a moment, I get my bearings and realize I'm in a hotel room at training camp and not in a fiery ravine. I sit on the edge of my bed, breathing deeply until my pulse settles, then drag myself out of bed and to the bathroom, feeling as sore as I did that night. I wash my face and drink some water before heading back to bed.

Knowing sleep will be elusive, I settle against the headboard and close my eyes, but I can still see wisps of the dream. Nightmare. Or is it a memory that I've repressed, one that's causing the retrograde amnesia? After all these years, I still don't know, no matter how hard I try to remember.

The last thing I recall before the accident is being at the lake, and the first thing after it is waking up in blinding pain, with the sound of Daphne's screams competing with the crackling of fire. I'll never forget the sound of her screams for as long as I live.

Or the sight of my mother, looking like a bloodied and broken ragdoll as she lay on the wrong side of the windshield, several yards away.

Daphne's screams and the image of my mother are what wake me up when I have the nightmare.

When the sheriff asked for my statement later that night, I'd realized I had no memory of the crash. For some reason, Victor was there that night and witnessed what had happened. It had been about three years since I'd last seen him. He'd told the sheriff he'd seen my mother intentionally drive off the edge of the road, just as she'd threatened to do after she almost ran over him and drove away.

But in private, he'd told me a different story, telling me *I* had actually been the one driving, and he'd lied to the sheriff to protect me.

And he's been holding it over my head ever since.

I don't know what the truth is. The recurring dream only adds to my confusion. Maybe I should call that psychologist that Joey mentioned and try the hypnosis thing, even though I doubt it will work.

The beginning of football season is probably not a great time to start therapy, but I'm desperate enough to ask Joey the next day for the number of the psychologist she'd mentioned.

When she texts me the information, I force myself to call Dr. Vandermeyer's office and leave a message asking for an appointment. Feeling better about the future for the first time in years, I video call Daphne.

"Hi, DeeDee. How are you, darling?" I ask when she answers.

"Hi, Luc."

My heart warms at hearing her shy voice and seeing her sweet face, even as guilt consumes me at seeing the scars that mar one side of her face.

Despite my efforts to avoid joy, having Daphne in my life, even with the physical distance between us, brings me immense happiness. She's the spitting image of my mother, in looks and character. She's turning into a little beauty despite the scars that are still visible. And she's a sweet, kind girl with the voice of an angel that no one else hears except for the few adults close to her.

Though our calls and visits are warm and loving, the infant whose diapers I changed and the toddler I tickled and read books to is, in some ways, a stranger due to the distance I had to keep between us.

After a few moments of patiently drawing her out, I listen as Daphne tells me about what she's been up to since we last spoke a week ago. At twelve, she should have a dozen friends her age that she could talk to. Instead, the closest people in her life besides me are her tutors and my aunt and uncle, who became her adopted parents after the accident.

She has been sheltered due to her physical and emotional trauma. She's been through so much in her young life that no one who loves her has the heart to force her outside of her social comfort zone. Homeschooling had been the only option while she'd been going through surgeries when she was of age to start school. It made her more introverted, and she refused to attend a regular school when she was older. She's been practically a hermit her whole life. I sometimes question my decision to further isolate her by hiding her away in rural Mississippi, but I felt it was best to keep her out of Victor's reach.

I only visit her a few times a year, taking extra precautions to make sure my trips are private and away from the eyes of the prying media—and Victor.

After hanging up with Daphne, I pick up the playbook to learn the latest plays, but my mind turns to the baby and how different his life will be from Daphne's. I wonder how she'll react when I tell her I'm going to be a father.

My thoughts continue to wander. What will the baby be like as he or she grows up? Will he be shy like Daphne or bold like Charlie? Will she have my curly hair and darker skin tone or be fair like her mother?

My thoughts inevitably turn to Charlie as I recall the softness of her creamy skin, the taste of her mouth, the feel of her clenched around me...

Feeling my sexual frustration grow along with my erection, I can't help but hope that the hypnotherapy will help me learn the truth about the night my mother died. If it can release me from the guilt, perhaps I can release myself from the vows I took to punish myself. And I can finally put a stop to Victor and move on with my life.

14

Charlie

I HAVEN'T HEARD FROM Luc since I confirmed the pregnancy a few days ago, but I did receive my STI lab results. Considering his reputation, I'm surprised to learn everything came back negative, thank god.

Training camp is over so he's no longer staying at the hotel. I tell myself not to take his silence personally since he's been busy preparing for the first preseason game.

Rather than dwelling on why a guy isn't calling me, something I never did even in high school, I put what energy I have into work. And right now, that means finishing the background interviews for Luc's segment.

At Mark's insistence, I've already spent a couple of days in Fontaine, getting several people from his high school days to talk about what Luc was like as a boy and what they think of his accomplishments. I also tracked down some of his more successful teammates to do the same.

The picture that's emerged is of a responsible and hard-working young man who loved football, fun, and his mother, not in that order. Everyone knew he was going to go far, but most were surprised at just how far.

One teammate commented, "I think what happened to his mama forced him to put all that emotion and attention to football when he went to college. In a tragic way, it's losing her that made him as successful as he is, but he'd give it all up to have her back instead. He loved his mama more than anything in the world, even football. That's just who he was."

It was hard to remain professional when I had a lump in my throat. I swallowed it down to ask, "And what about the little girl that was in the car accident with them? How are they are related?"

"Oh man. I forgot about her. His cousin, I think. Although..."

When he looks away, I know there's something more. "Although...?"

He shakes his head. "Nothing. It was just a rumor."

"Please, I'd like to hear it. I won't use it unless I verify whatever you tell me."

Despite his obvious discomfort, he answers. "Well, the way he loved that little girl, some people were saying he might have been her daddy...that he got a girl pregnant when he went to visit his aunt in Mississippi."

Could the rumor be true? Is this why Luc never mentioned her? Was she one of the secrets he was hiding? But why hide her? Where is she now? Who is the mother?

So many questions, but when I asked his former teammate a follow-up question, he'd just shrugged and said he didn't know what happened to the toddler. "She was taken to the hospital in the city and never came back. Saint left for college right after his mama's funeral."

Holy crap. No wonder Luc hadn't wanted me to go digging into his past. Why had no other journalist? Maybe his legal threats stopped them, and they were satisfied with what he gave them? They could still cover the human-interest angles from talking to current players and about his charity work, including an organization that helped pay for children's medical expenses. Did he choose that charity because of the girl who is—was?—somehow related to him?

I was still reeling from that interview when I knocked on the door of the closest neighbor. No one had been home when I'd gone there on the Fourth. The elderly woman who was home this time was more than willing to talk.

"Angeline kep' to herself when she moved here with Lucien. Wouldn't tell nobody who the daddy was. Well, I guess we found out at her funeral when that good-lookin' football player showed up, acting all concerned about the boy. 'Fore that, he'd sneak in and out of town every now 'n then. Said it was Angeline that wanted to keep quiet 'bout it so as not to put Luc in the public eye, but I say hogwash. I bet it was 'cuz he was married."

When I asked about the rumor supplied by the former teammate, the neighbor replied, "I s'pose I can see how people might talk since Angeline goes to Mississippi one summer and comes home with a baby, saying it's her niece. Hogwash, I tell ya. I bet that good-for-nothing football player got her pregnant on his rare visits and she was too ashamed for people to know 'bout it."

I don't know what to think about everything I learned. What's true and what's purely speculation?

I'd love to ask Luc about it, but I'm afraid of his reaction, seeing as he asked I not do these interviews in the first place. Perhaps Victor can clear some things up. He's my last interview before I fly back home, though I may need to extend my trip to follow some of these new crumbs.

I shake hands with Luc's father when he arrives at the hotel room in Las Vegas. It's just me, a local camera operator, and a sound technician. I'm conducting the interview without Tom, since I plan to use only soundbites to weave together the story of Luc's childhood.

"Thank you for doing this interview, Mr. Miller."

He smiles and holds onto my hand. "Of course. I wish more of my interviews were with a beautiful young woman like you." His charm is a part of his personality that came across clearly even in the photos and videos I've seen of him. And there's no doubt the man is handsome, as the neighbor said. I'm happy to note there's very little resemblance to Luc other than height and their eye color.

I pull my hand away to gesture to the chair where he should sit, maintaining a polite smile despite the phony vibe I'm getting from him. It doesn't help when he runs his eyes—so much like Luc's—over my body with an expression that clearly says he finds it lacking. I brush it off since his opinion means nothing to me.

I normally start interviews with softball questions, most of which are just to help the person become used to talking on camera.

With Victor, I start with his background. From everything I've learned about him so far, I figure he'd like it if he thought this was more about him than his son. As expected, he's happy to talk about himself, at least as it relates to football—anything else about his younger days seems to be off the table. Something father and son have in common.

I move on to his relationship with Luc and how he feels about his son's success, but it's still all about Victor. It quickly becomes nauseating to continually hear self-aggrandizing remarks.

"He gets all that talent from me. It's in the genes."

"I was teaching him about football while he was still in the womb."

"The first toy I got him was a stuffed football that I taught him to toss to me."

With every word that comes out of Victor's mouth, I have a clearer picture of what he was like as a father. He never uses words like "proud" or "talented" or anything positive unless he can tie it back to himself somehow.

Fuck it. I have to ask a question that's not on my list.

"So Mr. Miller, do you acknowledge that you are in fact Lucien Saint's father?"

He laughs, probably waiting for me to say "just joking," but I wait in unsmiling silence for his response.

"Of course I do. What kind of question is that?"

He laughs again, but his clenched fists indicate he's not laughing on the inside.

I'm not laughing at all. I continue, still in my hard-hitting *60 Minutes* reporter persona. "But you didn't claim him as your son until he was eighteen. Why wait so long?"

"Angie wanted it that way to protect Luc. As a well-known celebrity athlete, I attracted a lot of attention, and she wanted to keep him out of the public eye."

"I understand you were in Fontaine when the accident occurred. Can you tell me what happened?"

"You can find all that in the police report. Is that really what you want to talk about?"

"Police reports can't speak on camera, Mr. Miller." I smile and soften my tone, now that I've gotten under his skin. "Our viewers would much rather hear directly from you how traumatizing that experience must have been."

He settles back, satisfied with my more deferential tone.

"Yeah, it was very traumatizing. I'm just thankful I was there to call for help. Otherwise, I'm not sure Luc would have made it."

"Why were you there? Did you often visit Luc?"

He narrows his eyes at me, probably because I sound like a prosecutor questioning a defendant. I can't help it. There's just something about him that gives me bad vibes.

Perhaps Angeline did use the public eye thing as an excuse to keep Victor away. I would have had I been in her shoes.

I force a smile. "Just trying to set the scene."

"Right. Well, my boy had just turned eighteen, and I figured it was time to claim him as my own. He was old enough to learn how to be in the public eye, seeing as he was going to be in it when he started playing ball."

If this was a hard news show, I would have clapped back at Victor that he had been out of the public eye for years before Luc turned eighteen. No NFL team wanted to sign him due to his overly aggressive plays and history of injuring other players. Luc would have been five or six at most when Victor played his last pro game, leaving plenty of years to show up for your kid away from the media, especially in a rural town like Fontaine.

"Did Luc know you were coming? What was his reaction when he saw you?"

"I wanted to surprise him, but when I got there, he wasn't home. Angie was acting a little crazy so I left, telling her I'd come back later."

"Angeline was acting crazy? In what way?"

He shrugs, his gaze flitting around the room before coming back to me.

"Yelling, throwing stuff around."

"She was yelling at *you*? Throwing things *at* you?"

"Yeah, I guess."

"Why? Did you two have an argument?"

"Nope, no argument. At least not from me. I mean, she wasn't too happy that I'd married my wife, God rest her soul, before I found out Angie was having Luc. So she was always a bit testy when I visited my boy."

I remind myself I'm not a hard-hitting investigative journalist or a prosecutor. I need to move on, though I'm dying to keep pushing for the details and then match them up with the police report I'd already read. But I need to talk about the crash itself before he gets fed up.

"I understand. What happened when you returned?"

"When I pulled up, she was running out of the house, still acting crazy. She jumped into her car and Luc came out, telling her to stop. She started reversing the car without looking and hit my car. I got out, but she went forward to make a U-turn. Luc jumped into the car, trying to stop her, but she kept going. I ran in front of the car, waving my arms, hoping she'd stop."

He shakes his head and gives me a self-deprecating smile. "Someone said it was a brave thing I did, but I was just going on instinct. Looking back, it wasn't the smartest thing I've ever done. I mean, she just came at me full speed. When I realized she wasn't going to stop, I tried to get out of the way, but she clipped me good."

"Were you injured?"

"Oh yeah. A couple of fractured ribs and bruises all over. And hit this noggin pretty good when I landed." He knocks his knuckles against the side of his head and grimaces.

Giving him my best sympathetic expression, I continue. "So you didn't see the car crash?"

"No, I didn't see it," he says with regret. "When I came to, it took me a minute to get up and into my car. I called 9-1-1 and drove down the road until I saw the flipped-over car, on fire. I tried to run to it, but I could barely breathe because of my ribs. By the time I got to them, help had come."

"What happened to the little girl?"

"Little girl?" His whole body freezes as he realizes he'd forgotten to include Daphne in the story he was spinning. I'd already noted a couple of details that were different from his statement, not that it mattered, since anyone would say that memories can be fuzzy after ten years.

"Yes. A young girl, a toddler, named Daphne Deveraux is mentioned in the report. Can you tell me who that is?" I don't mention the neighbor's belief that he is the girl's father. The more time I spend with Victor, the more I understand why Angeline wouldn't have told him if that's true.

He scratches his chin. "Daphne Deveraux? I have no idea." Then his eyes clear. "Oh, you mean the br—uh—kid that Angie was babysitting?"

Babysitting? Angeline was definitely hiding Daphne from Victor. I nod. "Yes. Were they related?"

His eyes squint as he tries to remember. "I never saw the kid before so I don't know. All I remember now is how she was hanging onto Angie and crying. I could hardly hear myself think with all the noise she was making."

Callous bastard. Poor little thing was probably scared if there was yelling and things being thrown.

"Do you know what happened to her after the accident?"

"Honestly, I don't know. I was focused on Luc." He holds his palms up. "Sorry. Like you said, it was traumatic, and I try not to think about that night."

"Yes, I'm sure. Thank you for talking about that painful experience." I pivot to the topic of what he's doing currently and his future plans, only half listening to something about a big business deal.

Ending the interview, I thank him for his time. I take the memory cards from the cameras, thank my small crew, and return to the airport; I'm going to Mississippi to try to track down factual information from more reliable sources.

Over the next few days, I perform endless searches for articles in local newspapers and put together the tidbits I learned. I contact people mentioned in the stories and pull as much information from them as I can, which finally leads me to some of the answers I've been looking for.

15

Charlie

WHILE I'VE BEEN WORKING nonstop, I don't hear a word from Luc. My patience and my empathy for his busy schedule fly out the window when I scroll through social media and see photos of him with a woman. A woman whose ass he has his hand on while the other is tangled in her hair as they lock lips. I keep scrolling only to see a video posted by another player, talking about the Firebirds' first preseason win. He's panning the camera as he talks, at one point calling out a farewell to Luc who's leaving with the same woman, his arm on her hip as she kisses his neck.

I go down a rabbit hole, looking for more photos and mentions of Luc that don't pertain to football. My digging results in several photos of him with different women since our night in his hometown and one more of him since I called him to confirm the pregnancy. And these are just his hookups that are public.

Bastard.

I've never experienced jealousy in my life, and I refuse to acknowledge the emotion now. No, it's not jealousy or hurt. It's anger at being manipulated. Here I am, giving him the benefit of the doubt and believing his bullshit about not telling anyone he's the father, forcing me to keep secrets from my family. Now I know why. He'd look like an asshole for getting a woman pregnant and then continuing to fuck others.

My mood is as low as the lighting in the editing bay I sit in with Dave, my editor. I go through my logs for the approximate timestamps of noteworthy soundbites while he scrubs through the recordings to clip and place them for me in the video time-line.

I add in some of Victor's interview where we discuss a recent article that portrayed Luc as the ideal of America's melting pot. Where Angeline's ancestry consisted of Haitian Creole, French, and Scottish blood, Victor's was Mexican and a mix of several Eastern European countries. But he brushed off his Latino heritage saying, "My mother's family has been in Texas for generations. I think we can consider that part of my American heritage at this point."

Focusing on the clip Dave had cued up, I have a hard time holding back a snort when I hear again Victor's claim to have passed down his football prowess to his superstar son.

"Guy's a sleazy schmuck," Dave says. "He never threw a ball in the five years he was in the game. He was a freakin' linebacker who played dirty."

Dave's words echo my research. Victor paid out tens of thousands in fines due to dirty hits almost every year and was even sued by one of his own teammates for ending his career due to an injury caused during a practice. Who does that?

"His only positive claim to fame," Dave continues, his lip curled in disgust, "is recovering a fumbled ball in the last few seconds of a Super Bowl, allowing his team to win. And he only got it because he was knocked down and fell on the ball."

"Yes, he does seem to be holding on to his glory days." Afraid Dave's criticisms are going to escalate into a full-on rant, I direct him back to the work at hand. "Let's just stick to the part where he talks about how proud he is of Luc's success."

"Gonna be hard to find a sentence that doesn't include himself," Dave retorts, but turns back to his monitors.

When I come in to work the next morning, there's a message from Mark asking to see me right away. *Shit.*

I knock on my boss's open office door to grab his attention. "You wanted to see me?"

He waves me in but doesn't ask me to sit. "What's with Saint's segment? I thought you were going to look deeper into his background."

My hands become clammy with stress. "I did. His segment has more personal stuff than any of the other pieces I've done."

"But there's nothing in there that justifies the legal document he sent us. There has to be more."

I hesitate for a split second too long to verbalize a denial. Mark jumps on it.

"There is something. What is it?"

"I'm sorry, Mark, I don't feel comfortable adding in anything more than I already have."

"It doesn't matter what you're comfortable with, sweetheart."

Ugh, I hate when he uses nicknames and endearments, but this one is without its usual peppy "good job for a girl" undertones. This time, it's overtly condescending.

"That's not your call to make," he continues, his gaze unyielding. "You've spent a lot of time and the station's money traveling for this piece. There needs to be something to show for it."

A drop of sweat runs down my back. I'm about to be fired. I'm sure of it.

"Now tell me what you found out," he demands.

I stare at him, unsure of what to do. This job doesn't pay a lot, but it's my only source of income—and health insurance, which I'll be needing more than ever. And if Mark fires me, I doubt I'll be able to use him as a reference for another job. I don't want to be dependent on my family or Luc for years while I raise a child as a single mother.

Filled with trepidation, I tell Mark about Luc's financial support of Daphne Deveraux and her medical care, and her adoption by Luc's maternal aunt.

"Adopted? Why? Who are the biological parents? What happened to them?" he asks in rapid fire succession. "And what's the relationship between Saint and this girl?"

"There's no information on the father, but the mo—"

"Are you sure Luc's not the father?" Mark's eyes light up at the possibility.

"What? No. I mean, yes, I'm sure." Never mind that the thought crossed my mind and, according to his former teammate, several others'. Even if it's a possibility, I don't want Mark going down that road. He'd sensationalize it for ratings, and that's not something I could live with. I don't work for a gossip show. "Neighbors have said she's Angeline's daughter."

"That's not proof." He waves off my comment, still lost in thought.

He's right, but the law prevents me from accessing Daphne's birth certificate or adoption records. Corroboration by multiple neighbors who saw a pregnant Angeline at the time is the only proof I have.

I try again. "Mark, I don't think we should put any of this into the segment. At least, not until we give Luc—Saint—an opportunity to comment."

"He had the opportunity to talk about it. If we give him a heads-up, he might find a way to stop the piece altogether. We'll use what you've found. I don't see what the big deal is anyway. We're not saying anything negative. It's human interest, and it makes him even more likeable."

He finally seems to see my distress and says impatiently, "Look, if you can't finish the piece, hand over everything over to me. I'll give it to another producer to finish, and we can talk about whether being a producer is the right career for you."

I'm torn. Do I refuse to do as asked and risk getting fired, or do I finish the segment in a way that protects Luc and Daphne as much as possible?

Mark answers his phone and waves me off, not waiting for my answer. I agree what I found doesn't appear to be a big deal. In fact, it would help to soften Luc's playboy image by showing what a caring person he is. He's been supporting Daphne and his aunt and uncle since his first NFL paycheck. He'd paid for her expensive reconstructive surgeries and even founded—not just supported, I discovered—a charity to cover children's medical expenses.

But even though I have yet to find out why, I'm pretty sure revealing information about Daphne is going to be a big deal to Luc.

Keeping that in mind, I work with Tom to script and record his voiceover and with Dave again to lay it down over the video. I try not to feel guilty as I do my job, which is to create content that will attract more viewers. If I didn't have the personal connection with Luc, would I think twice about it? Recalling how Luc begged me in that tortured voice, I'm pretty sure I'd still have issues with going against his wishes.

I decide to look at Brent's segment to see how the producer handled his—our—tragic past.

"Let's stop here for now," I tell Dave. It's already well past quitting time. "We'll finish the rest tomorrow. Thanks for staying late."

"No problem, Charlie. This is a great piece. And I like working with you."

I appreciate the compliment and ignore the underlying tone. I'm too tired to wonder if there is more to the look he gives me before heading out. Being too busy and too tired have prevented me from pursuing a relationship since I started this job.

I pull up Brent's episode that the other producer has finished and loaded to the server. I've already gone through the interview he and Luc did together to pull out what I wanted. Not wanting to remind everyone at work that Brent is my brother, I'd stayed away when he was being interviewed.

The producer did a good job with the episode, covering Brent's career, his playboy lifestyle, and our personal family tragedy. It's not something he or any of us like to talk about, but he didn't hide it from the producer or threaten to sue the company if she included it. The only information not included is his relationship to Joey, which he's hiding because they work together.

I text him.

ME: *Hey. Got a minute?*

It's a couple of minutes before Brent responds.

BRENT: *Not really. What's up?*

ME: *Can you call me?*

The phone rings a few seconds later. "I'm a little busy here, Charlie," he says, annoyed, when I pick up.

"If Joey's right there, I don't want to know what you're so busy with."

That makes him laugh. "Okay, I won't tell you."

"Shut up. Is Joey really there? I need to ask you something."

"She went back to the kitchen, so thanks."

"The kitchen? You sound like a caveman, dude."

"Just ask whatever it is you need to ask me."

"Fine. Once Joey is done filling in at the Firebirds, are you guys going to make your relationship public?"

"What are you talking about?"

I scoff at his pretense of ignorance. "You're an idiot if you think I don't know about you two."

"Jesus, are there no secrets in this family? First Mom, now you."

"I haven't talked to Mom about it. And Joey's barely told me anything. But that's my question, Brent. Why are you keeping it a secret, at least from family?" I wince at my hypocrisy.

He sighs. "Well, obviously because of the job. But I also didn't want any of you on my ass if—when—if...this doesn't work out."

I wonder at his floundering. Is he not sure he wants it to end? Or does he not want to admit to me that he plans to end it eventually, thereby hurting my friend?

"And because," he continues before I can ask him to clarify, "I never want her to feel like she can't be around our family after. Our family is her family."

Okay, that is not what I was expecting him to say.

"Aww. You are such a good man, Brent. I love you."

"Love you too, Barbie. Now fuck off so I can get back to Joey."

He hangs up before I can yell at him for using the childhood nickname.

My smile falls away as Brent's words cement my growing belief that Luc is also motivated by his need to protect Daphne and possibly himself.

My growling stomach reminds me I missed lunch, except for a couple of caramel candies I found in my desk drawer. It's well past dinnertime and I'm hungry when I reach home, but I have no desire to eat, the nausea somehow worse on an empty stomach. However, for the sake of the baby, I force myself to heat up some of the casserole Mom left in the fridge for me.

"Please tell me you already ate dinner at work, honey, and this is just a snack."

I turn when my mother enters the kitchen and heads toward the stove and the old tea kettle that's been a fixture there for as long as I can remember.

I grimace but force another bite. "I lost track of time," I admit, preparing myself for a lecture.

Thankfully, she just shakes her head and sighs, saying only, "You need to eat."

"I know. It's just really busy right now with the NFL season starting, the US Open Tennis Championships coming up and—"

"Sweetheart, there's always going to be something at work." She brings two mugs of steaming tea to the table, setting one next to my plate before sitting beside me. Hints of lavender and chamomile waft up, the familiar scent soothing me more than the actual tea.

"Tell me what's really on your mind, honey."

I pick up the tea to avoid looking at my mother while I determine how I can gain her wise counsel without giving away too much. She waits, full of patience as always. Finally meeting her concerned gaze, I say, "I'm interviewing someone who's asked me not to include certain aspects of their personal life, but my boss is adamant that I do. Despite the player's threats to sue the studio."

"Do you have much say in the matter if your boss has already made the decision?"

"No. In fact, he said he'd give it to another producer to finish it if I don't. But I'm not sure I should have dug that deep when he, the interviewee, asked me not to."

"Why did you then?"

"Because it's my job?" The guilt of lying by omission makes me defensive.

"Then what's the problem?"

I shrug. "I feel like I should warn him."

"And if you do, all the hours you've put in, all the money the company has spent, is for nothing if he prevents it from being aired."

"Exactly."

After a quiet moment while she takes a sip of tea, she asks, "Is it something that the public needs to know, something criminal or unethical?"

"Not that I can see."

"Why do you think this person doesn't want it part of the episode?"

"He didn't say."

"So why is it necessary to include it?"

I shrug. "Honestly, Mom, I think it's for ratings. It's information that's never been revealed. They're already putting together promotional teasers hyping the episode." I'm glad that's not my job anymore. I never liked making them, having to create sensationalism, even where there was none, to lure viewers.

"Hm. Well, that is the studio's mission. Without the viewers, there's no money. No money, no jobs. And if they're willing to risk the legal threats, it must be worth it to them."

"You're not helping here," I whine. "What should I do?"

She pats my hand. "I haven't told you kids what to do for a while now. All I can advise is to examine the character of the person and follow your own gut. That's assuming that you even have a say in what happens at this point."

I finally fall into bed, expecting to drop into sleep right away. Instead, my thoughts go to Luc, and my conscience wars with the image of him kissing some random woman.

My anger rises once more, as does a sense of betrayal. Why did he extract a promise of secrecy and then continue to ignore me for weeks? Doesn't he care that I'd find out he's sleeping with other women?

Don't be stupid, I chide myself. *He doesn't owe you anything.* There is nothing more between us than a quick fuck and an accidental pregnancy.

Which means I don't owe him anything, either.

My conclusion doesn't bring me any relief from the guilt I've been feeling since working on editing Luc's segment.

Probably because I'm not following my mother's advice.

16

Luc

"WE'VE BEEN DIGGING PRETTY deep," Gabe says, sliding a folder across his desk in his midtown office. When I reach for it, he presses down on it with his fingertips so I can't pull it away.

"The stuff in here is intense," he cautions. "Are you sure you want to delve into all this now? We can wait, continue to collect more information, and go over everything when the season ends. It's only a few months."

I tug on the folder, silently demanding he release it. I've put up with Victor long enough, and I don't want to wait another second to see if I can kick the man out of my life for good. He's called a few times already, leaving messages asking when I'm sending the money.

Gabe sighs and takes his hand away. I take the folder, but before I can open it, he says, "You can read it all later, but I'll give you the highlights. My investigators were discreet, but it wasn't hard to find people who had a lot to say about Victor—and none of it good. We started with his recent activities, but each time we found something, it forced us to keep going back further because one thing led to another."

"What is it? Spit it out. I can handle it," I prompt when Gabe hesitates.

"Okay. You probably know that your grandparents, your mother's parents, were killed."

"Yeah, when they came home while their house was being robbed."

Gabe just cocks an eyebrow while I wait for him to continue. When he doesn't, I lean forward in my chair. "Wait. Are you trying to say it wasn't random? That Victor had something to do with it?"

"No one was ever arrested for the crime, and the investigation went cold. There's still no evidence, only a few suspicious dots based on conjecture."

Victor is an asshole, but I'm not sure I want to believe my father is capable of that kind of evil. What would that say about the DNA I carry?

"Keep going."

"A source said your mother tried to have Victor looked at as a suspect, but no one took her seriously. And Victor had an alibi."

Before I can process that bit of information, Gabe continues.

"Now, going back even further, you already know he married his wealthy wife just before you were born. They married against her father's wishes, according to one of her friends. The father threatened annulment, but she got pregnant. Unfortunately, she miscarried and they never had any kids. The father changed his will so that Margaret was technically cut out of it. He set it up so that she'd receive a certain amount each year. This prevented her from naming Victor as her beneficiary."

"Sounds like he didn't trust Victor with the money," I note.

"Or that he didn't trust him not to hurt his daughter to get his hands on her inheritance."

Okay, that fits better with what I know, firsthand, of Victor's character when it comes to money, and why I've instinctively protected Daphne since the beginning. I stand and pace in front of Gabe's desk, unable to sit still while my mind spins.

Gabe stays silent this time, allowing me a moment to take in what he's told me so far. When I stop and meet his eyes, he arches a brow. "Ready to hear the rest?"

"Yes, go on."

"Unfortunately, there are more suspicious dots. Margaret's father died when his gun accidentally went off while he was cleaning it. An investigation resulted in no evidence of tampering."

What Gabe leaves unsaid is that it doesn't mean there wasn't any.

"After her father died," he continues, "Margaret threatened divorce because she, correctly, suspected Victor of cheating, but the threat sent him running back to her side. Without his NFL salary, he didn't have much and needed her to support him. He must have been some charmer, because she took him back."

Gabe shakes his head. I can't tell if his look of disgust is for Victor's actions or Margaret's forgiveness.

"Yeah, shit just seems to roll off him," I say, resuming my pacing.

"Unfortunately for Margaret, she died from cancer a few years later, right around the time you graduated high school. Her brother-in-law was running the family business by then, but Victor forced his way into some of the decisions, which turned out to be bad ones. There were whispers of embezzlement, but the person who spoke to us thought the board decided not to prosecute since it would damage the company's reputation if it became public. Victor tried suing the family for a stake in the company. They gave him some to make him go away, after signing a document promising not to ask for more."

I stop at this piece of news. Was it that easy? Why didn't I think of that?

Gabe concludes, "Of course he tried again, but didn't make it very far. The company is doing fine now that his hands are out of it. But we weren't able to find any meaningful source of income once he ran out of the life insurance money and whatever the family gave him. By then, his cachet as an NFL player was nonexistent so he couldn't use that to trade for endorsements or TV gigs. He's been living mostly off gambling money if he wins or women he can charm. And the money you've been giving him." He raises an eyebrow and asks, "Anything you want to tell me about that? The amount you give him goes beyond familial duty. And it goes up every year."

I hesitate to respond, not ready to admit it's more blackmail than duty. It's partly pride, not wanting anyone to know I've given in to Victor's threats. But mostly it's fear of what he'll do and the consequences.

"Luc, it would help if you told us everything."

"I've told you everything that matters."

His raised eyebrows tell me he's not buying it. I ignore him and go to the window to stare down at the streets, congested with rush-hour traffic.

"Right," Gabe says, letting me off the hook. "Well, despite all the money you've given him, he's up to his eyeballs in debt. Seems he's trying to raise a pile of money for a business venture and using gambling as a means to acquire it. Not only did he lose the million you recently gave him, he borrowed more."

"Do you know how much he owes?" I ask.

"Over two million."

Over? Has he gotten into more debt since he called me? Pride keeps me from telling Gabe about Victor's latest demand. "How the hell did anyone let him borrow that much?"

"Victor likes to pretend he's still the football star, yet he uses your celebrity as collateral when he's gambling at the high-stakes tables. He's been throwing your name around and borrowing quite a bit from unsavory types."

"So much for learning his lesson. Fucking idiot. You'd think he'd stop gambling or get help for his addiction, considering how bad he is at it." I blow out my breath in frustration. "Okay. Is that it?"

Gabe shakes his head. "Sorry, no. One more thing. He's using. Some of that money is going up his nose, likely contributing to his debt."

"And his tendency to lose. Shit. Okay. Please tell me that's it."

"That's it, except for whatever it is you're not telling me."

Despite Gabe knowing everything about my father, it's still hard to admit just what a fucking piece of shit he is. I take a deep breath and let it out.

"He's been low-key blackmailing me." I have to pause before I admit, "It's getting a little more in my face."

"Blackmailing? About what?"

I force myself to face Gabe before admitting, "I was driving the car that killed my mother."

He straightens abruptly in his chair.

"What bullshit is this? I've read the police reports. Your mother was driving."

I shake my head. "That's what Victor told the police."

"And why would he do that if it wasn't the truth?"

"To protect me. My future."

"I'm not following."

"My future in football," I explain. "If I was arrested, it might have impacted my chance to make it to the NFL."

"That seems uncharacteristically unselfish of him."

I smile without humor at Gabe's sarcasm.

"Blackmail is more his style," he continues. "What is he threatening?"

I'm able to sit back down now that it's all out in the open. "He preyed on my guilt in the beginning, but now he's threatening to go public, saying I killed my mother."

Gabe's eyes narrow and he leans forward in his chair.

"I call bullshit," he says, his tone harsh with anger. "He can't go public without putting himself at risk. He'd be an accomplice after the fact, not to mention facing charges of obstruction in all sorts of ways. You're not the one who lied since you couldn't remember."

"But I could still be charged. There's no statute of limitations on vehicular manslaughter. An ambitious prosecutor could accuse *me* of lying about my memory. It doesn't matter so much financially if I go to jail now, but I needed the football contract and the money back then. For Daphne. I couldn't risk anything happening to me until I knew she was taken care of. At least Victor still doesn't know about her."

"How does he not know about her?"

"He wasn't around when she was born, and it seems my mother told him she was just babysitting that night. I had my aunt take Daphne away and legally adopt her. Victor never bothered to check into it. She wasn't important to him. Then. But I was always afraid if he found out about her, he might find ways to cash in somehow. Now, after all the stuff you've just told me about him, I'm afraid of what else he may do."

"You were right to keep her off his radar." Gabe stares off into space for a moment then focuses on me again. "Okay, here's what we're going to do. We'll put eyes on him. Not just to make sure he stays away from Daphne, but also to see if we can catch him doing something that can get him locked up for a while."

I take the folder from Gabe's desk when I leave but don't look at it while Reggie drives me home. Sensing my need for silence, Reggie keeps his usual commentary on idiot drivers to himself. I ignore his occasional looks of concern in the mirror, staring out at the gridlocked traffic as we head downtown past Times Square and Penn Station.

I consider everything Gabe said, especially his point that Victor can't expose the fact I was driving without risking himself. It solidifies my decision to do what I can to remember what really happened the night of the accident. It could be the key to not only easing my guilt, but also stopping Victor from harming anyone else. If I can evict him from my life, I can see Daphne and Charlie without worrying about their safety.

How I'd love to see Charlie again. I've only interacted with her a few times, but they were almost all life-altering interactions. I hardly know her, yet she feels like an integral part of me, and I have this urge to see her again. Can you miss someone you barely know?

17

Charlie

"**Y**OU LOOK LIKE HELL," Stevie says when I walk into the kitchen, dressed for work. She recently returned from a month-long road trip through New England and will soon be getting back on the road, to the Midwest this time.

I'm not a morning person to begin with, and my sister's comment raises my crankiness another notch. The NFL segments are done and waiting to be aired, but that means we're finishing up the tennis players and getting ready to move on to hockey and basketball. Another late night working, combined with morning sickness, adds to my foul mood, causing my next words to come out before my brain can catch up and stop them. "Thanks, sis. We can't all take off and travel indefinitely."

I see the hurt in Stevie's eyes before she turns her back to me. I kick myself and go over to hug her rigid body from behind. "I'm sorry, honey. I didn't mean that. I'm just tired and being bitchy."

Stevie shrugs. "Well, you're just doing what comes naturally...bitch." She turns as I release her and gives a small smile.

I feel horrible. Stevie was always closer to Georgie when we were younger, having more in common with my twin sister than I did, but I love both of them. And I know the sacrifices my older sister made when she was still a child herself, and I truly appreciate her for it.

She bore the brunt of the day-to-day family responsibilities when Bobbie was born just months after the death of our father and brother. Mom was busy with the baby, who'd needed round-the-clock care due to her congenital heart defect and subsequent surgeries.

A few years later, Mom suffered a stroke and Stevie lost her chance to go to college. And to top it all off, she had her heart broken around the same time as well.

She deserves to do whatever the hell she wants. The last three years of travel don't come close to making up for the years of her life she'd sacrificed for the family. She could do nothing at all if she chose to, and no one in our family would say a word. Except me, apparently, in a moment of sheer carelessness.

"I am a bitch," I agree, "and you're the best big sister in the whole wide world." I give her another hug, and she playfully pushes me away when I try to plant a big wet kiss on her cheek.

Both of us laughing, we turn to the sound of our mother's uneven steps entering the kitchen.

"What a wonderful way to start the day, seeing my girls getting along," she says, smiling. "You two were always bickering when you were little."

"No, she used to fight with Georgie. I was always trying to be peacekeeper."

"Ha!" I scoff as I pour a cup of coffee from the pot Stevie had made. "Peacekeeper, my ass. Mom, remember when they told me I was adopted and not really Georgie's twin because we didn't look alike?"

Stevie laughs while Mom just smiles as she makes her tea. "We had you convinced too. RJ heard you crying and yelled at me for making you cry."

Mom's smile turns sad at the mention of her eldest child.

"Hey!" I protest. "I was like six or seven when you tried to trick me."

"My point is, it was you who couldn't get along with us. Georgie and I were fine."

"Ugh. I take back what I just said about you being the best big sister." I mock-glare at her.

Stevie smiles, then sobers. "But seriously. Are you okay? You really don't look too good."

I look away from her piercing gaze, so much like Mom's, and focus on taking out a piece of bread and popping it in the toaster, though I probably won't eat more than a bite of it. "I'm fine. Just tired from working all the time." Still avoiding her eyes, I take out a spoon to add sugar to my coffee.

"How far along are you, honey?"

The spoon clatters as I drop it. My head swivels around in shock at my mother's point-blank question. I try to form an innocent expression under my mother's knowing stare. My mouth opens, but I can't form a word.

"What?" Stevie asks into the silence. "You're pregnant?"

"No, of course not." Unable to lie to my mother's face, I turn to Stevie. But even to my ears, my denial sounds pathetically weak.

"Charlotte Jayne."

My shoulders hunch around my ears automatically as they always do when my mother says my name like that. Her stern voice deflates what little resistance I have, and I sigh in defeat. "Okay, yes, I'm pregnant."

"How far along?" she asks again.

"Ten weeks." I'm relieved to finally admit it. I hated hiding it from my mother.

"Ten weeks," she repeats flatly. "When were you going to tell me?"

The disappointment and concern in my mother's voice stabs at my conscience. I really should have told my family sooner but hadn't wanted to deal with the questions that are sure to follow.

Ones that I can't answer, bound as I am by my promise to Luc. I curse him for forcing me to prevaricate.

"I'm sorry, Mom. I wanted to, but it's complicated."

"Life often is. What's so complicated that you can't tell your family something this big?"

I go with the easiest explanation, one that's not a lie. "I don't want Brent to know yet, so please don't tell him. And I'll tell you everything as soon as I can."

Stevie says nothing, appearing shell-shocked. My mother, on the other hand, goes on matter-of-factly. "Alright. Have you gone to the doctor yet?"

I nod. "Yes, and I have another appointment set two weeks from now."

"Taking your vitamins?"

"Yes, but I don't know how much good they're doing since I'm puking them up again."

Mom limps closer and takes my hand. Feeling my mother's unwavering love and support makes my eyes well.

"I remember the morning sickness well. I'll make you some ginger tea. You can have that with saltines instead of coffee, which you should cut back on anyway. And make sure you eat something healthy as soon as the nausea passes. You need to take care of your body so it can take care of the baby. Go sit down."

I kiss my mother's cheek, keeping my lips there for an extra second. "I love you, Mom."

"I love you, too, sweetheart." She pats my cheek then moves away to make the tea. "And just because you're too old for me to ground you, doesn't mean you're off the hook. I still want to know how you got yourself in this predicament because I haven't seen or heard anything about a man since you parted ways with that college boyfriend of yours."

Trying to lighten the mood and avoid answering the question, I tease, "Surely you've heard of Tinder, Mom?"

She narrows her eyes at me. "Not funny, Charlotte. I hope you're joking."

I wipe the smile off my face. "Yes, I'm joking. I met him through work."

I bite my lip, not sure what else I can say, and look at Stevie. "Is he ghosting you?"

I wonder at the edge of bitterness in Stevie's voice, but I don't have the bandwidth to think about that right now. I look down at my hands and shake my head, though I'm not sure. He texted once to ask me how I was feeling, but didn't reply when I told him the date of my next appointment.

I hate keeping secrets from my family. And I need them to help me through this, emotionally. My eyes burn with tears, and I quickly blink them back.

Stevie reaches across the table to clasp my hands. "Oh, honey. Forget him. You don't need him. You have us. And if you decide to—" She breaks off and looks at my mother, who pins her with a look. She turns back to me and continues, "If you decide you're not going to have the baby—"

I pull my hands out of my sister's grip. "Of course I'm having this baby. How could you even think otherwise?"

Stevie flinches. "Check your privilege, Charlie," she says, her voice tight. "Some women have no other option but to think *otherwise*." She pushes back her chair and gets up, walking out without another word. I look after her in bewilderment and turn to my mother, who is also looking in the direction that Stevie has gone. "What was that about?"

Mom shakes her head and says, "Your tea is ready."

I stand and take it from her. She brings her cup, and we sit at the kitchen table.

"Now tell me when you're due and what your plans are."

Happy to finally have confided at least the pregnancy to my mother, I blow on the tea and take a sip before I start talking, leaving out any mention of Luc. And that I slept with him within five minutes of meeting him.

There are some things you can't tell your mother, no matter how grown up you are.

Now that my mother and Stevie are aware of my pregnancy, I have to tell my other sisters and Joey. I'll hold off on telling Brent until the season ends. Hopefully I can hide it from him until then.

It takes three tries before I'm able to reach Georgie.

"Hello, Charlie."

"Georgie, you're alive."

"Why wouldn't I be?"

"Um, because we haven't seen you in forever. Seriously, we've been getting worried. And a little pissed. You missed this year's memorial for Dad and RJ again, and I can't even reach you on the phone anymore."

Family is the most important thing to me, so I don't understand how Georgie could have not made time for the memorial for two years in a row.

"I swear I would have been there if at all possible. I just...I really couldn't. I'm sorry." Georgie's voice is suddenly thick with tears.

I sigh. I have no idea what's going on in her life, though not for lack of trying. She changed after the deaths of Dad and RJ—we all did, but she pulled away whereas I needed my family more than ever. Though we're twins, we're as different as could be. And we definitely don't have twin ESP, though right now, I wish we did.

"Are you okay, honey? What's going on?"

"I'm fine. Everything's fine. It's just Connor's campaign is in full swing, and it's been so stressful for all of us."

Connor, Georgie's husband, is from a prominent family in southern Missouri and running for governor after a short stint as the state attorney general. His father and maternal grandfather have been long-serving politicians in the state, and according to Georgie, he's feeling the pressure from his family.

I don't understand how my sister ended up marrying into an uptight, wealthy, uber-conservative political family. Ours is a working-class family that's more traditional than conservative. She never had any interest in politics or, frankly, anything academic. Her only priority had been dance, which she'd seen as a path to leaving our small hometown for the bright lights of the big city—any big city.

And somehow ended up in the rural Midwest.

"How are you doing, Charlie? How's the job?"

"It's busy. Doing a lot of traveling."

"Dad would have been so proud of you."

"He'd definitely get a kick out of me meeting so many pro athletes. But I think he'd be even more excited to become a grandpa."

Silence greets my news. When Georgie still doesn't say anything, I glance at my cell phone screen to see if the call has been disconnected. Nope, still there.

"Georgie?"

"Yeah, sorry. I'm just...confused."

"I guess I was a little too subtle for you. I'm pregnant, dummy."

"Oh. Wow. Okay. I had no idea you were seeing anyone."

"Hm, I wasn't, but how would you know? We haven't really talked in while. Anyway, it kind of just happened."

"Kind of just happened?" Georgie parrots.

"It's a long story, and I'll tell you if you come visit. I miss you."

"Sure you do," Georgie scoffs.

"Well, I don't want to live under the same roof with you again," I tease. "But I've matured and could stand to be with you for a few days. Or at least a few hours. Hey, maybe I can make a detour if one of my work trips is anywhere near—"

"No!"

I stop, surprised by the vehemence in her voice. "What do you mean, 'no'? Why not?"

"It...it's just not a good time, Charlie. I'm traveling all over the state with Connor. Who knows if I'd even be free if you came? I'd hate for you to make a wasted trip."

Something isn't adding up, and I become suspicious. "What's going on, Georgie?"

"Nothing. I told you, I'm busy. Speaking of, I need to go. I was in the middle of getting ready to leave. Connor's waiting. I'll talk to you later, okay? Love you."

She hangs up before I can say anything else. Concerned, I call Stevie, who left that morning to start her cross-country road trip. I relay the conversation to her.

"Yeah, she's hung up on me like that a couple of times, too, when I pushed to visit her. I've already mapped out my route to see her, whether she likes it or not."

I recognize that tone of voice, developed from years of having to deal with me and Georgie while our mother was busy with Bobbie. It sounds just like our mother's.

"Let me know when you go, and I'll see if I can swing a trip at the same time."

My opportunity to tell Joey my news, which I'd wanted to do in person, comes over Labor Day weekend when she and Brent come home to Connecticut for a friends and family cookout. The two of them pretend they are nothing more than friends in front of everyone else, but have been lax when it's only family. They just can't help with the looks and small touches.

Joey turns the table on me when I ask her about their relationship and instead asks me about my one-night stand. I stop chopping basil and glance out the kitchen window. Mom and

Bobbie are putting tablecloths and paper goods on the tables while Brent preps the grill.

"Okay, don't be mad at me," I warn her, "but I have to tell you something, and you can't tell Brent."

At my serious tone, Joey stops dicing tomatoes.

"Of course I won't."

"I know but...I'm pregnant," I blurt out.

Joey just looks at me as if I've said something in a foreign language. "What?"

"That one-night stand will soon result in a lifetime fixture."

"You're getting married?" she asks in confusion and shock.

"No, Joey!" I lower my voice. "I'm having a baby."

"What?! Charlie!"

"Shh," I caution her, glancing out the window again.

She doesn't say anything, apparently doing math in her head, because she whisper-shouts, "But that means you're almost two months along. How long have you known?"

I sigh and cover her tomato-smeared hand with my basil-stained ones. "Okay, remember I told you not to be mad at me? I couldn't tell you sooner because—well, it's complicated."

She turns her hand over to clasp mine. "How do you feel about this? I mean, I assume you're keeping it."

There's a reason Joey is my best friend. She knows me and understands me better than my sisters.

"I'm not sure it's really hit me yet."

"Does your mom know?"

"She figured it out. I've been puking my guts out every morning before I leave for work."

"Oh, Charlie. I wish I'd known." Joey pauses. "Does the one-night stand know?"

It's my turn to hesitate, but after a moment, I nod.

"Who is it?"

I purse my lips and shake my head. "I'm sorry, I can't tell you. It's—"

"—complicated," Joey finishes with me. "It's a player, isn't it? Someone on the team? That's why you don't want Brent to know."

Of course, telling Joey to keep it from Brent has clued her in to the fact that it's someone from the team, so I simply say, "I can neither confirm nor deny at this time. Wow. I'm finally the one to say that instead of having it thrown at me when I try to pry information out of people."

"Charlie!" She suddenly squeals in excitement and pulls me into a tight hug. "You're going to be a mommy!" We sway together in each other's arms, teary-eyed and sniffling with happy tears. We jump apart when Brent opens the patio door.

"If you're done with your mushy girl talk, can a man get something to eat around here? What can I start grilling?" he asks, hanging onto the doorjamb and leaning in.

I hope my expression doesn't appear as guilt-ridden as Joey's. He narrows his eyes at us, but it's Joey's tear-stained cheeks he notices.

"Why are you crying?" he asks her, straightening. "Are you okay, baby? What's wrong?" He steps inside to rush to Joey.

"Nothing's wrong," I answer for her. Past experience has taught me what will stop my brother from asking any more questions. I give Joey a mischievous look, then turn to Brent. "Hormones. It's that time of—"

He stops in his tracks and spins, hotfooting it back out without another word, leaving us laughing.

We finish the bruschetta topping and slice the Italian bread that Brent will toast on the grill, but before I can take it outside, Joey stops me. "Charlie, I respect that you can't tell me who the father is, but is he at least supportive?"

Does one text asking how I'm feeling count as being supportive?

"Your silence either means no or it's a complicated answer. Okay, how about this? If you need anyone to go to the doctor appointments with you, will you promise to tell me?"

This one I can answer without reservation. "Yes. And I love you. Now let's go before Brent gets hangry and starts gnawing on his knuckles."

18

Luc

"**W**HY DIDN'T YOU TELL me we had another member in our little family, son?"

I stare at the phone in confusion. I'm in no mood for any of his games or demands. I just got back from Miami where the guys had insisted I go party with them before the season officially kicks off next weekend. I'm exhausted from the thirty-six-hour trip during which I maybe got six hours of sleep.

"What the fuck are you talking about, Victor?"

"I'm talking about the interview I just watched. I even made an appearance. I didn't think that pretty blonde thing liked me. She was all uppity and snooty-like, but she made me look pretty good. Did she interview you too? I bet you got a piece of that after—"

My brain tries to make sense of what he's saying.

Another member in our little family...Pretty blonde thing...

Charlie? She met with him? And told him of the baby out of some misguided notion of us being one big happy family?

I shake my head to clear it. "Shut the fuck up and tell me what in the hell you're talking about."

"I'm talking about a little girl named Daphne Deveraux. The one your mama said she was just babysitting. You have a sister. Who's the daddy?"

"Not you. And she's not my sister." I can't give him any opportunity to think he can control me using her.

"Then the rumors are true? You started mighty young, son, if you have a twelve-year-old child. I'm pretty sure I didn't scatter any seeds around at that age. Was it your first time and you were too eager to bother suiting up?"

I let him ramble while I recover from the whiplash of thinking he was talking about Charlie's baby to the fact he means Daphne. *His—Victor's*—daughter, a fact my mother kept secret to keep him out of Daphne's life and away from his control. I'll continue to keep the secret from him. If he finds out, he'll use it to control me even more, knowing I'll do anything to keep her safe and away from him.

"She's my cousin. What difference does it make to you anyway? You've never cared about family."

"Don't make no difference to me at all, son. So long as you send me the money I asked for. Otherwise, I might just go to Mississippi and—"

"You stay away from her, you mo—"

He chuckles. *Fuck.* I should know better than to let Victor know how much I care. It's another thing for him to hold over my head.

"I don't know," he drawls, his voice lighter now that he has me where he wants me. "Sounds like she means a lot to you. You sure have spent a lot of money on her medical bills."

I try again to brush off his suspicion. "Unlike you, I care about people other than myself. Like I said, she's my cousin—Aunt Celeste and Uncle Pierre's daughter."

"I'm starting to not believe you. I think you doth protest too much. Is that how the saying goes? Which makes me think—"

"I'll send you the goddammed money," I say before he can come to any conclusions. "Just stay the fuck away from her. She's already suffered enough."

"I knew you'd see things my way. And let's double it since you've made me wait so long. Four million. If I don't get it in the next forty-eight hours, I might have to take a trip to Mississippi to check things out for myself."

"You stay away from her! I'll send the fucking money. Go even within a hundred miles of her, and you'll never see another penny." I realize it's a mistake to say the words even as I'm saying them, but it's a knee-jerk reaction to keep him away from Daphne.

I hang up and pull up the segment on my phone and watch the entire thing.

What the fuck? How could Charlie do this? Not only did she expose Daphne's whereabouts, but she'd interviewed Victor, which means she was in the same room with him. And the way it was presented leaves my relationship to Daphne open for speculation.

I try to calm myself down with the fact that at least he doesn't know about me and Charlie or the baby. She's safe. Daphne, on the other hand...

I call Gabe and let him know Victor knows about Daphne and her whereabouts.

"They didn't give out an actual address, did they?" he asks. "That would be the height of stupidity, and legally—"

"No, but they named the town. It won't be too hard to find out exactly where in a town of a few thousand."

"Don't worry. We have eyes on Victor so we'll know if he takes even a step in her direction. But I'll send someone down there to check things out and make sure security at your aunt's is updated."

Trusting Gabe to keep Daphne safe, I call my business manager to transfer the funds. The quicker Victor gets his money, the quicker he loses interest in Daphne.

For the first—and last—time in my life, I call my father. When he answers, I say only, "I'm sending you your last request. That's it. No more. I'm done. Don't ever call me again." Without waiting for an answer, I hang up.

Damn, that felt good.

Last, I text Charlie, too angry to talk to her directly.

19

Charlie

WE'RE FINISHING UP AN early dinner, the last Sunday family gathering with Brent for a while, when I receive a text. I pull out my phone to check the message.

LUC: *What the fuck did you do?*

Confused, I start typing, asking him what he's talking about.

LUC: *You crossed a line with the segment.*

My heart starts pounding with anxiety. The video aired earlier, but since I was the one who'd produced it, I had no need to watch it again. What line is he talking about? Before I can even think of a response, my phone dings again.

LUC: *Come to my place. ASAP.*

"Charlotte."

I nearly drop my phone at my mother's stern voice. I look up, trying not to show my panic, but the phone signals another text.

LUC: *Since you're so good at digging, I'm sure you can find my address. But for the sake of time, here it is.*

"Sorry," I say before my mother can rebuke me. "It's work. There's an emergency." I hold her discerning gaze, signaling an apology for the lie. "I'm sorry. I have to go."

Another ding, this time with his address in the West Village.

She gives a slight nod, and I stand, relieved she won't call me out. Once in the car, I call Luc but it goes straight to voicemail. I text him to let him know I'm on my way from Connecticut. It'll take me at least ninety minutes to reach his place—too much time to think on the drive.

Other than the one text from him asking me how I was feeling, I haven't heard from him. I've fought back my desire to contact him, partly because of the photos of him with other women, the latest one from this weekend. No more kissing ones, thank fuck, but in every photo, a beautiful woman is usually plastered to his side with his arm around her.

I was also afraid I'd warn him about his segment, something I desperately wanted to do, despite being angry and hurt about him continuing with his life as if nothing has changed. But alerting him would mean the station possibly not being allowed to air the segment. I'm not sure what all the consequences of that would be, but I'm pretty sure being fired is one of them.

My only hope is that Luc won't be too upset about the segment, since it displayed only positive details about him, guaranteed to generate compassion for what he's been through. I didn't include anything too specific about his relationship with Daphne. I suppose I'll find out soon enough exactly what pissed him off about it.

Thankfully, the traffic is lighter than usual with most people staying put for one more night of the holiday weekend before heading back home tomorrow. I easily find a parking space on his street and walk up the stone steps of Luc's impressive brick row house. I wipe my clammy hands down the front of my capris before pressing the doorbell.

I avoid thinking about the upcoming confrontation and marvel instead that he has *two* garages at the ground level of his house. It was rare to have even one in Manhattan. What strings did he have to pull to obtain a permit for that? I wonder idly what kind of car he has.

My mind goes blank when the door opens to reveal an unsmiling Luc. His mouth is tight, and his eyes glitter. He really is angry. Furious, actually. And incredibly gorgeous. I have the urge to tell him he's beautiful when he's angry. I bite the inside of my cheek to stop myself from giggling inappropriately.

Though I'm nervous about seeing him and he's obviously not happy with me, my body is very happy to see him. My breasts peak, my thighs clench, and my heart beats faster.

Get a grip.

While I've been puking my guts out every morning, he's probably been waking up next to some other blonde who can fill a bra better than I ever will.

I open my mouth to speak, though I'm not sure if I should apologize or display some anger of my own. Before I can decide, he pulls me in and shuts the door, then faces me, hands at his waist. "What the ever-lovin' hell were you thinking, Charlie? I specifically told you to stay away from my past."

I knew he'd be upset, but I hadn't expected rage...and something else I can't identify. Panic? To ease my guilt, I remind myself that he hasn't even asked me how I am or about the baby. My blood starts to boil.

"Wow, Luc. You've really got a way with greetings." I feel a quick spurt of satisfaction when the muscles in his jaw jump. "But too fucking bad you're not my boss and have no power over me. Since I work for Mark, he's the one I need to listen to, not you."

"Jesus, Charlie. This has nothing to do with power." He turns away then whirls back. "You don't know what you're getting into, what you're stirring up. The segment was supposed to be about me playing football, and yet you brought my personal life, my *sister* into this. And to suggest we're related without making it clear how? People are insinuating she might be my daughter and I'm hiding her away because I'm ashamed of her scars. What the fuck?"

What the fuck is right. I did no such thing.

"Daphne is just a kid. Why the hell would you do that?"

"I swear I didn't. Mark must have had someone else re-edit the segment after I uploaded my final version, even though he threat—"

He's too angry to hear me as he continues to rage. "And you met with Victor. Good God! He doesn't know about you and me or that you're pregnant, does he?"

"Why would I tell him about that?" My guilty conscience at his distress rears its head again. My defense mechanism kicks in, and I go on the offensive. "Anyway, I was beginning to wonder if you remembered that I was."

"Of course I remember."

"Right. Your one text message of four words was very touching. Thank you. I guess your hands were too busy fucking a woman to handle another message. Was that the real reason you didn't want anyone to know you were the baby daddy? Would we be cramping your style?"

I glare at him. He stares back at me, confusion all over his face.

"Busy fucking...Cramping my..." Luc sputters. He's thrown off by my counterattack.

Good.

"Come on, Luc. Let's be honest with each other, okay? I realize there's no relationship between us, but I'd like to know what I'm dealing with. If you're—"

"Charlie, stop." He puts up his hands, palms out, as if trying to hold off my barrage of words. "I'm not fucking other women. I haven't been with anyone since you."

The photo evidence says otherwise.

"So you just go around shoving your tongue down random women's throats?"

Luc eyes me blankly for a moment before he realizes what I'm referring to.

"Shit." He rakes his fingers over his short curls and sighs before gesturing for me to follow him. "Come and sit down. We need to talk."

He leads me through a doorway into a large living room. Despite the formal décor and heavy drapes, the room is inviting, with its warm tones, comfortable-looking seating, and large marble fireplace.

Luc gestures to one of the sofas, and I sit gingerly on one end. He sits at the other end, leaning forward, elbows on knees. He stares down at his clasped hands and blows out a breath.

"Everything happened so fast with us," he says without looking up, "right when I got busy with football. I wasn't ignoring you, and I didn't forget you or the baby. I just didn't want to leave any messages that could give our relationship away." He finally meets my gaze. "Because we do have one, Charlie. You're pregnant with my baby, and that automatically links us together. I should have explained things to you, but—"

He stands up to pace. "I know I have a reputation, but it's one I've intentionally developed. None of the women you see me photographed with are going to admit I didn't sleep with them, because I purposely pick ones who benefit from everyone thinking they have." He pauses before admitting, "You're the first person I've had sex with since the night of the accident ten years ago."

I stare at him in utter disbelief, too shocked to even scoff at that whopper.

He glances at me, and the corner of his mouth tilts in a self-deprecating half-smile. "I know. You don't believe me. That's because I work hard to keep up appearances. I just didn't think about how it would appear to you. I'm sorry."

I see the sincerity in his eyes and nod, though I'm still not sure I believe him. "Okay, but why do you need to keep up appearances?"

"For several reasons."

When he doesn't say anything more, I prod him. "Care to enlighten me on those reasons?"

Luc glances at me, then shakes his head. "It's complicated, Charlie. And not relevant. I just need you to understand that keeping you at a distance is to protect you and the baby. Who else knows about us?"

"No one. I did tell my family, except Brent, that I was pregnant—but not that you were the father," I add before he can ask. "And I told Joey yesterday. I trust her not to tell Brent."

Luc takes a deep, calming breath. Apparently, it doesn't work, because he rakes his hands over his head again and turns away. He walks to the bay window overlooking the street, hands in the front pockets of his jeans. I try not to notice how the denim tightens around his perfectly shaped ass. I force my eyes up to his shoulders. Seeing how tense they are brings the guilt back in full force.

"Maybe it's not too late." He turns back to me, hands coming out of his pockets to gesture as he asks, "Can you take the video down? Or at least remove the part about my sister from the segment?"

"Luc, please believe me that I tried to keep her out of the video altogether, but Mark was going to give the segment to someone else. He was going to demote me or maybe even fire me if I didn't put something in. He must have had another producer re-edit it. I swear I hardly put in any mentions of her at all except as it relates to your charity, and that she's your cousin."

"That's not what was implied in the video. I'm begging you to have it taken down or fixed. It's important. Probably even a matter of life and death."

God, that tortured voice I hoped to never hear from him again. It kills me to tell him, "The video is already out there. It's probably been shared thousands of times by now. Networks have likely already obtained permission to use clips. I'm not sure it would make a difference anymore."

A horrifying thought occurs. "Please tell me they didn't use photos of her or share her location? I only said she lives in Mississippi."

Luc turns back to the window, fingers clenching and unclenching at his side. "No pictures of her, thank fuck. It mentioned the town. Damn it. This is why I didn't want you digging. Now I'll have to deal with the repercussions."

"What repercussions? Luc, I don't understand."

"I know you don't," he says, his voice and demeanor softening with exhaustion. "You were just doing your job, and you did warn me you were good at it." He shakes his head and faces me again. "But dealing with Victor has nothing to do with your job, so can you promise me you'll stay away from him from now on? It's dangerous to have anything to do with him. He's not to be trusted, and you need to avoid him at all costs," he reiterates, pinning me with his stare and waiting for me to promise.

"No." As guilty as I feel for whatever I've done to make Luc so worried, I'm not going to just blindly follow his orders. I clearly wasn't very good at that anyway. "Not unless you tell me why."

He turns back to the window. He sighs, his head going back as if he has no energy to hold it straight. Finally, he speaks. "Until the video, just a handful of people knew where Daphne was, and only so they can protect her."

"Protect her from what? The paparazzi?"

"No." He draws the curtains closed on the impending twilight as he continues, "From someone far worse and much more dangerous. You might have put her in harm's way by revealing her whereabouts." He walks to the fireplace to lean against the mantle with one hand.

I stare at him, shaking my head, unable to accept that I'm responsible for doing that to someone so innocent, one who has already suffered too much. My research, digging through paperwork, and persuading people to talk had led me to a young girl who still has scars on her face and body from broken glass and being trapped in her car seat while flames licked at her. It's a miracle she survived and even more wondrous that she had the strength to make it through her endless surgeries and rehabilitation.

"I don't understand."

"Victor is her father. He doesn't know about her. My mother never told him, afraid he would use Daphne to control us. Luckily, he didn't come back after he...after Daphne was conceived."

My stomach turns over at his tone and phrasing. His poor mother.

What have I done?

"Oh my God," I gasp. "Luc, I'm so sorry. But why would he want to hurt her? She's just a kid." Only a couple of years younger than Bobbie.

"Because she's my heir, and he won't let anyone stand in the way of his own selfish needs. If he finds out he's her father, he could try to claim her and use her to control me, my money." He shudders. "She was safe as long as he didn't know where she was or that I had anything to do with her."

I'm having a hard time processing everything he's telling me, but the guilt coursing through me is clear. "Luc, if I had known you were only trying to protect Daphne, I wouldn't have gone digging so hard. I only did it because I needed to know what you were hiding for the sake of this baby." I run a hand over my still flat belly. "Family is everything to me, so despite what my job entails, I would never put a family at risk."

"You're very close to yours, I guess."

I think I detect a note of envy in his tone. "Yes, we were always close, but after my father and oldest brother died, we became even closer."

"Daphne and my aunt—my mother's older sister—are my only remaining family. I may share DNA with Victor, but he is not family." He dismisses the connection with a sneer.

"But you never refute anything he says about you—how proud he is of you, and how close you two are."

"It's all bullshit. He's got his own appearances, illusions to keep up. Just like I do."

I narrow my eyes at him. "Don't you dare say 'like father, like son.' You're nothing like him."

"I hope to God not, but you don't know that. You hardly know me."

"I know you're not a bad person, and I think I'm a good judge of character. I'm sorry I didn't remember that before I ignored your request to not dig into your past."

When he doesn't say anything, I continue. "But I still don't understand, Luc. You've told me he's dangerous and he'd harm your sister—and me—but you haven't said why. It makes no sense that he'd do it just because of your money."

His short laugh holds no humor. "Actually, he really would do it just for the money. He's selfish and greedy. And one who has a history of violence, on and off the field."

"Oh, Luc." I don't know what to say, because I understand exactly what he means.

"On his rare visits, he used to beat my mother black-and-blue and bloody for the smallest imagined thing that someone else did to him. It would have enraged him that she'd kept the truth from him, even though he would have done nothing to actually support Daphne. I got her away from him so he'd never hurt her the way he did m—my mother."

Though he's unable to admit it, I sense that he has also suffered at the hands of his father. He stares unseeingly into the unlit fireplace and says in a pain-filled voice, "At least her death saved her from more abuse."

My heart aches for the burdens he's been carrying all these years, and I wonder if he's ever revealed how he felt to anyone else. I doubt it.

I want to hear the rest of it, but more importantly, he needs to talk about it, to get it all out.

When I stand and walk to him, taking his hand, he focuses his gaze on me. In my flat sandals, I have to tilt my head back a bit to meet his eyes.

"Will you tell me the rest?" I ask softly, bringing my other hand to his cheek.

20

Luc

Charlie's touch startles me, and I realize just how much I've revealed. A squeeze of her hand on mine brings my attention back to her. She looks at me with compassionate gray eyes, and I discover I want to tell her all of it. My burden already feels slightly lighter with the little I've told her. There's so much more.

I turn my palm and enfold hers securely, giving her a little tug. "Come on. Let's sit down again. This is going to take a while. Want a drink?"

She tilts her head and gives me a wry smile. "I'd love some wine, but alcohol is not in my future for a while. But don't let that stop you."

"I don't drink. I have—"

"Don't drink?" Charlie gives me a disbelieving look. "You were drinking the night we...met."

My lips quirk at her word choice. She recalls as well as I do we did a lot more than meet. "That one night is the exception. Sit," I instruct. I go behind the bar in the corner and pull out a couple of water bottles from a hidden fridge. Handing her one, I sit next to her and take a long swig from my own. Never have I wished more for something stronger. I'm not sure if I can lay bare my past. My soul.

As if sensing my thoughts, she asks me gently, "How did Victor and your mother meet? From what I saw of your hometown, it doesn't seem like a place he would visit."

I sigh. "No, it's not. She'd gone away with friends for a long weekend in New Orleans, out from the watchful eyes of her parents for the first time in her life. They were very strict, and she'd thought it was because they were extremely devout. She realized too late it was partly to protect her. But she also blamed them a little bit because being so sheltered made her very naive and prey to the likes of Victor. She was only eighteen when she caught his eye. He'd just started playing in the NFL."

I pick at the label on the water bottle while I recall the bits and pieces my mother told me as I got older. My aunt filled in the rest for me after Maman died.

"He seduced her, then forgot all about her until she tracked him down when she found out she was pregnant with me. Easy to do since he'd bragged how he played football for New Orleans. He refused to acknowledge I was his and didn't give her a penny to help her out, even when her parents threw her out for getting pregnant without a husband."

Seeing the mess I'm making with the bits of paper I've peeled off, I set the water bottle on the console table behind me. I lean forward, clasping my hands and resting my elbows on my knees, so Charlie can't see my face.

"A part of him must have known I was his—she'd sent him a photo of me, and I have his eyes—so he kept tabs on us. He'd come by every once in a while, usually during the season, when he was playing and living in New Orleans while his wife stayed at home in Houston.

"I don't know when he started hitting my mother. We were close, and she told me almost everything, but she didn't talk about that. I just found out about it one day when I came home from school and he was there, passed out drunk while she was icing a black eye. I realized then that all the accidents she'd had—a broken finger, a bruised cheek, sore ribs—were not accidents at all. I was too little at the time to do anything about it."

Unable to sit while I talk about the most painful time in my life, I stand and walk around the room while I continue.

"He would usually be drunk and belligerent during his rare visits, so he may have hit her before, and she hid it from me. I think she did it for my sake. Maybe she thought if he accepted me as his, he'd eventually stop hitting her and start taking care of us. He started showing more interest in me once I started playing Pee Wee football and showing promise as a good player. By then, he'd been forced to retire from football."

Still not looking at Charlie to see her reaction, I shrug. "His playing days were over, and I think he started living vicariously through my success, but he still never claimed me as his own. That would mean having to support me financially. But he did claim my victories as his own and blamed my mother for the failures. Once I found out he was hitting her, you can bet I did everything I could to win so he wouldn't lay into my mother. Since I wasn't big enough to take him on, it was the only thing I could do to try to protect her.

"I'd put myself between them because I knew he wouldn't hurt me badly enough to injure me and keep me from playing. It wasn't until I was as big as he was and stronger that I was finally able to fight back. He stopped coming around then, which was fine by me. My mother was safe and it kept him from finding out about Daphne."

I've been intent on getting my story out, the most I've ever told anyone, and I blocked out Charlie's presence in order to do so. When I finally look at her, I'm surprised to see tears on her cheeks. Knowing she's crying for me, something inside me loosens. I sink back onto the sofa and hold out my arms.

"Come here, darling." When she shifts closer to me, I wrap my arms around her, and she rests her cheek against my chest. "There's no need to cry. It's all in the past."

"Your poor mother." Charlie's voice is thick with tears. "It's so unfair that she had to bear so much."

I wonder if I could stop here and not say anything more. Surely, what I've already told her would be enough to make her understand the need to stay away from Victor.

"Why didn't the media ever pick up on this, on Victor's abuse or that you were his son?" she asks, always curious to know more.

"He threatened her if she tried to tell anyone about it. Threatened to take me away from her, to kill her parents and her sister if she ever went to them. He's a master at threats, so she never reported him or pressed him for child support and begged me not to report him."

"We need to expose him. It's not too—"

I grip her shoulders and hold her away from me so I can look into her face. "Charlie! You're not listening to me. He's dangerous, and you don't even know all that he's done. I keep telling you that you need to stay away from him, and you want to run headlong toward the monster."

"Yes! Because he is a monster and people need to know that. He's out there acting as if he raised you into the successful man you are today when, in fact, he did less than nothing."

I look at the fire in her eyes and feel the tenderness again. "You're so sweet. I wish..." I stop and lean forward so my forehead rests against hers.

"What do you wish?" Charlie whispers, her hands coming up to cup my face.

"Too much, but there's no point." Still, I can't help closing the distance between our lips and giving her a soft kiss.

I mean it to be a quick kiss, but Charlie presses closer and parts her lips. What else can I do but accept the invitation? I sweep inside and taste her. Sweet, just as I remember. I shift so I'm lying against the arm of the sofa and pull her down with me without breaking the kiss. I've waited too damn long to feel her mouth on mine again, to hold her body close to me.

We both moan when Charlie straddles my legs to settle against my growing bulge, and I rock her against me. God, that feels so fucking good! I want to feel her skin, gaze upon her body, feast on her honeyed sweetness. I want to take my time doing all that, something I wasn't able to during our brief encounter.

It wouldn't be against the self-imposed rules, right? As long as I don't get off...

With lust influencing my reasoning, I hold on to Charlie, still kissing her, and reverse our position so that she's lying on the cushions and I'm hunched over her. I kiss my way down her jaw and neck, my fingers busy on her shirt buttons. My mouth follows the skin I reveal, sucking on her collarbone patiently while I undo the bra hooks. Moving the loosened fabric out of the way, I lower my lips to her delicious breasts. I take my time tasting her, licking, sucking, flicking my tongue against her tight nipples until she's moaning and lifting her hips to grind against my erection.

I let go of one breast to take care of the fastening to her pants. Her pelvis rises in anticipation of my touch, but instead of reaching into the loosened waistband, I pull on the fabric from the back and work the garment down her hips. She lets go of me and helps, her movements rather ungraceful in her desperation to get closer, to consummate. It makes me feel guilty for leading her on, because this isn't going to end the way she expects it to.

Not this time. Not ever again. I'm keenly disappointed that the last time, the only time, had been too hurried. Powerful. Explosively satisfying. But over much too quickly. Had I known how it was going to be and that it would be just that once, I would have gone slower, lingered and savored every moment. Savored her.

But I'll take my time now, to satisfy her. To touch her and taste her as I didn't before. My mouth kisses its way down her concave belly—where my baby is growing—to the top of her pelvis. I press soft kisses against her hip, down her thigh. I lift her leg to lick behind her knee and gently bite her calf.

I continue my exploration with my mouth all the way to her toes, kissing each one before making my way back up, skimming over her mound and repeating the journey on her other leg, ignoring her disappointed protest when I don't put my mouth where she most wants it. When I shift her leg to gain access to the back of the knee, my mouth waters at the glistening treasure between her legs, but I resist the urge to rush in, continuing instead down her long limb.

"Luc, please."

Charlie reaches for my head, futilely trying to grasp strands of my hair to pull me to where she wants me to go. But my hair is too short to grab onto, and I smile against her ankle when she groans in frustration. A second later, I grunt in surprise when she grabs my ears.

"Not so funny now, huh, ace?" She gives my ears a gentle tug, and I finally relent, moving up to her pussy. My mouth waters at the sight, anticipating her taste. But instead of diving right in to feast, I circle my thumb over her clit and press first one finger and then another inside her wet heat to bring her to the edge over and over again, until she's panting and begging for more.

I look at her, her head thrashing, face flushed, eyes closed. My cock pulses, desperate for its own release. If it wasn't for years of practicing self-denial, I'd have come in my pants already.

"Look at me, darling." I wait for her eyelids to flutter open, then remove my hand from her slick flesh.

"Luc, hurry." She grips my shoulders, pulling at me, urging me to move up and consummate the moment.

Instead, keeping my eyes on hers, I dip my head and use my mouth to bring her back to the edge one more time. I watch as her eyes roll back and flutter closed again. I pause until she opens her eyes.

When they do, I reward her with a hard suck of her clit. This time, her eyes stay open though they're blind with passion. Every ounce of her attention is on the knot of nerves that is my sole focus. I can tell she's reaching her peak when her hips undulate wildly, forcing me to hold her in place against my mouth as I lash her faster with my tongue. Her low moans end in a short scream just as her body freezes before it spasms with the force of her orgasm.

I keep my mouth on her, allowing her to ride the wave against my tongue. When her movements slow, so do mine, until I'm soothing her gently, leisurely.

"Come inside me, Luc," she whispers. Her hands on my head tug slightly, beseeching me to move up and inside her.

"Again," I say against her heat, renewing my efforts. She's delicious, and I could feast on her forever. I'm hard as a pike and almost come from just the taste of her, from the sounds she makes, louder this time as another orgasm builds. I ignore my own need and concentrate on bringing her pleasure, determined to satisfy her so well that she'll be too sated and tired to demand anything more of me.

21

Charlie

I LAY BONELESS, MY fingers limp on Luc's head, still between my legs, as he gently kisses and laves, bringing me down slowly once more from the highest peaks I've ever climbed. He brought me to the edge and over, again and again, ignoring my pleas to take me, fill me with his hard cock. I wasn't even able to touch him except for grabbing his head to try to move him away...to bring him closer. Good thing he doesn't let his hair grow long enough to be gripped, or he'd likely have a few bald patches now.

Luc moves his kisses to my inner thighs, up my stomach, to curl his tongue around one sensitive nipple then the other before finally reaching my mouth to kiss me.

"You are delicious," he murmurs against my mouth before moving off me and standing.

His words, his gaze on me as he looks at me spread before him, bring on a rare, full-body blush and galvanize me into snapping my knees closed and sitting up. As foolish as it is, I take a throw pillow and hold it against my chest. I've never been shy, so I feel like an idiot for hiding myself.

"Bathroom's down that way if you want to clean up."

I look at him in confusion. "That's it?"

Luc smirks. "That wasn't enough? I lost count, but I'm game for another round if—"

"That's not what I meant, and you know it! What about you?" I look at his erection, right at my eye level, big and hard and straining with need behind his zipper.

Luc turns away. "I'm fine. This was about you." He walks to the bar and behind it.

"I don't understand. You're obviously still...Are you one of those players who do weird superstitious things during the season?"

Luc unscrews a bottle of water and drinks half of it before answering.

"Uh-huh. I guess I am." He flicks a glance in my direction before looking away.

That is not the answer I was expecting. And he is obviously lying. What the hell?

"Bullshit! I loved what you just did, but I wanted you to fuck me," I say bluntly, gazing right at him when he turns to look at me. I continue, not sure why I'm angry at him when he's taken his time to satisfy me. It isn't my problem if he chooses to suffer. "You're a...a cock tease!"

Luc looks at me for a second in shock before bursting into laughter. Enraged, I throw my pillow at him, missing him by a mile, and stand up to dress, my movements stiff and disjointed. For some reason, I feel rejected. I pull on my capris and adjust my bra. When I look over at him, he isn't laughing anymore. He's eyeing me hungrily. Instead of righting the bra, I unclasp it from my body, letting it fall to the ground.

He watches me warily as I saunter toward him, my hips swaying. I hold my shoulders back, chest out, so that my breasts, as small as they are, thrust out with the uptilted nipples pointing right at him. I'm gratified to see his eyes locked on them. His lips part slightly with a faint gasp when I cup my breasts and run my thumbs over the tips. The way he looks at me takes away all the self-consciousness caused by an ex-boyfriend who I over-heard making jokes about my "tiny tits" with his friends.

"I loved when you used your mouth on me here. And down here."

I leave one hand on my breast and slip the other one inside the loose waistband of my pants, which are still unfastened.

"And your fingers..."

I can see Luc's eyes follow my hand and stay there to stare at the movements it makes under the fabric.

"Can't you just imagine yourself pushing your cock inside me? Feel how hot and tight I'd be all around you, squeezing you, as you slide all the way inside and then pull slowly out? Ohh yeah." I lick my lower lip and bite it. "Mmm, I can feel it."

I make a sound of excitement even though my fingers don't feel nearly as good as what he was doing earlier. "Do you re-member how it was that night in Louisiana? You were so big and hard and hot inside me."

Luc makes a sound, like a groan of pain.

Yeah, I bet he's in pain.

He definitely isn't laughing now. I pull my hand out of my pants and move toward him, going around the counter. Luc stands frozen, one of his palms cupped against his fly as if the pain is too much. I reach for his hand, bringing it to my mouth to kiss. Placing my hand over his hard bulge, I give it a soft squeeze. With my other hand, I unbutton his jeans and pull down the zipper. He makes a move to evade me, but I hold on to his belt loop.

"Charlie, don't. I can't." His voice is guttural and low, his eyes squeezed shut.

"You don't have to do anything," I reassure him, desperate to touch him. To taste him. To give him as much pleasure as he'd given me. "I just want to return the favor. You're hurting. Let me help you." I slip my fingers inside the opening and have barely touched his erection when he catches my arm roughly and holds me away from him.

"I said no!" He takes his hands off me and grips the edge of the counter, his head down, his breathing fast and harsh.

I'm left feeling as if I was about to molest him. Humiliated, angry, I rush back to the sofa and grab my shirt, pulling it on roughly, foregoing the bra. I grab my sandals and hurry toward the front door, buttoning my shirt as I go.

"Charlie! Charlotte! Stop!"

I ignore Luc and open the front door, but he comes up behind me and puts his hand on it to shove it closed again.

"Let me go, Luc." Embarrassed tears are choking me.

He presses up against me so I'm caught between the cool door and his warm body. His arms slip around my waist, and he nuzzles my neck with his nose and lips. "I'm sorry."

I just shake my head, eyes closed tightly to prevent tears from leaking, but they're escaping anyway. One drips onto his forearm.

"Ah, darling. I'm sorry. Please don't cry. My problems have nothing to do with you, and I'm trying to keep you away from them. I don't want you hurt in any way." He rests his chin on my shoulder and presses his cheek to mine.

"I don't understand." I sniffle.

"I know, darling." He kisses my jaw and straightens, turning me around and holding my hands. "I'll tell you the rest of it if you'll come back with me."

I look at him, unsure if I want to keep myself open and vulnerable to this complicated, confusing man.

22

Luc

I GUIDE HER BACK through my house again, this time taking her to the staircase leading down to the family living area, consisting of an open space with a large kitchen and breakfast area on one side and a sitting area on the other. Through the glass sliding doors, exterior lights reveal a patio covered by a pergola that's draped in wisteria, providing privacy.

"Make yourself comfortable. Are you hungry?"

Charlie shakes her head and sits in the corner of one of the couches. She folds her legs against her chest and crosses her arms tightly around her knees, staring at her still-bare feet. She fixed her clothing as she walked back downstairs with me but left her shoes by the door. Somehow, the pink-painted toes make her appear even more vulnerable.

She's so bold and confident that it doesn't feel right to see her like this, or crying and hurt as she had been a few minutes ago. Then I remember her tears from before, when she'd heard about my mother, and realize she's soft and emotional under the tough exterior she displays. No, not soft. Caring and compassionate.

I pour two glasses of iced tea and bring them to the sitting area. I offer her one, then sit next to her when she takes the glass. I have no idea how to start this conversation. How do I tell a woman I've been intimate with twice now that I can't have sex with her? Before I can think of the words to begin, she asks me baldly, "So are you going to explain to me why you can't fuck me now when you did in Louisiana?"

There she is, my bold Charlie. I laugh. "Wow. Okay. Right to the point, huh?"

She looks at me, eyebrows raised. "Why do you pretend to be a man whore in public when you're far from it in private? And why would you pay to have sex when you could have any of those women, any and every night of the week?"

I open my mouth to answer, but Charlie isn't done yet. She's no longer subdued. No, she's back in spitfire mode, making me want to smile again. I resist, knowing she'd probably come flying at me. She's facing me now, legs tucked under her, and leaning toward me.

"Do you know how far-fetched it is to hear you say you haven't had sex in ten years when you have been seen with probably hundreds of women? And you're doing things to them that look an awful lot like you're about to get down and dirty with them."

"A sham. All of it done for the cameras. For my image. Do you know how easy it is to fool a public that already has a preconceived notion of you?"

"But why?"

Her insatiable curiosity and inability to accept superficial answers is probably what makes her so good at her job. And her persistence in searching until she finds the answers.

Keeping my eyes on the glass I'm holding, I finally say, "It's penance."

"Penance? For what?"

"For killing my mother. And for ruining my sister's life."

Charlie gasps. "What are you talking about? Your mother died in a car accident. You weren't even driving; she was."

I shake my head. "That's what Victor told the sheriff so I wouldn't be arrested, but he said I was the one actually driving. I was the one who caused the crash."

Charlie's eyes widen but not in horror as I expected. Instead, she squeezes my hand in sympathy. "No, Luc. Even if you were driving, it was an accident...Wait a minute." Her eyes narrow. "Victor said? Why don't you know?"

I shrug. "I don't really remember much of that night. Nothing at all about the crash. All I know is what Victor told me."

"And what else did he tell you?"

"Apparently, I tried to run him over."

"Do you believe him?"

"That I tried to run him over? Yeah, I can believe that." I give her a half smile.

She's not amused. "I don't believe anything that comes out of his mouth. There's something about him that makes my skin crawl, and his words have a layer of...slimy shit." She waves her opinion aside. "What was the last thing you remember before the accident?"

"I remember I was at a party at the lake. I had driven myself there. I remember having a few beers early on but planned to keep it to a minimum since I was driving back. But I have no memory of getting home or anything until after the crash. I was trying to recreate that night when you showed up at my doorstep in Fontaine. I was expecting a couple of..." My neck starts to heat at the thought of having to admit the next part to her.

"Two sex workers. I know. I saw them on their way to you after I left."

Her flat voice and narrowed eyes let me know exactly how she feels about that, so I quickly continue. "I did not have sex with them. You left, leaving me wanting you even more. I had zero desire for them. I couldn't go through with it. Couldn't even start it."

Her lips curve and her eyes soften. I run a hand over her head, tucking a strand of hair behind her ear. She leans into the touch for only a moment. She straightens and asks, "What does any of that have to do with no sex for ten years?"

I pull my hand from her and face forward. "As I said, I was trying to retrace my steps and recreate what I could remember of the night. And the last memory I have until after the crash is..."

Charlie tenses, alerted by my hesitation. "What?"

"Having sex," I admit. "With two girls. Separately." Looking back, I am disgusted at the thought I'd been on my way to following in my father's womanizing footsteps.

Charlie clears her throat lightly. "Okay. So what do you think happened between...that...and the accident?"

"I'm not sure. I've had dreams over the years, snippets of things, but I don't know if it's real. They feel real, like they're memories. I don't know." I sigh. "Maybe I've just dreamed them so often that they feel like memories now."

I hope Charlie can't sense my torment and helplessness at not being able to know for sure.

"What about your friends? What do they remember? What did they tell the sheriff?"

"My friends were three sheets to the wind and didn't remember if I was drunk, but said I had dropped a couple of them off before heading home. There were no other witnesses besides Victor."

Charlie is quiet for a moment, deep in thought, her brow furrowed. "Okay. No witnesses. Only Victor, who said you were trying to run him over, but he told the sheriff your mother was driving in order to cover for you. Why? What was he protecting you from?"

"He wasn't protecting me from anything. He was protecting *his* future. He couldn't let anything take me away from football, and if it was discovered that I had been driving the car, I would have been arrested and probably rotted in prison. At the very least, I would have lost my football scholarship, and then there would go my chance to make it to the NFL. He claimed he did it for me, but I was his meal ticket, and he couldn't afford to let me take the blame."

"I only met Victor once, but it was enough to know I wouldn't trust anything he says."

I smile. "Reggie would agree with you there." My expression becomes resigned. "But my only choice is to accept what Victor said. I did black out, then I woke up with the mother of all hangovers, proving how drunk I must have been."

"Or that you hit your head during the accident. Maybe that's why you can't remember."

My body stiffens with tension, but I don't say anything. I'd never considered that as a possibility. I'd brushed off the EMT who tried to examine me, my focus on Daphne and trying not to fall apart at seeing my mother's body covered by a sheet.

"You don't know that you were drunk. They didn't do a Breathalyzer."

When I look at her with surprise, she says, "I read the police reports, read Victor's statement, and interviewed him. Something felt off, and even more so now. So why no Breathalyzer or field sobriety test?"

"Victor told the sheriff I wasn't driving so no need, I suppose."

She narrows her eyes in thought. "Do you remember how you felt when you woke up?"

I close my eyes, recalling the pain I had felt from head to toe. "My head felt like it was going to split in half...or explode. And I felt like I was going to throw up, seeing my mother taken away in a body bag."

"Headache. Nausea. You might even have been off-balance, confused, and had dilated pupils. Things that might have been passed off as shock, but are also symptoms of a concussion," Charlie points out.

Her words stir an emotion in me I haven't felt in so long that I hardly recognize it—hope.

"I should have gone to the sheriff when Victor told me I was the one driving and turned myself in, but I was in shock from my mother's death and worried sick about Daphne. By the time I could think, Victor had convinced me there was no point. That I'd be throwing my life away when nothing could be changed. My mother would still be dead, and I'd be in jail. He would be, too, since he'd lied to the sheriff, and I wasn't sure what he'd do if I said anything that would implicate him in a crime. I felt so guilty about killing my mother. And Daphne was—"

Charlie points a finger at me. "Stop right there, pal. You did not 'kill' your mother. If you were driving—and there's still the question of where you were going in the middle of the night—something must have happened to cause the accident. You said you didn't drink a lot. Maybe someone slipped something into your drink that caused you to black out. Maybe you were trying to avoid Victor, not run him over. He might have caused the accident by jumping out in front of you and is covering up."

"Stop it, Charlie! There's no point in going over all the 'maybes' and 'what-ifs.' Trust me. I've done that for years already. *If only* I'd been home that night instead of partying. *If only* I hadn't drunk anything at all. *If only* I hadn't taken the car, leaving my mother stuck there alone. I've already been there, done that. It doesn't change the fact that she's gone."

"Luc," she says quietly, shifting closer and putting a hand on my shoulder. "You're still there and still doing that, by blaming yourself."

I find a deep well of compassion in Charlie's eyes, and I have to turn away before my own burn with emotion.

"Because you're feeling guilty, for something that might not even be your fault, you're punishing yourself."

I'm so tired of feeling the guilt, of closing myself off. But it's soul-deep and won't leave because of simple logic. I try to explain it to Charlie. "Because of the guilt, misplaced or not, I feel like I don't have the right to enjoy my life. Uh-uh," I admonish when she's about to interrupt, holding up my hand. "Let me finish. My mother was gone and my baby sister had not only almost died, but was left with severe pain and trauma and without a mother to raise her. What right did I have to keep on living my life and go off to college as if nothing had happened? But I forced myself to go, to do it for Daphne. I had to make it through college so I could afford the surgeries she needed, but going on with my life felt too much like I was getting away with what I'd done. So I decided my punishment was going to be no...personal joy. I gave up drinking, sex, any thought of a normal relationship. And that's why I can't—won't—have sex with you now."

Charlie's hand, which had been rubbing my back, takes ahold of mine and squeezes. "I don't mean to belittle your feelings, but I think you've gone too far. First, you're feeling guilty for something that wasn't your fault. You didn't kill her on purpose. Even if you caused the crash, I'm sure it was just an accident."

"How do you know that for sure?"

"Because, like I said, I'm a really good judge of character, and I have great intuition when it comes to people." Charlie smiles softly. "And my intuition says you're a good man who loved his mother. A mother who loved you in return and wouldn't want you missing out on life because then it would be like you died with her. I think she'd be devastated to know that you won't allow yourself to be happy, don't you?"

She lifts our clasped hands and kisses the back of mine. Her gesture and her words have me biting the inside of my lip and blinking away the burning in my eyes. I'm moved and stunned by her words. But she isn't done.

"If you had been arrested for the supposed crime that night, you'd likely already have served your time by now, if you were even convicted of anything. It's been, what? Ten years? As an eighteen-year-old, you'd probably have been out in five years, seven or eight at the most. You put yourself on trial and came up with a guilty verdict, then gave yourself a life sentence that a real judge or jury would never have given you."

I don't think a few years is enough punishment for killing some-one, but I've never thought of my self-imposed sentence in terms of criminal justice. I look at Charlie, my eyes welling with...tears? I blink and drink my iced tea, looking away from her knowing gaze. I haven't cried since my mother's funeral.

She seems to know I need to be alone for now, because she gets up from the sofa.

"I need to go back home. It's late." She hands me her glass and leans over to kiss my cheek. "Thank you for being honest with me and telling me everything. It couldn't have been easy."

Pulling myself together, I say, "I'll drive you home."

She shakes her head. "I have my car, and I'll need it to get to work in the morning."

"Right. Okay. Promise you'll me text when you reach home."

After she leaves, I wrestle with my thoughts for a long while. About Daphne. About the baby. About Charlie and how much I'm beginning to like her beyond how she makes my body react.

23

Luc

THERE'S NOTHING LIKE THE roar of the crowd when our team comes out of the tunnel for the home opener. However the prior season ended, the first game is filled with brand new possibilities and boundless optimism.

Waiting in the tunnel for the announcement, my teammates and I jump around and shout like a bunch of little boys. We give each other chest bumps and roar, almost knocking each other over with the force of our enthusiasm and energy. One by one, they leave the tunnel. At the signal, I run onto the field last, a wide grin splitting my face as I look out at the sold-out crowd. I skip and wave through the aisle created by my teammates before jogging over to the sidelines.

By the fourth quarter, the energy and enthusiasm have waned as we practically limp around on the field like the walking wounded. I've been sacked once, had a late hit that knocked the breath out of me, and my body is fucking sore.

Hutch left the game with less than four minutes to go, his ankle in question. Despite his two touchdowns, he and I did not fall into the groove we had when we played together on the Sailors. I don't know if it's the Seahawks' defense or if we're unable to connect on the field because I haven't come clean with him about my connection to his sister.

I ignore the aches and pains and try to hear the play Coach is calling through my helmet speakers. The crowd is fired up with the game tied and less than a minute to go. Hutch's last catch before he was injured got us a first down. We've run the ball and managed to gain another first down despite a holding penalty, but it's third down and we're still a few yards from kicking distance of a field goal.

Coach calls for a passing play that I'd be more confident about if Hutch was still on the field. I take my position behind my center, half crouching with my hands at his balls, waiting for the handoff as I call out my cadence.

"White 80! White 80! Set!"

Shit, the defense adjusts. They know which side we're about to send the ball down.

"Rip! Rip!" I shout, telling my receivers to adjust the route.

"Set! Hut! Hut!"

I grab the ball from my center, take a step back, and fake pass to my running back. He takes off, not fooling anyone as the defense is still trying to smash through my offensive line. I scamper back three steps and pump my arm, waiting for my other tight end to open up, but he's got a safety all over him. I scan the field for an open player, scrambling as a linebacker comes at me. The tips of his fingers reach my arm, but I'm able to evade him.

Fuck! The clock is running down. I need to leave enough time for the field goal kick. Seeing a hole in front of me, I tuck the ball into both arms and run. Somehow, I make it through for a first down, but there's not enough time to set up again and spike the ball to stop the clock. I have no choice but to keep going.

Out of the corner of my eye, I catch a glimpse of a white Seahawks jersey coming at me from my left. I veer to the right, see CJ running at me from where he'd gone deep as a decoy. He's open so I toss the ball to him. He grabs it and whirls, sprinting for the end zone. I run after him, pushing off stride anyone who tries to go after him. He twists and whirls away from Seahawk players trying to catch him. One of them is about to grab his jersey as he reaches the end zone, but CJ holds the ball out in front of him and dives across the line.

Touchdown!

All the tiredness evaporates as I jog to him while he celebrates with his typical arrogance, posing with the ball for the cameras—and the ladies. I rush him and jump as he does the same.

"Fuck, yeah!" I yell as we collide in the air. "That's the way to do it!" We land on the turf and I give him a congratulatory smack on his helmet.

A great way to start the season. Can't wait to end it the same way, with one last win at the Super Bowl, preferably in a less dramatic way.

Despite hearing we'll lose Brent for the next few games due to his ankle injury, I'm still riding the high from winning the first game of the season while I wait for Charlie to come out from her doctor's appointment. I feel like a stalker, hiding behind the tinted windows of the SUV Reggie drives me around in. It's been over a week since I saw her, the day the segment aired and we talked for hours. After which I feasted on her.

Nope. Can't think about that anymore. It was a one-time thing. It happened because my emotions were high and my walls were down. I'm in control again.

I didn't tell her I was coming today when she texted me about her appointment. There was no way I could go with her without the media finding out about it within hours. The best I can do to support her is be here when she's done.

Other than the text, we haven't communicated. I've been feeling a bit raw after everything I'd revealed to her. And I was focused on preparing for our first game. Hopefully, she's not pissed at me for not reaching out.

My heart skips a beat when she exits the building. It jumps into my throat when she stops and sways as if she's going to fall. I grab the door handle to leap out, but Reggie locks the doors.

"I got her, boss. You stay here."

He's out of the SUV before I can protest, and I watch helplessly as he strides to where she's leaning against the brick wall of the building. She glances my way, but she can't see me through its darkly tinted windows. Reggie takes her arm and leads her to me. He unlocks the vehicle with the remote and opens the back door for her. When she slides in next to me, he shuts us in and stands outside to give us privacy.

"Hi," she says, sounding shy for the first time since I've met her.

"Hi," I echo, feeling a little uncertain myself. I want to reach out and touch her, pull her into my arms. "Sorry I couldn't come to the appointment. I wanted to, but—"

"You couldn't. I understand. Great game. Congratulations." She smiles but her pale face dims the usual sparkle.

"You okay? How was your appointment?"

"It was fine. The baby's doing well." She pulls out an ultrasound picture from her purse and hands it to me with a trembling smile. "You can keep this image if you want."

I take it and stare at it without saying anything, unable to form a coherent word. I feel the way I do when I've taken a hard hit on the field—dazed and unable to breathe. Because the reality of a baby has just hit me as I stare at the evidence of it. And then a rhythmic swooshing sound accompanied by a rapid heartbeat fills the space between us.

My gaze darts up to Charlie, who is holding her phone out in front of her.

"Is that...is that the baby's heartbeat?"

She nods, her eyes welling with emotion as we listen to the life-affirming sound in the close confines of the SUV. There's a life growing inside her, and I helped to create it. The thought is powerful and overwhelming and fucking scary.

Then I think about how it must be for her, actually carrying that life inside of her. I have to protect her, no matter what.

"Can you send me that recording?" I ask, my voice hoarse as it pushes past the emotion clogging my throat. I carefully put the picture in my shirt pocket.

"Sure," she says, her voice husky. As she tilts her head down to her phone to do so, I notice how pale she looks. When she lifts her eyes back to me, I see the shadows under them.

"How are you doing, darling? What did the doctor say about you?"

She manages a smile. "She said I need to eat and rest, though I'm not sure how I'm supposed to manage that when I'm still having some morning sickness."

"Just the morning?"

She grimaces. "And most of the afternoon."

I move closer and put a hand on hers. "I'm sorry."

She shrugs. "It's getting better. At least I'm not throwing up all the time. I only feel like I'm going to."

"What else did she say?"

"That I've lost weight."

"Does that mean something's wrong?" My hand tightens involuntarily around hers. I have an urge to scoop her up into my lap and hold her tight. But I don't want to give her the wrong idea, that we could have a real relationship when that's impossible, so I resist and clasp her hand instead.

"No, it just means I need to eat more. The ultrasound shows everything is fine with the baby."

"And you? Besides the weight, which we'll have to do something about, everything is okay with you?" I bend my head to look at her since she's staring down at her phone. "Charlie?"

She takes her time lifting her eyes to meet mine. My heart tightens like a fist at the vulnerability I see. Her lips quiver before she bites down on the bottom one.

"Honestly? I'm scared."

I give in to the urge I've had since I saw her walk out of the building and pull her to my chest, wrapping my arms around her slim torso.

"Shh. It's okay. I'm here." I allow myself to hold her close against me, to breathe in the floral scent of her hair, her skin. I don't know who moved or if we both did, but our lips meet in a slow kiss, sensual and deep. My body immediately goes up in flames, and I lift her on top of me, bringing her knees on either side of my hips. I wrap my arms around her and let my hands roam from her head to her ass, pulling her close to my growing erection. Her skirt has ridden up, and I can feel her heat against my slacks. She moans and rubs herself against me.

Fuck, yes!

Without thinking, I bring one hand between her thighs and slip it under her panties. She gasps when I brush over her mound. I lose my own breath when my fingers move down to her opening, finding it slick. I easily slide in a finger, which she immediately starts riding. I want nothing more than to bury myself inside her wet heat, feeling her tightness around me again.

Nothing else matters in this moment. I've forgotten all the reasons I can't have Charlie, a family, joy.

I move my hand to my zipper and discover Charlie is already there, struggling to undo the belt. I'm about to help her when a knock sounds loudly on the window.

Both of us freeze and come back to the present. Charlie practically flings herself off me and fixes her skirt. "Oh my God! What are we doing? In the back seat in broad daylight?"

I look at her face, flushed now and no longer pale. Her eyes are wide and filled with lingering passion. Her lips are swollen and wet, just like her pussy.

Remembering the feel of her, I want nothing more than to hold on to that sensation. No, I want more than that. Much more. But I can't have it. All I can do for now is sample her sweetness again. I raise my finger to my mouth and suck it clean. Charlie watches me, eyes even wider now, mouth parted.

Another knock on the window breaks the moment. I hold her hand before she can open the door.

"Don't be scared," I say, continuing our conversation. "I'll make sure nothing happens to you."

She shakes her head. "If you mean Victor, that's not what I'm worried about."

I narrow my eyes at her, irritation at her stubbornness pushing away the remnants of lust that are slow to fade. She damn well should be worried about Victor, and I don't know how to make her understand.

But I tamp down my frustration and ask, "Then what are you worried about?"

She continues, "It's how everything changes now. My whole life, for the rest of my life. Almost every decision I make from now on, I have to make with this baby in mind. I have to think about how this impacts my career, who's going to care for him or her while I work, how—"

"You know I'll take care of everything financially, Charlie. You'll never have to worry about that, ever."

She gives me a brief smile. "It's one of the things we'll need to talk about at some point."

There's no discussion required since it's already decided in my mind, but I let it go. Instead, I ask, "One of the things?"

She nods. "But not now. Not here."

"You're right. Let me know when you can come over to my place so we can talk."

Her eyebrow rises, and I reiterate, almost sternly, "Just talk."

Giving me a mischievous grin, she exits the vehicle.

Reggie takes his place in the driver seat and meets my eyes in the mirror, his full of apology. "Sorry, boss. You were in there a while, and we can't stay parked here forever, especially if it was going to start rockin' and rollin'." He grins. "You might want to see about getting a limo if you want to meet in a car, so you two can have your privacy while I just drive around."

Now there's an idea, except a limo always garners attention. Though my resolve to avoid sex is still in place, I'm quickly becoming addicted to tasting and pleasuring Charlie. I just have to do it without losing my head as I almost did a few minutes ago. If it hadn't been for Reggie's knock, the SUV would have been bouncing, right there in broad daylight.

"Why don't you start driving, wiseass." My logical head is glad Reggie interrupted, because the one below my belt is howling in agony. I'm not sure how long I'll be able to maintain my self-control and stay true to my vows.

24

Charlie

WHEN I GET HOME from work that evening, it's to find my mother eyeing a pile of food containers.

"What's this, Mom? You went on a cooking spree?"

"Someone did, but it wasn't me. This was delivered a few minutes ago. Did you start a food delivery service?"

"No. Are you sure it was meant for us?" I take the paper my mother hands me and see that it's addressed to me by name. It's from a restaurant in Manhattan, with an address near Luc's neighborhood. "Is there a note or anything?" I ask, even though I know the answer. He wouldn't risk giving away his identity with a message.

Mom confirms there is no note, but of course it's Luc who sent this...care package. My heart warms at his thoughtfulness.

"I take it by that smile you know who's responsible for this?" Sandra asks.

How can I explain without telling my mother too much? Deciding there's no harm in answering the question without giving any details, I nod.

"The same person who's responsible for the other gift?" my mother asks, gesturing with her chin at my belly.

I grin. "Yes." I take out the second ultrasound picture I got from my appointment and hand it to my mother, knowing it's guaranteed to stop this line of questioning.

"Oh, Charlie." As expected, she forgets everything as she stares at the picture, her eyes turning soft and misty. "He's just beautiful. Perfect."

"If you say so. It's so fuzzy. And how do you know it's a boy?"

"I don't, but I'm not calling my grandbaby 'it.'" She sniffs and dabs at her eyes.

I play the recording of the heartbeat as well, causing her tears to flow once more. While she's occupied, I pull out the containers of food and find baked chicken, roasted vegetables, rice, and bread rolls. Looking at it makes me realize just how hungry I am. I read the heating instructions, wash my hands, and warm up the food, calling Bobbie down for dinner.

While we eat, I deflect questions about the father, saying only that I will tell them soon. To turn the conversation again, I distract them with another bit of news. "So I think I'm going to quit my job."

"You're going to be a stay-at-home mom?" Bobbie asks.

"Why do you say *stay-at-home mom* like it's a bad thing? I would if I could, like Mom did."

Bobbie sends a chagrined look at our mother, then grins. "Yeah, but that was the old days."

I roll my eyes. As a fourteen-year-old, she thinks anyone over the age of thirty is old. According to her, I'm practically middle-aged.

"Very amusing, Roberta," my mother says, shaking her head.

"I'm just kidding, Mom." Bobbie leans over to give Mom a kiss on the cheek. "Besides, if you didn't stay home to take care of me and homeschool me early on, I'd be going to regular school and not able to graduate early." She shudders as if it's her worst nightmare.

"Excuse me," I say, giving her a mock-glare. "We were talking about *me*."

Mom puts a hand on Bobbie's arm, stopping her from responding with that simple gesture. I hope I develop superpowers like that by the time my peanut becomes a teenager.

"Why are you quitting, honey?" she asks me.

"Yeah, I thought you loved your job," Bobbie adds.

"I think I loved the challenge of it and the excitement of meeting famous athletes. And I liked learning more about each of them on a personal level when I researched them for interviews."

"So what's changed?" Mom asks.

"Remember the interview that made me uncomfortable? Where I was asked to put in private information that the person didn't want included?"

I continue when Mom nods. "Mark added in things I'd left out. And didn't even tell me."

"Wow, that's pretty underhanded of him," Bobbie comments.

"Yes, it was. And the way he twisted things for ratings made me lose respect for him."

Mom slips a spoonful of veggies, which I hadn't taken on my own, onto my plate. "I agree it was a terrible thing for him to do, but has anything like this happened before? Why now with this interview?"

"Probably because the interviewee insisted we not look into his past. It made our antennae go up, wondering what was there." I stab a piece of a Brussels sprout and eat it. Hm. Not bad. I spear another one.

"Yeah," Bobbie agrees. "If someone told me to not to look in a closet, you know it's the first thing I'm going to do."

"Which is why I never tell you where I hide presents," Mom tells her.

Bobbie and I share a look and grin. We already know Mom's hiding place.

She catches us and huffs. "I guess I have to find a new place. Or maybe stop with the presents since you're all old enough."

"Mom!" Bobbie protests. "That's not fair! *I'm* not old enough. They've had at least ten more years of presents than me."

Mom just raises her eyebrows at her and turns to me. "Before you quit, make sure you consider whether you'll be able to find another job, especially when you start to show. You'll need health insurance. Having a baby in the hospital is expensive, and God forbid there are any complications."

Shit. I'd forgotten about the insurance. She'd know better than anyone what it's like to have a baby with health complications and no job. Even Dad's death benefits weren't enough for Bobbie's heart surgeries.

"And if you tell your boss you're pregnant, he can't fire you," Bobbie adds.

No, but he could demote me since my job requires frequent travel, and I won't be able to do that in the last month or two. I guess I'll wait to quit until after the baby is born.

Leaving Bobbie to clean up after dinner, I go up to my room for privacy and call Luc.

"Thank you for dinner, Luc, though you didn't have to do that." Sprawled on my bed, lying on my stomach with my bent legs swinging behind me, I feel like a teenager talking to her boyfriend.

"Just making sure you follow doctor's orders and eat."

"Trust me, I love to eat. I've just been too nauseated or too tired lately." I flip onto my back, wondering if it's still okay to lie on my stomach.

"I bet the traveling doesn't help. Have you told your boss yet that you're pregnant?"

"Not yet. Though I'll need to soon. I just don't want to face all the speculation when I don't mention who the father is."

"Right. I'm sorry."

I sigh. "Even if you hadn't told me not to, I wouldn't have jumped to tell everyone that it's you. Not exactly the professional thing to do in my field, to sleep with a player, especially since we aren't even dating or anything."

"I don't know about the 'or anything' part," Luc says, a smile in his voice.

His words ease insecurities I didn't know I had. "Well, I'm ready for more *anything*," I tease. "Just say the word. When I don't feel like throwing up, I'm hungry—for more than food."

Luc chuckles. "Patience, darling."

"Not my strong suit. But fine. I just wanted to call and thank you for the food. However, it's fueled curiosity about your identity so you should probably stop."

"Tell them it's a secret admirer. Speaking of secret admirers, I heard you were mine for a long time. Or was it a long time ago?"

I gasp. "How did you find out? And I'll have you know, it was ages ago, and my crush didn't last very long," I fib.

His low laugh sends shivers through me. "If you say so. Let's add that to the list of things we can talk about over dinner. Tomorrow? I'll have Reggie pick you up so you can take a nap during the drive. Doctor said more rest, right?"

"Right, but I have a couple of interviews out of town. I won't be back until Friday."

"Okay, if you're back by dinnertime, let's do it that night." We arrange for Reggie to pick me up directly from the airport, but neither of us is ready to hang up.

"What are you doing right now?" I ask.

"Looking at a couple of new plays since it looks like your brother is going to be out for a few games."

"Yeah, he's pissed about it. Hasn't missed a game in years and to have it happen during the first game of the season..."

"Well, I'm sure with Joey helping him with rehab, he'll be back soon, better than ever."

"I agree. She's really good at her job."

"You're also very good at your job, darling. A little too good, remember?"

I search for signs that he's still mad at me, but all I hear is a hint of humor. Nevertheless, I change direction.

"Joey's known since high school what she wanted to do. I didn't know what I wanted to be even while in college, so I took the job that sounded the most exciting instead of something practical. I wasn't thinking about the future, and the job is not exciting anymore."

"You know..." There's hesitation in Luc's voice, making me brace myself for whatever he's about to say next. "If you don't want to work anymore, I can provide—"

"Stop right there, pal. Don't say whatever it is you were about to suggest."

"Charlie, it's my responsib—"

"Uh-uh. I'm serious. I need to know I can stand on my own two feet. I saw what my mom went through when my dad died. Everything that could go wrong, did. And she was helpless to do anything about it except rely on others for as long as they were willing and able to help, and lean on her two older children. I see how it's impacted Brent and Stevie. Georgie too. She and I were too young to be of much help, but old enough to know how difficult it was for them. I don't ever want to be in that position."

"But you wouldn't be. I'd make sure you and the baby were taken care of."

"No, you don't understand, Luc. My brother paid for my college and my car, and I live in a home he's paid for. I'm not even allowed to pay the electric bill. I want to be able to support myself, because God forbid, if something went all wrong again, I need to know I can take care of this child."

"Okay, darling. I just don't like seeing you so exhausted. If it becomes too much, especially as you...grow...pregnanter—"

I snicker at his attempt to avoid saying "bigger."

"—don't feel like you have to do it at the risk of your health or the baby's. Or if you don't want to go back to it after the birth—"

"I don't plan on going back. I'm actually..." Saying the words out loud makes me feel a bit foolish.

"Tell me what you're thinking," he coaxes.

"I'm thinking of going back to school. It'll be tough for a few years, school and taking care of a baby, but it'll be an investment in a career that can accommodate having children."

"Sounds sensible. What's the career?"

Luc didn't laugh. In fact, he sounds genuinely interested.

"I'm thinking of becoming a counselor. A therapist." In case now is the time for him to think I'm being impetuous, I add, "I've just started researching the idea. Maybe it's not a good idea, but I think it would be the perfect career for me. No travel, most importantly. I can be somewhat flexible in my schedule. My therapist helped me process some of my grief, and I'd like to be able to help others do the same. I don't know..." I haven't done my usual level of research yet for a decision this big, making me feel uncharacteristically hesitant. "I think...I might be good at it."

"I think you'd be phenomenal as a therapist."

"Really? How do you know?"

"Because you are caring and compassionate and...curious. And because I don't think you'd give up on anyone who needed your help."

Wow. His words fill me with the confidence I'd been lacking, and my heart swells with tender emotion. I'm still basking in them when he pivots the conversation with a rush of words.

"I've started seeing a therapist."

"You have?" I ask when my brain catches up. "That's great!"

"Yeah, I've gone to her a couple of times so far."

"I'm so glad."

"Let's see what happens," he says, tempering my optimism. "At the very least, I hope she can help me remember what really happened so I can get Victor off my back and stop his blackmail and threats."

"What? You've never mentioned blackmail before. What threats?"

I'm shocked when he tells me about Victor's blackmailing over the years and his latest demand for money.

"What a complete and utter asshole!" I'm outraged on Luc's behalf. "The bastard didn't give you or your mom a penny when you were a kid, but he has the nerve to ask you—no, to guilt you and threaten you into giving him money?"

"Easy, tiger." He laughs.

"It's not right," I huff.

Luc is quiet for a long moment.

"What are you thinking?"

"I'm thinking about what an amazing mother you're going to be."

Everything fades but his words, spoken in that tender and drawling voice. God, I wish we lived closer. Even if he can't make love to me, I want to be with him, cuddled up next to him, talking or watching TV together or just breathing each other in. The last week and a half have felt like a month.

I don't know what to say back, too full of emotion. Damn hormones.

"Alright, you need to go to bed and get some rest now. Call me tomorrow night."

Several hours later, I lay in bed, hungry but not for food. Exhaustion and a good meal allowed me to fall asleep right away, but erotic dreams and unfulfilled passion awakened me a couple of hours later. I'd read in the pregnancy books that, besides swinging emotions, sexual appetite might increase due to elevated hormones. Or it could just be the unfinished job from earlier.

I resist the temptation to finish that job myself. It had been the norm for the past three years, whenever the infrequent urge arose...except for the incredible quickie that night in July and the satisfaction Luc had given me at his house.

I fling off the sheet, and the early autumn air, cooler once the sun goes down, breezes through my open window to soothe my over-heated body. My nipples immediately tighten even more painfully with the added stimulation. I roll over and groan into the pillow.

Luc hadn't touched my breasts this afternoon. He'd kissed me like he wanted to swallow me whole while his hand had gone straight to my overheated core. And I'd ridden him like—

I groan again. What must he think of me? I'd had sex within minutes of meeting him, had allowed him to go down on me, and was ready to ride him in the back seat of a vehicle—in public, with someone standing right outside the SUV, less than a couple of feet away!

I stop myself from groaning again in embarrassment, though it's unlikely Bobbie would hear me since her room is down the hall. Stevie is traveling again, and my mother has her own suite downstairs. I focus my thoughts on the changes to my childhood home to distract myself.

Brent wanted to buy another house for us once all our debts had been paid off, but Mom refused. She agreed to renovate instead, expanding the downstairs to include a stair-free suite for her. And a bigger kitchen. Ignoring her protests about the cost, Brent had also added a gym and indoor pool and had the upstairs extended and remodeled.

Mom assured me she'd be fine if I wanted to move out, but I loved staying in my family home. The commute to work is a little long but not that bad. The only downside right now is the distance to Luc's place, which is at the farthest end of Manhattan.

With my current situation, I'm glad I didn't move out. It al-lowed me to save money, which I'll need when I go back to school. While I accept that I'll have to allow Luc to provide some financial support for the child, I'm glad I won't have to be completely dependent on him, not when I know what the consequences are if the support is abruptly cut off for some reason. And I don't want to ask any more of my brother than he's already given me.

Waiting for sleep to overtake me, I think about when and how I should tell my boss about my pregnancy and how it will impact my job. Even when Luc is ready to reveal himself as the father, I'm not sure it's something I want to broadcast while I'm still working at the studio, not when we don't have a defined relationship. He's in the public eye so much that there's bound to be speculation, especially if he's seen pushing a stroller around the neighborhood with a baby...assuming he'll want to be that involved.

One more thing to talk about at dinner.

Thinking about my upcoming evening with him, I wonder if I can squeeze in a visit to Andi. She is another stray, like Joey, that our family took in. She lives in Stamford now and owns a dress boutique in Greenwich. I'll stop by and see if I can pick up something irresistible to wear to dinner at Luc's.

But first, I have to get some more sleep. I punch my pillow, then turn onto my back. Thoughts of an uncertain future aren't going to help me fall asleep anytime soon. I pick up my phone and play the recording of the baby's heartbeat, looping it so it plays continuously as I finally drift into sleep.

25

Luc

I LOOK AT MY watch: 7:20. Waiting for Charlie to arrive is turning me into a teenager on his first date. Not that I'm considering this a date. I've taken women to functions, "hooked up" with them at nightclubs, and hung out with them in groups. But I've never had a woman to my house for dinner—or other activities.

No, I can't allow myself to think of this as a date because Victor is still very much a threat. And I'm still filled with too much guilt to allow myself to move on with my life as if nothing happened. But what Charlie said the last time she was here has stuck with me.

"I think she'd be devastated to know that you won't allow yourself to be happy... You'd likely already have served your time by now, if you were even convicted of anything..."

I repeated those words to Dr. Vandermeyer when I saw her at my session earlier today. She praised Charlie as a "wise young woman." But she also acknowledged my feelings of guilt and said it was important that I be prepared for whatever I remembered under hypnosis, which she wouldn't do until she'd had at least a few sessions with me first.

"I want to have a better understanding of your current mental health," she explained, "before I return you to a time in your life that was so traumatic your brain has chosen to forget it." Her words gave me pause, but I don't think my guilt could be any worse.

I'm waging a mental war with myself, trying not to look at my watch again and focus instead on cutting up vegetables, when I hear the security ding of the garage opening. I drop the knife and catch myself when my hand nervously goes to my shirttail to fix it. I wipe my hands on a kitchen towel, then bound down the hallway to the door leading to the garage Reggie uses.

When I open it, I lose my breath. Charlie steps out of the SUV, looking beautiful. Stunning. Stunningly beautiful. *Jesus.* I really do feel like a sixteen-year-old, though I'm pretty sure I had more game with girls back then.

"Come on in," I manage, opening the door wider and stepping back. She smiles and brushes by me, and I lose my breath again when I catch the scent of her perfume. It's light and musky. Sexy.

I'm about to shut the door when I notice Reggie standing a few steps away with Charlie's overnight bag.

"Thanks, Reg," I say, taking the bag from him. "I'll drive her home." Shutting the door, I lead Charlie to the family room. I put the suitcase down and turn to her.

"I'm sorry I'm late," she says. "I decided to clean up and change at the airport lounge before showing up here for dinner. You like?"

She hands me her purse and twirls around slowly. Her form-fitting black dress reveals no signs of her pregnancy. Though it has long sleeves, the wide scoop neckline shows off her sexy shoulders and collarbones—I've never thought of those as sexy before—and the short length exposes long, slim legs. And her heels—fuck me—bring her almost eye, and mouth, level to me.

Charlie looks at me expectantly, that mischievous look in her eyes. Minx. She knows the effect she's having on me.

"You clean up nice," I say, turning away to go to the kitchen. I catch her look of irritation at my lack of response when I glance back at her and smile. I have to bite back a groan as I watch her walk toward me, her hips swinging, each movement outlined by the fit of the dress.

"Something smells good."

"I hope you're hungry. But even if you're not, I'm going to make sure you eat."

Charlie smiles and surprises me by reaching out to take my hand. "Thank you." She holds onto my hand and walks to the stove. I'm learning that Charlie is much more comfortable than I am at initiating casual touch. I like that about her. It's not the same as the grasping hands of hangers-on with whom I usually surround myself.

"You cook?" she asks in surprise.

It takes me a moment to answer. My mind is on her soft hand holding mine and how I want to feel it instead on other parts of my body.

"Yes, I do, though not as much during the season. And I didn't make everything tonight. It was an early practice today, but I had an appointment afterward." I reluctantly let go of her hand and finish the salad I was making when she arrived. "I used to help my mother in the kitchen. She taught me how to make my favorite dishes. She said it was so I could always have them whenever I wanted. Of course, they never taste quite the same as when she made them."

Charlie stands watching me, her hip leaning against the counter, arms crossed. "I know what you mean. My older sister did most of the cooking when she lived at home, and the long hours when I started working meant I didn't get a lot of practice. When I do get the chance to make one of my mom's recipes, it never tastes as good as when she makes it. She once told me 'mother love' was the secret ingredient."

I toss the salad. "Mother love. I like that. I think mine would have agreed." Picking up the wooden bowl, I say, "Come on. Sit down."

I lead her to the table, put down the salad, and pull out a chair for her. The table is already set, and I just have to bring over the serving dishes from the oven that's keeping the food warm.

We talk about her trip while I bring them over, ladling lobster bisque into two wide bowls for us before sitting down.

Charlie closes her eyes and makes a satisfied noise after the first bite that reminds me of how she looked when I was satisfying her. I want to be the one to put that look on her face again. Maybe I'll get the chance someday soon. But for now, I enjoy looking at her while the food gives her a different type of pleasure.

While we make our way through the meal, conversation between us flows. I can't remember ever talking to a woman so easily, so openly. There's no hidden agenda, neither of us looking for anything more than just each other's company. There's something about Charlie's open, straightforward manner that inspires trust, but despite my attraction to her, I remind myself that she dug deep into my background for the story even when I asked her not to.

"Everything okay?"

Charlie's question makes me realize I've been lost in thought and quiet for some time. She's picking at her dessert, poking the spoon into the crunchy burned sugar of the crème brûlée. I've finished my own without even realizing it.

I meet her eyes and decide to ask her about what's bothering me. "Why did you do it?"

She tilts her head. "Do what?"

"Why did you keep digging into my past when I asked you not to?"

Charlie bites her lip and reaches for my hand. "I'm sorry, Luc. I had no idea it would hurt you so much or that it would have an impact, a dangerous one, on you or your sister. But"—she pauses and shakes her head—"I'd like to blame it on my job. To say that

Mark made me. I'm pretty sure I would have been either fired or demoted if I refused."

Charlie glances away, and I know there's something more. "What?"

She looks back at me and grimaces. "But if I'm going to be completely honest, I wanted to know what you were hiding. You were going to be a part of my life, my child's life, and—"

"*Our* child."

Her breath catches at the correction, but she continues.

"I know I had no right. We'd made no promises to each other, but I just...I couldn't help..." Charlie stops and sighs. "I don't know how to explain it." She pushes away from the table and gets up. I follow suit. She crosses her arms in front of her and walks to the patio doors to look out.

I walk up behind her and put my hands on her shoulders. She feels so slight under my big palms despite her height. I rub my thumbs over her shoulder blades, and she leans back against me and sighs. We look at each other in the reflection in the glass door.

"Tell me."

After a moment, she tries to explain. "You and I hardly knew each other. A few weeks ago, we knew even less about each other. And yet, we created a life together. A baby. A child that's going to forever link us, for better or worse."

26

Charlie

*F*OR BETTER OR WORSE.

The phrase makes my heart skip another beat. At this rate, I might develop a heart condition. It's bad enough I've been getting emotional about making a baby, which in reality is nothing more than biology. It's not as if we knew each other for more than five minutes before we started on the miraculous deed. It's not as if we consciously set out to have a child, to create one out of love.

I'm not naive enough to think that's the only way children are made, but it's the way I've always wanted them. It's what I grew up with and aspired to for myself. Maybe I'm attaching emotion to simple biology in order to try to make reality match my fantasy. Or am I trying to turn my fantasy into reality?

I slip out from under his hands and walk toward the sofas. When I look back at him to see if I've freaked him out with my choice of words, it doesn't appear I have. He's looking at me, waiting patiently for me to continue.

"I was angry at you for not trusting me or sharing more of your life. I felt I had the right to know who my baby's father was. And to see you in the tabloids kissing other women...I know it wasn't right for me to use my job as an excuse to go about getting the information. I am good at what I do, but I didn't need to be that good at it. Mark wouldn't have known any different if I hadn't tracked down Daphne. I'm sorry."

Luc comes to me and takes my hand. He sits and pulls me gently down next to him. When I settle beside him, leaving a few inches between us, he shifts closer and puts an arm around my shoulder, holding me to him.

"I understand. Thank you for telling me."

"You understand?"

"Of course. It makes sense. And you're right. I should have told you more about why I needed to keep things private. I should have trusted you."

Now that he's not angry with me anymore, I'm able to laugh. "No, you were right. Trust a woman you just met, one who works for a sports show? I don't blame you, especially after what you've told me." I lean back against him. "But you know you can trust me now, right? I mean, now that I know why and now that we're...I mean..."

Shit. I've done it again and duck my head to hide my embarrassment. I can still hear my mother telling me what happens when you make assumptions. Well, I certainly feel like an ass right now.

Luc leans back to look at me, and I reluctantly raise my head. "Yes, we are...something. I'm not yet sure exactly what either. But I'm working on figuring it out, darling, I promise you."

"What you said before...your vow of celibacy...Does that mean we're never going to have sex again? Ever?"

"Like I said, I'm working on it."

"Good, because I really want to have sex with you again. I was trying to give you a little demonstration that day of what you were saying no to," I say, as much as it pains me to remind him of what a fool I made of myself.

"Trust me, darling. I didn't need a demonstration. I was painfully aware."

We're quiet then, each lost in our own thoughts.

"Hey. You falling asleep on me?"

I jerk awake, realizing I had, quite literally, fallen asleep on him. Or at least the entire left side of his body. Between the long travel day, the delicious meal, and the comfort of his warm body against mine, I'd dropped into sleep in an instant without realizing it. I must have been truly exhausted to have dozed off when the body I badly wanted again was literally at my fingertips.

Sitting up, I push my hair off my face while discreetly checking for drool. "I'm sorry. I don't know what happened."

"You're exhausted. Why don't you stay the night and get a good night's sleep, and I'll have Reggie drive you back in the morning? I would, but I have an early practice."

I look at him, wondering—hoping—if he's changed his mind. Reading my mind, he shakes his head. "Sleep only. And as much as I'd love to have you sleep next to me, I don't think I could take the torture. I wouldn't sleep a wink, and Coach will strip my hide if I half-ass practice tomorrow, even if it's just a walk-through. I think I have at least five guest rooms you can pick from."

"You think? You don't know how many rooms are in your house?" I'd be lying if I said I wasn't disappointed that he wasn't offering the use of his bed. Though I'm exhausted, it wouldn't take much for my body to wake up.

"My financial advisor convinced me this was a great investment. The previous owners were a Hollywood couple who were going to use this as their second home if one of them was filming a project in New York. Allegedly, one of them used it for something more and they split."

"Are these two rowhouses combined into one? It's huge."

"Yeah. Apparently, after living in their mansion out West, they couldn't possibly survive in a three-bedroom here."

"Oh. How many kids did they have?"

"None."

I laugh at his dry tone. "Says the guy who's now living alone in a who-knows-how-many-bedroom bachelor pad."

"Touché." He laughs and I just stare at him, forgetting what we were talking about. He's always gorgeous, but when he laughs...

"I got a great deal on it since it was sold with the renovations not even half done. I hired an architect to redesign some of it with the intention of selling it for profit before putting it on the market. She did such a great job, I ended up keeping it. So? What do you say?" he asks.

When I look at him blankly at the non sequitur, he raises his eyebrow at me. "Stay here tonight?"

It makes sense to do that instead of making the ninety-minute drive back home. While I could sleep if he drove, he would have a three-hour round trip. I don't want him to lose his rest before practice.

"Okay," I agree. "But on one condition. I sleep in your bed." I start to walk out of the room.

Luc stops in his tracks, but I keep going, looking over my shoulder, eyebrows raised in challenge.

"Charlie, you know that—"

"I know," I interrupt. "Just sleep. I promise." Not only do I want to be close to him, to his strong lean body, I also want him to get used to my nearness. It would be an added bonus if he felt tempted into doing something.

He catches up to me and cups my face in his big palms. "You're a siren, you know that? Tempting me to my death."

I huff. "Your death? I thought it was to paradise. Unless you mean *le petit mort*. In which case, yes, I am." I smile seductively.

He groans and leans his forehead against mine. "Charlie, I'm working on it. Trust me, there's nothing more I'd love to do than experience paradise with you again."

I can't resist, and I lift my mouth to close the gap between us and press a soft kiss on his beautiful lips. "Okay, but work faster. I had a three-year drought before you, and I'm dying for another drink."

Luc leans back in shock. "Three years?"

I shrug. "I broke up with the guy I was seeing in college, got busy with my new job, and it was just too much effort to go through the dating ritual for sex. Obviously, I don't believe in abstinence before marriage, but despite how you and I fell into bed within minutes of meeting, I don't believe in casual hookups either." I grin. "It was a lot easier to take care of it myself if I felt the urge."

Luc groans again. "Jesus, darling. You really are trying to kill me here."

"Good. Now you know how I feel."

He takes my hand and kisses my temple before taking me on a tour of his home. We work our way up each level, starting with the garden level where the kitchen and family room are, as well as a bedroom suite that was likely used by a housekeeper.

On the first floor, he says, "This is called the parlor level. It's perfect for entertaining guests with the large parlor and formal dining room as well as an office for business meetings."

"They must have had some big parties because these rooms are huge."

Luc shrugs. "Maybe. The guys on the team come over every so often. It's enough space that it doesn't feel crowded."

We take the elevator to the next two levels. Part of the second floor is basically a man cave with billiards, a poker table, flat screen TVs, and leather recliners. There's even a small bar stocked with top-shelf liquor, presumably for when his teammates visit.

This level also has an empty room that looks like it was meant to be a kids' playroom based on the storybook murals, another office, and a library with a fireplace and gorgeous built-in bookshelves with plenty of room for more books. The perfect place to spend a rainy day cuddled under a cozy blanket with a book and...Luc.

Four roomy bedrooms, two double-vanity bathrooms, a nanny suite, a bright and spacious open area, and a laundry room take up the third floor. I'm pretty sure my eyes and mouth have been wide open in amazement during the entire tour. Luc's house is made for a large family. It makes me wonder if he chose it for that reason subconsciously, despite his vow of celibacy.

"The house is way too big for me with all these bedrooms," he admits, "but I like the layout and I like the neighborhood. And I'm hoping Daphne will be able to come live here with me someday."

"It's perfect. Whoever designed the remodel built it for daily family living, as well as entertaining formally and informally."

The top floor is where the primary suite is located. Besides the bedroom, which has a large sitting area and giant his and hers walk-in closets, there's yet another office and a magnificently huge bathroom with a jetted tub and a shower that can each fit a half-dozen people comfortably. The shower with its mosaic tiles has multiple shower heads sticking out from the ceiling and walls.

"I think I've entered paradise. You have a beautiful home, Luc." Besides the size and design, I love the tray ceilings in almost every room and fancy molding and medallions throughout the house.

"Thanks. A little big, but I like it, at least the parts I use. I do use the rooftop, but we'll skip it for tonight. There's a greenhouse and a hot tub up there."

"Perfect for stargazing," I say dreamily.

He laughs. "Okay, country mouse. You might see a handful of stars. I hate to burst your bubble, but you're more likely to see lights from planes and helicopters."

It doesn't matter. I love the house and its separate areas for entertaining, relaxing, and family living. I had thought all the residences in New York City, especially Manhattan, were small and cramped. Even the luxury homes I've been in were small compared to their equally priced counterparts outside of the city. Although, his place is technically two homes.

His bedroom is large and has a giant bed centered against one wall and a fireplace opposite it. I'm surprised to find the room decorated in shades of blue and green rather than the typical bachelor-pad color scheme of metallics and neutrals, like Brent's. Luc had mentioned he'd hired an interior decorator...someone who must have noticed the color of Luc's eyes. I wonder if it was a woman, perhaps the female architect he'd hired, who'd hoped to share the bedroom she'd designed? Despite knowing what I do about Luc's ten years of celibacy, a stab of jealousy pierces me at the thought of him giving another woman the kind of mind-numbing pleasure he's given me.

There's a sofa and a thick, soft-looking rug in front of the fireplace. I can just picture making love with him in front of it when the fire is going and then curling up in his arms afterward.

I shake the image away, knowing that's not going to happen tonight. No point in getting myself any more worked up.

"Since my bag is mostly full of dirty laundry, could I borrow a T-shirt?"

"Sure." He gets one out of a dresser and tosses it to me. "I'll be back. I'm going to clean up the kitchen and lock up."

"Let me come help you. I just assumed you had someone to do that. I'm sorry." I really need to work on making assumptions.

Luc is already shaking his head. "I do have someone come in a couple of times a week, but I'm capable of loading a dishwasher. You get to bed. I can see the circles under your eyes now."

I think about insisting, but he's already left. Anyway, the early morning start and the travel have taken their toll. I text my mother and Bobbie to let them know I won't be home tonight, then get my makeup bag and toothbrush out of my carry-on to wash up.

Minutes later, I crawl into the middle of the big bed since I'm not sure which side he usually sleeps on. I figure he'll have no choice but to sleep close to me, whichever side he chooses. I settle cozily under a down comforter on soft sheets, wrapped in one of Luc's T-shirts. I press my nose against his pillow and breathe in, reveling in the hint of his masculine scent. Snuggling in deeper, I drop into sleep.

27

Luc

WHEN I COME UP to bed, it's to find Charlie snuggled in the middle of it. Fuck, she looks good in my bed, her blonde hair spread over my pillow.

I slide in beside her, trying not to wake her, but she's so tired she doesn't even move. I don't know what I'll do if she scoots closer to snuggle against my back, her small breasts with the sensitive nipples poking into me.

I hold in my groan but squeeze my eyes shut. *Three years?* She's obviously ready to get back into the game. And oh, how I'd love to play with her.

If I keep up this line of thought, I'm not going to get any sleep tonight. I mentally go over my playbook to get my mind off Charlie and her warm body.

A hand on my shoulder is shaking me. "Luc."

I snap my eyes open and realize I had fallen asleep, though for how long I'm not sure. Charlie is hovering over me. I can just make out her face in the dim light of the streetlights filtering in between the blinds.

"Hey. Are you okay?" I ask.

"Me? You're the one hyperventilating in your sleep." She brushes a hand over my forehead. "The dream again?"

I stir, sitting up to lean against the headboard. She pulls herself up next to me, her leg brushing against mine. My body immediately reacts, and I'm glad I decided on pajama pants so I can't feel her silky, bare skin against me. Being near Charlie puts me too close to the edge of losing my control as it is.

To get my mind off having her half-naked in my bed, I decide talking about my recurring dream will douse the sexual flames.

"Yeah. But like I said before, just snippets that don't fit together."

"Tell me about them." She picks up my hand and entwines her fingers with mine, then lays her head on my shoulder. "What do you dream?"

Sighing, I rest my head against the leather-covered headboard. "It always ends with the night of the accident, Daphne screaming and my mother, broken and bloody. The rest is just bits and pieces with big gaping holes in between...Daphne crying in terror while Victor beats our mother." I close my eyes, admitting, "I'm afraid it's just my subconscious making up this stuff to help me ease my conscience, because I can't stand the thought that I killed my mother." I hate the yearning note in my voice and hope Charlie can't hear it.

"You need to try to get those memories back."

"I know. I'm just..." I shrug and look at her.

"Afraid of what you'll remember?"

How does she understand me so well?

"Luc—" Charlie sits forward and twists to face me, one hand on my chest. "What if it's true? Can you go to someone, like a—"

"Hypnotherapist?" I interrupt.

"Yes!"

"The therapist Joey recommended, the one I'm seeing, does hypnotherapy."

Charlie frowns. "Joey? My Joey? She knows about this?"

Do I discern a note of jealousy along with the confusion?

"No, she doesn't know all of it. Just that I have dreams and don't remember what happened that night. Don't worry, Green Eyes. You're the only person I've told the whole story to."

Charlie looks at me in annoyance. "I think you need to be checked for color blindness. My eyes are gray."

I grin. "I know." I can't help but kiss her when she realizes my meaning and scowls at me. I hear her breath hitch and pull away before she can deepen the kiss.

"Luc," she breathes.

Knowing what she's asking with just my name, I shake my head. "Not yet, darling."

"Well, that gives me hope." With a sigh of resignation, she puts her head on my shoulder again and asks, "So are you going to do the hypnotherapy?"

I nod. "Yes." I put up a hand when she lifts her head again in excitement, about to bombard me with questions. "She hasn't put me under yet. She wants to get to know me first before bringing me back to that night, to make sure my mental state is stable enough to handle whatever I might learn. Her words."

"Oh, Luc. That's..." She stops to search for the right word.

"Scary," I fill in for her. "And nerve-racking. And just a little bit of a relief. Like I might finally be able to put it all to rest when I know and move on with my life, once and for all."

"Liberating."

"Yes, that too. Or at least I hope it will be. Let's see what comes out of it. As the doc said, it could open a whole new can of worms that I'll have to deal with."

"But at least you'll have something to deal with, once you know what it is. You can face it, overcome it."

God, I hope she's right. I don't tell her my biggest fear is that I'll get confirmation of my guilt or discover something even worse.

I look down at Charlie when I hear her yawn. Of course she's tired. It's still the middle of the night.

"Come on, darling. Back to sleep now."

Charlie shifts to lie down again, and when I settle back in my spot, she scoots closer and puts her head on my shoulder.

She's going to be the death of me, I think as I breathe in the scent of her hair. "Charlotte, I need you to move over a little."

She snuggles in closer and murmurs, "Mmm. Why?"

"Because I'm dying here," I groan.

"Good." Pressing a kiss a little too close to my nipple, she moves up and folds her arms on my chest, putting our mouths just centimeters apart. "Fine, I'll move. But will you kiss me first? I love the way you kiss." She bites her bottom lip while staring at my mouth, making me want to free her luscious lip and soothe it with my tongue. "You kiss amazingly well," she continues, moving her gaze up to meet mine. "I guess you had a lot of practice with all those women you were seen with."

By the time she finishes talking, my mouth is on hers. I'm helpless to resist. I love kissing her too. And touching her. She's so responsive, her body sensitive to my slightest touch. My hands roam over her back, down to her slim hips, and under the thin T-shirt. Her nipples tighten into hard points and jut into my naked chest.

Between the tongue-tangling kiss and her mouthwatering breasts, I'm lost.

It takes all the willpower I have and then some, but I resist taking her as I did our first time. That had been too fucking fast. Instead, I allow myself the pleasure of pleasuring her, taking my time and savoring the feel and taste of her. I kiss her mouth endlessly. I hadn't realized how much I loved to kiss, slow and deep, tongues stroking against each other. I've kissed other women in public for show and sometimes in private when I couldn't avoid it, before making excuses for not being able to finish what I started. I won't be able to finish what I start with Charlie now, either, but she knows that. I don't have to make any excuses.

By digging deep for self-control, I'm able to help her fin-ish—twice—using my fingers the first time while I took turns kissing her sweet breasts and sweeter mouth. The second time was as much for myself as for her as I pulled her up to sit on my face. I kissed her pussy as deeply as I did her mouth while she hung onto the headboard and made the sweetest sounds of pleasure. When I finish drinking in every last bit of sweetness, she slides limply to the bed, sated and exhausted. After giving me a kiss of thanks, she turns over and gives me space as promised.

Fuck that. "Get over here." I flip her toward me and pull her close. So much for needing distance from temptation.

She burrows into my chest and drops into sleep in an instant, her head resting on my shoulder, her leg flung over my hip. Hesitantly, I tangle my own limbs with hers and force my body to relax. She feels too good to let go.

The familiar guilt starts to creep in, warring with the content-ment I'm feeling while lying with Charlie and holding her in my arms. I haven't cuddled with a woman or slept with one in so long that I can't remember when the last time was. Possibly never. As a teenager, it was usually quick, in the back seat of a car or the bed of a truck or against a tree at the lake. There wasn't the time, or the desire frankly, for cuddling afterward.

I lie there, listening to Charlie's soft breathing, feeling her warm exhales on my chest as I hold her close. But the guilt—and the torment of a raging hard-on—eventually force me out of the bed.

I pick one of the guest rooms I offered her and pass the remain-der of the night in restless sleep, thankful it will be a short practice in the morning.

28

Charlie

I AWAKEN SLOWLY, FEELING more rested than I have in months, even well before my pregnancy. It must have a lot to do with the satisfaction Luc provided during the night. A woman could get used to the endless pleasure he gives me. I'm definitely spoiled for anyone else. No one will ever compare to Luc. I hope I never have to find out.

I sigh, knowing I'm getting ahead of myself. Just because he has a talented mouth and my crush is back full force doesn't mean he's my Mr. Right.

Feeling the cold space beside me, I figure he's left for practice long ago. Dragging myself out of bed, I head for the shower. Despite the deep sleep, the morning nausea drives away my rested feeling. I take an anti-nausea pill the doctor recommended, which I use only when absolutely necessary.

When I spy the note in the kitchen that Luc left, I sigh gratefully. I hate to bother Reggie, but I don't think I can make it through the long train ride home, afraid that the motion sickness might push me over the edge into actually vomiting.

"Hey, little girl. You're finally up," Reggie says when I call him.

"Yes, I slept a lot longer than I expected," I say, ignoring the 'little girl' comment. I suppose I am little to him, and I don't think he's trying to demean with the words. "I hate to bother you, but Luc said that you'd be able to drive me home?"

"I would have, but Luc's on his way back now and he said he'd take you. He should be there in a little while."

"Oh. Okay. Thanks."

I hang up and go back to Luc's room to tidy it up and bring my travel bag down. Not sure how long a little while might be, I head to the kitchen to try to force myself to eat something. Luc finds me not long after, trying to swallow some oatmeal.

"Hey. You're up," he says, then frowns in concern. "You okay?"

Putting a hand to my stomach, I grimace. "I was trying to eat this oatmeal and not gag. Sorry, I just can't." I bring the bowl to the sink and rinse it out, flushing the remaining oatmeal into the garbage disposal. "I'll have lunch when I get home."

"You better." He gives me a stern look, then says, "Let me quickly change and then I'll drive you."

"No, it's okay. I'll take the train." With a makeshift barf bag with me if I have to. I don't want to put him out when he has to get back to the stadium later to fly out to an away game.

"No way. I'm taking you. I'll be back in two minutes," he calls out over his shoulder as he jogs out.

By the time he comes back, I'm relieved to note the nausea is receding. The pill is doing its job.

Luc takes my suitcase and my hand. "Come on." He leads me down a short hallway off the kitchen and opens a door.

When I enter the whitewashed garage, twin to the one Reggie parked in last night, I take a second to enjoy the sleek and sexy classic Corvette. It's bright red against the stark walls.

"Gorgeous car," I say, settling into the luxurious black leather seat while he stows my bag in the narrow space behind his seat.

"Thanks. She's a '67 Stingray," he says, sliding his long legs under the steering wheel. "I don't get to drive her often—and I'm probably not supposed to since I've been told I shouldn't get too many miles on this baby."

"My father would have disagreed with you and whoever told you that. He loved old cars and said if he ever got one, he'd drive it all the time. He didn't understand people who bought something for a ton of money just so they could look at it or say they owned it."

"I agree with him." He pulls out of the garage carefully, looking for pedestrians before pulling out into the street. I note a man standing across the street with a camera taking pictures.

"Luc," I start to warn him.

"It's okay. I had the windows tinted, another sacrilegious thing to do, I'm told. He won't be able to see you."

Relieved, I settle back. I think about what my father might have said about Luc. As a die-hard New England Patriots fan, he would have had a lot to say about the team he played for, none of it good. But he would have respected Luc as a talented football player and rooted for him, even while hoping for his team to lose. I'd like to think my dad, as a father, would have been able to offer Luc some wisdom about his troubles.

Despite the tragedy and difficulties in my family, I'm lucky to have had my father for the few short years I did and to still have my mother. What kind of a man would Luc be today if he'd had a better father or been able to spend more years with his mother?

Would things have been different for the two of us if that had been the case? I wouldn't have tracked him down and gone to his house that night. We might still have met through Brent or my work. Would we still have felt this sizzling chemistry between us? I'm sure I would have because I've always been attracted to him, even before I met him, but I'm not anything like the well-endowed, sexy women he pretends to be with. If he really had been with all those women, I'm not sure if he'd have even noticed me.

The thought makes me uncomfortable, but I brush it aside because the reality is right now. And right now, he's sitting next to me. Based on his inability to keep his hands off me when I get too close, even knowing he isn't going to be fulfilled in the same way, I like to think he would have still felt the instant attraction.

I genuinely like Luc, and I hope he works through his issues soon because I want an actual relationship with him. And I want to make love with him again, for real. Desperately.

The yearning builds within me, and my body begins to ache in memory. I squirm and squeeze my legs together to try to ease the torment.

"You okay there? Should I pull over?"

I start and turn to find him looking at me with concern. His gaze flicks over me, and I bite my lip, hoping he can't tell how turned on I am, just thinking about having sex with him. He isn't even touching me. No man has ever made me feel this way, and I'm beyond frustrated that it's with a man who won't allow himself to fully follow up on what he makes me feel.

Something in my face must have given me away because his eyes blaze as they flicker over my body again. My face feels warm. I look down to see my nipples have beaded against my thin sweater. I resist the urge to cover them, both to hide the evidence of my desire and to ease the ache I can feel there too. I'd much rather have his big hands on me. Better yet, his warm mouth and talented tongue.

God, his tongue. What he could do with it, not just on my breasts but between my legs. A moan builds in my throat, and I take a quick breath to stop it. It sounds like a gasp.

"Darling, if you don't stop that, I'm going to have to pull over."

Yes, please. The thought is so loud in my head, I look at Luc to see if I've said it aloud. His jaw is clenching, his cheeks tinged with color. Both of his hands are clasping the steering wheel tightly. My gaze falls to his lap, and I can see he's suffering as badly as I am.

I don't believe in suffering.

"Then pull over," I tell him, turning my body to face him and shifting as close to him as the seatbelt and center console will allow me. I wish we had a good old-fashioned bench seat right about now. At least his seat is pushed back to accommodate his long legs and the gearshift is higher up on the console, so I'm able to lean over between the seats without impeding his shifting. I lean against his seat with my left arm while my right hand reaches over to touch his thigh.

He looks at me suspiciously. "What do you think you're doing?"

"If I'm feeling sexually frustrated despite what you did for me last night, I can't imagine what you're feeling. Let me ease some of that." I give him what I hope is a sexy siren smile as my palm rubs up and down his thigh, getting closer to the bulge that speaks of his desire.

"Darling, you better keep your hands to yourself right now. There are too many damned people on the road who suddenly forgot how to drive in the rain."

The hint of his Southern drawl deepens just as his voice does. He has to downshift for a slower car ahead of him that refuses to move over to the right lane. His thigh tenses and releases under my hand as he works the gas pedal. I stroke the spot above the muscle a little more firmly, and it tenses again.

I glance out through the tinted windows and see we've passed Yonkers and are on the Parkway. Traffic is congested as usual, but it's moving at a decent speed for once, despite the drizzle that has just started. Until a few minutes ago, Luc had been zipping efficiently around cars to move even faster.

"Find a place to pull over," I plead in a low voice. Giving in to an unfamiliar urge, I bite his bicep through his shirt, desperate to taste him.

I rest my hand just next to his erection and use only my thumb to touch his long, hard length. He curses and tenses, but I give him credit for shifting smoothly into high gear again as he finds an opening to zip around the oblivious driver ahead of us. I return my attention to stroking him, watching his erection grow with every pass over it. It has to be getting uncomfortable being trapped in his pants.

When the car slows down, I glance out the window to see he's pulled off the exit and onto a side street. My hand grows bolder and covers him entirely, my fingers tracing his shape and my palm pressing against him. Another curse followed by a groan. "Fuck, Charlie."

For a moment, I wonder if I'm pushing him past what he's comfortable with, given his vow. "I'm sorry. I shouldn't—"

His mouth covers mine in a punishing kiss. My moment of doubt turns into a feeling of joy when his hand traps mine over his pulsing erection, silently asking for what I've been dying to give him.

My fingers squirm beneath his to find the zipper tab to his dark khakis and draw it down slowly. Once I have it opened all the way, his hand falls away as I worm my fingers into the opening, feeling his heat and hardness through a thin layer of cloth.

"Mm, silk. It feels so good." The fabric makes it easier to slide my fingers across until I find the opening of his boxers. Reaching in farther, I finally feel soft skin over hot steel. "Mm, you feel even better." Wrapping my hand around him, I gently pull him out.

"Jesus fuck, Charlie." He releases my mouth to utter the words. I take the opportunity to shift in my seat so I can lean closer to his lap.

As I work my fist over him, I use my other hand to release my seatbelt and fold myself over the console. His hand tangles in my hair, but he doesn't pull me away or push me closer. Instead, his other hand curves over my back to my breast.

Angling him just right, I take him into my mouth just as he rolls my nipple and pinches it. I moan at the zing that travels straight to my clit. Fuck, that feels good.

In return, I try to give him as much pleasure as he's given me so many times already. I use my hands, my lips, my tongue...

Taking him in as deeply as I can, I hum in appreciation at the clean musky scent of his skin as I breathe through my nose. He groans at the vibration, and his hand fists in my hair. He's rubbing and playing with my over-sensitive nipple as if it's my clit, which is throbbing as if it can feel his touch directly.

"Fuck, Charlie. I'm going to—"

It isn't a warning, it's a request for permission, and I hum my agreement before suctioning my lips around his head, working his hard length with my hand. He tenses and a second later, he jerks his hips in tiny movements against my mouth. His fingers tighten almost painfully on my nipple and a wave washes over me. I moan at the forceful throbbing between my legs.

"Ah, God. That feels so fucking amazing," he growls, lifting his hips to push himself farther into my mouth.

I take all of him and wait to release him until he loosens his tight grip on my hair. He runs his hand over my head as he relaxes back against the seat. I slowly work him out of my mouth, licking as I go, loving the taste and feel of him. The wet pop as I let go of him sounds loud in the enclosed space of the car.

I ease myself up, licking my lips in satisfaction and wiping the tears caused by taking him so deep. The moment feels so much more special because he hasn't allowed himself this pleasure in years. And I was the one he allowed to give it to him.

"I was a little out of it, but...it sounded like you came?" he asks, sounding awed and still trying to catch his breath.

I grin. "I did. It's never happened before, but you playing with my nipple did it."

"That's fucking hot. Can't wait to make it happen again." He cups my face and kisses me softly, thumbing away the remaining tears. The look of tenderness in his beautiful hazel eyes undoes me. I smile at him, suddenly shy, an emotion I rarely feel. To counteract the discomfort it causes me, I shake my head at him in amazement.

"Kudos to you for having the wherewithal to find an exit onto a quiet road." Quite a feat on the parkway, not too far outside the city. Since a car like his would draw a closer look by passersby, we're lucky the lack of houses nearby and the rain have kept the road mostly free of cars.

"Yeah, well, I would have needed a hell of a lot more 'wherewith-al' to stay on the road if I tried to drive with your mouth making me lose control." He adjusts himself and zips up his pants.

"You're welcome."

He shakes his head, smiling. "You're a menace. Now put your seatbelt back on."

I settle back into my seat, locking the belt into place.

"Luc..." My fleeting doubt from earlier returns. "I hope I didn't...I mean, you wanted this, right?" I ask. I'm such an idiot. It's something I should have asked before, not after it's all over.

He takes my hand and kisses it. "Hey. You didn't force me to do anything I didn't want from the moment I saw you. Is this going a lot faster than I expected? Yes. But never doubt I want you, to be with you. With every fucking fiber of my being."

And just like that, my heart tumbles headlong into love. I can only hope Luc will eventually catch and protect the fragile organ and not break it into tiny pieces.

29

Luc

F OR THE REMAINDER OF the drive to her house, Charlie be-
haves. While a part of me is feeling guilty for the pleasure
she's given me, the rest of me is feeling somewhat sated and deeply
content. I decide to deal with the guilt later and to just enjoy the
drive with her.

She calls her mother to let her know she's on her way home with
a guest, without mentioning my name. When she hangs up, she
tunes the radio to a classic rock station, then casually warns me that
I'll be meeting her mother, who'd told her to invite her "guest" in
for lunch.

"She'll know you as Brent's teammate and that I interviewed
you, but there's a good chance she'll guess who you really are. I
mean—"

"We'll deal with it if she does. If you take after your mother, I'm
sure it'll be best if I lay out the cards for her."

I'm surprised I'm able to smile and tease Charlie at the possibility of her mother learning I got her daughter pregnant.

"Tell me more about your family," I say.

She tells me about how everything changed for her family in
one night, like it had for mine, when her father and brother died

fighting a fire, and how her family struggled after Bobbie's difficult birth, followed a few years later by her mother's stroke.

I have no idea how they had survived through all of that and seem to have come out of it stronger than ever.

I understand when I meet Charlie's mother, Sandra. Despite her limp as she comes out to the wide porch to greet us, her bearing indicates she is the strength and the glue that has held the family together.

I experience a pang in my chest as I remember my own mother, who had the strength to raise me with so much love and to survive Victor for too many years.

Trying not to squirm as Sandra gives me the once-over with knowing eyes that seem to penetrate my soul, I smile and take her hand to kiss the back of it.

"It's a pleasure to meet you, Mrs. Hutchinson."

"You're quite charming, aren't you? Please, call me Sandra."

As Charlie leads me through the house, I'm surprised to find it homey despite the size. There are photographs on much of the wall space and knickknacks on most of the surfaces. Having been to Brent's loft once, which was contemporary and spartan, I'm surprised by the contrast.

The yeasty smell of fresh warm bread greets me when we enter the kitchen.

"Lunch is almost ready," Sandra says.

"Mom, you didn't have to cook—I could have put something together when we got here."

"You're bringing a young man home for the first time since high school. We never even met your college boyfriends. Besides, Bobbie helped me before she left with her friends."

"Well, you go sit at the table and I'll finish up. Luc, you too."

Charlie brings both of us glasses filled with iced tea, then moves around the kitchen. Since Sandra sits at one end of the oval table, I choose a seat in the middle, where I can watch Charlie as she sets the table. I'm hesitant to face the older woman, feeling a rare

SHEFALI PREM

case of nerves from having to make conversation with a girl-friend's mother.

Girlfriend. Is that what Charlie is? I'm not sure yet, but she is definitely...something.

I needn't have worried about Sandra. She doesn't pry or ask awkward questions. Instead, she asks about football, how playing with Brent now is different from the first time we played together, and where I grew up.

Charlie carries the soup tureen to the table, interrupting us before the conversation can get too personal. I smile at her gratefully when she sits between me and her mother.

The meal of pasta fasul and homemade bread isn't fancy, but it is truly delicious and filling.

Charlie keeps the conversation flowing, steering it toward general topics. But just as I put my spoon down after eating every last bite of my second helping, Sandra calmly asks, "So, Lucien, are you the father of Charlotte's baby?"

Charlie's fork clatters onto her plate, and she starts coughing on the sip of iced tea she'd just taken. I'm glad Sandra waited until I'd finished swallowing my last bite, or I would likely have inhaled it and choked.

"Mom!" Charlie gasps.

"What?" Sandra asks innocently. "I'm sure it's not a coincidence that you stayed overnight somewhere in his vicinity last night, which is why he's driving you home, or that he's the only man you've brought home in years."

Charlie gives me an I-told-you-so look and shrugs but doesn't answer her mother. She waits for me to take the lead on this.

I give Charlie a small smile, then look directly at Sandra. "Yes, ma'am, I am."

She raises an eyebrow when I don't expound beyond that. I shift uncomfortably when she doesn't look away, and I break under pressure. "I'm sorry, Sandra. I asked Charlotte not to tell anyone because I have personal issues I need to take care of before this information can become public."

"I am not the public, young man. I'm that baby's grandmother." Her voice is still calm, but there is a thread of steel underlying it.

The corner of my mouth curls up in unexpected humor. I can see where Charlie got her fire and temper from. "Lucky baby." I stand up and walk around the end of the table to sit on the other side of Sandra. I take her hand and hold it in both of mine.

"I'd like to ask that you please keep this to yourself for a little while. I wouldn't have asked it of Charlie if it wasn't a matter of safety. It's only—"

"Is my daughter in danger?" she demands.

I curse inwardly, clearly not having thought this through. I glance at Charlie, who is watching us silently, and back to Sandra. "I'm not sure. But there is the possibility that if my connection to Charlie and the baby became public knowledge..." When her hand tenses in mine, I squeeze gently to reassure her. "Don't worry. I won't let anything happen to them, but it's easier to do that if we keep this to ourselves until I can remove the risk."

Sandra searches my face, and I wonder what she is looking for. Whatever it is, she apparently finds it, because she nods. "Okay. Not that I had any intention of gossiping about my daughter's business."

I smile again at her acerbic tone. She's almost opposite in personality from my own mother, but the need to protect her offspring is the same. I'm glad Charlie has her.

I leave shortly afterward since I'm scheduled to be a guest on a sports show that afternoon before flying out with the team. The phone interrupts my thoughts of the drive earlier in the day—and of Charlie's mouth on me.

Fucking Victor. I should have blocked his number. I'm tempted to ignore his call, but he hasn't called me, not even to acknowledge the money I sent. I need to know what he knows about Daphne and where his head is at.

"What do you want, Victor?" I ask unceremoniously.

"Always straight to business with you, boy. People probably let you get away with it 'cause you're a superstar, but that ain't gonna work when you're done playing ball."

"Don't worry, I use my manners with those who matter." I can't help goading him.

There's a long moment of silence before Victor speaks again. But it isn't vitriolic as it usually is when I push his buttons. It sounds like he's doing his best to hold on to his patience. I'm not sure what to make of that.

"Well, that just plain hurt, son. But I'll let you make it up to me. I'm going to let you in on a sweetheart deal. I have a business opportunity and I need a little seed money."

"No way. I told you that was the last time. In fact, *you* told me it was the last time."

"Let's make *this* the last time, because I'll be set for life after this huge business deal. It's practically guaranteed to quadruple what I put in, so the more I put in, the more I'll make."

"And how much are you looking to put in?" I ask out of idle curiosity, not because I have any intention of giving him a dime.

"Ten mil."

I can't help laughing at his audacity. "You're out of your fucking mind." The gall of him to ask me for that much money and say he's doing *me* a fucking favor.

His voice turns cajoling. "Come on, son. Think of it as a loan. I'll pay you back when I reap the returns."

Yeah, right.

If my mother had been alive, I would have given her that and more, no questions asked. But the difference is, she was always there for me growing up, whereas Victor didn't want anyone to even know about me until it was convenient for him.

"I need you to send the money to me right away. Could you do that for me, son?"

How many times has he said son now? He's emphasizing our blood tie, as if that would make me more likely to agree. But I'm done going along with the blackmail, emotional and otherwise.

"Sorry, no can do. Actually, I'm not sorry. It's not my fault you can't manage the money I give you or that you can't earn any on your own. Unfortunately for me, you're still relatively young, and I'm not doing this for the rest of your life. You know, I might have taken care of you in your old age if you had taken care of me or my mother at any point."

"Have you forgotten everything I've done for you so you could follow in my footsteps and become a football star?"

Victor's control is slipping. His voice is tight from restraining himself from going off on me like he wants to.

Even knowing I'll pay for the jibes, I can't resist needling my "good ol' daddy."

"I think I've outgrown your footsteps, old man. My star is bigger and shinier than yours ever was."

I've pushed him over the edge. His breathing becomes harsh, and his voice blazes with hate. "You son of a bitch! You got your talent from me, and don't you ever forget it, boy. You owe me for saving you from jail. You owe me for giving you football. You owe me for your fucking life and don't you fucking forget it!"

I smile with grim satisfaction at hearing Victor lose control—and lose his fake drawl. Before he can catch his breath and launch into another tirade, I say, "Fix your own fucking mess this time, and don't call me again."

"You're gonna be sorry, you son of a—"

I hang up and block his number. The vitriol has come across loud and clear in those two seconds, and I don't want to hear any more.

My heart is racing at what I've done without thinking everything through. I should have been more patient, trying to find out what Victor knew, but I just couldn't bear to listen to his voice calling me son one more time. Not being able to get through to me is going to piss Victor off even more. Desperation can make people do irrational things, especially if they're already teetering on the edge.

I send a text to Reggie to keep an eye out for Victor in case he comes around and another to Gabe to let him know of the latest conversation.

Nevertheless, I need to be ready for the consequences of pissing off Victor and to counter whatever he might do with ammunition of my own. The best way to do that is to try to remember what really happened the night of my mother's death.

30

Luc

"I WANT YOU TO listen to the sound of my voice as I count to ten. With each number, you'll feel more relaxed. Your eyes will feel heavy and want to close. Just let it happen. You are safe."

I listen to Dr. Vandermeyer's gentle voice as she guides me into deep relaxation. As soothing as it is, there's no way I'm going to be able to let go. I doubt very much this hypnosis thing is going to work, but I have to try. To get rid of the shadows, the guilt. To get Victor out of my life and move forward.

"Eight...nine...ten."

Between one breath and the next, I find myself at the lake by the bonfire, one hand holding a beer and the other caressing the ass of a girl in a bikini. I'm feeling so carefree, like I'm on top of the world. High school is done, and I'm going to college to play ball on a full ride. I've just had fun with one girl, and this one wants a turn next. Could life possibly get any better than this?

But in the blink of an eye, I'm standing outside the tiny house I lived in with my maman and Daphne. I hear the bastard's voice shouting and my mother's whimpers, my sister's crying.

The sound of flesh hitting flesh, a thud. I wrench open the screen door and run inside to see Maman cowering on the floor, doing her best to keep Daphne behind her with one arm while the other is raised to ward off more blows.

"Who the fuck do you think you are, telling me to get out! I'm going to fucking kill you. And the brat. Who is she? She better not be yours, you filthy whore!"

Victor's voice, mercifully absent for the last few years, is angrier than I've ever heard it before.

"No, please. She's not mine. I'm just babysitting. I swear it."

The monster draws back his foot to kick Maman, but I fly at him with a roar, knocking Victor against the wall. He doesn't stand a chance, as surprised as he is by the attack. My relentless blows land on him, wherever I can reach as he tries to evade me. He slides down the wall and cowers, slumping over to protect himself from my fists and kicks.

"Stop, Lucien! Stop!" Maman's hand is tugging at me, pulling me out of the blinding, pent-up rage. "Come on now, my love. We have to go. We need to get out of here. Lucien, darling." Her soft, scared entreaties finally penetrate, and I stare down at the still form of my father at my feet. Is he dead? God, I hope so. I'd happily go to jail for the rest of my life and give up my future if I knew Maman never had to worry about the asshole again.

Unfortunately, Victor is still alive. As he stirs, I back away and take the whimpering Daphne from Maman's arms. We rush out of the house to the pickup truck I'd left running. I open the back door to put Daphne into her car seat, but she is still terrified and begins screaming, not letting me put her seatbelt on, her body writhing to get back into the comfort of my arms.

Maman slips into the back with her. "Shh, my darling. Shh. You're okay, my love."

Daphne turns to Maman, and I jump into the front and drive over the grass, not bothering to reverse out of the driveway when Victor staggers out of the house. Too busy looking in the rearview mirror, I clip the mailbox, knocking out a headlight. My remaining headlight is too dim to see the dark, tree-shrouded road very well.

I'm forced to slow down around the curves as I alternate my gaze from the road to the mirrors to see if he's following.

Keeping my eye on the road as I round a curve, I don't notice when Victor suddenly comes up behind us and rams into the back of the truck. I speed up despite being unable to see more than a few feet ahead of me. A quick glance in the rearview mirror shows no lights. Did he stop? Go off the road? Or maybe his lights went out when he hit the truck. Afraid it was the latter, and he's behind us, I speed up a little more.

"Put your seatbelt on, Mama!" I shout at my mother, putting my own on with one hand, keeping my eye on the narrow, dark road ahead of us.

Without warning, the sound of a firecracker goes off at the same time as the tire blows out. I can't control the truck as it veers sharply, hitting the guardrail of the bridge we were about to cross, the one that goes over a wide, shallow creek bed that's almost always dry. The truck is suddenly airborne. Time slows. The world is spinning—upside down and around. There's a crash, another spin. A forceful impact sends a lightning bolt of pain through my body, straight to my head, causing the darkness to swallow me.

Through the dark silence, I hear Dr. Vandermeyer's voice guiding me back from the black hole, her soft voice counting again, backward this time, urging me to come back and assuring me I'm safe. I open my eyes slowly and blink awake.

"How do you feel, Luc?"

I focus my gaze on her, trying to get my brain to come out of the visions that seem to hang in the air around me. Did I fall asleep and have my nightmare again?

"Was all that real?"

"Tell me what you remember."

I go over what I'd just experienced.

"Based on what you were describing while you were under, it appears as though you had a blow—or several blows—to your head during the car crash that caused you to lose consciousness.

This could also be the cause of your memory loss. That combined with the trauma and grief of losing of your mother."

"Victor was telling me the truth. I was driving, not my mother. I caused the accident." I didn't realize until that moment how much I'd been hoping it was a lie.

"You were driving, Luc," Dr. Vandermeyer said. "But I don't agree that it was your fault. You were trying to get away from someone who said he was going to kill your mother and sister." She pauses before continuing. "You also said you heard a firecracker at the moment the tire blew out. Do you recall the sound?"

I close my eyes as the sound I remembered echoes in my mind. A random firecracker? Or something else? Like...a gunshot.

I open my eyes wide. "Are you sure these are actual memories?" I'm afraid to believe. "How can you be sure I didn't just fall asleep and dream again...dream what I wanted to see, so I could get rid of this guilt that's been eating away at me?"

She shakes her head. "You haven't been just dreaming all these years, Luc. It was fragments of your memory, your subconscious giving you the truth. Your guilt appears to have been determined to keep it suppressed."

I am numb. My mother's death, my sister's injuries, weren't my fault. Victor caused the crash—he must have shot out the truck tire, causing me to lose control. And he used my lack of memory to his advantage for years. That thought brings a rush of feeling back into my body—pure, unadulterated rage. Through the red mist coloring my thoughts, I barely hear what the doctor is saying.

"Also, you talked me through the event while you were under. You answered my questions, described it as you were reliving it. Tell me what you're feeling."

I don't know what I'm feeling. Everything. Too much. Relieved that I finally know the truth. Grateful that I hadn't been directly responsible for my mother's death. Hopeful that I can finally move on with my life, free to experience all the joy it has to offer.

And resentment and rage at Victor for putting me through hell all these years.

"You said you video recorded the session." She asked for my permission before we started.

"Yes, but I advise you to give yourself some time to process what you've learned before putting yourself through it again." Her kind face is full of concern, but I have no intention of watching the video.

"Can I take the recording to the police?" I want Victor to pay.

"While it can't be used in court, you may be able to use it to reopen the investigation into your mother's death."

I'm torn between immense relief that I wasn't directly responsible for my mother's death and an overwhelming desire to cause Victor's. I wouldn't feel one shred of remorse for killing Victor. No, I'd feel relief, elation, a sense of satisfaction. Justice.

I need to get out of here. I have to think this through clearly. As much as I'd love to go straight to Victor and choke a confession out of him, I have to think about Daphne, Charlie, and the baby.

31

Luc

I WAIT TO GET home before taking out my phone to call Charlie and tell her what I've remembered. Before I can, the doorbell rings. I switch over to the app to check the security camera feed. A chill goes through me at seeing Victor standing on my doorstep. I had hoped to have more time to decide what to do about him before having to confront him.

While I debate about pretending to not be at home, Victor rings the doorbell again. Deciding to get it over with, and not wanting the paps to take photos of him on my doorstep, I open the door. I'm loath to let him into my home, but it's better to have this conversation inside in case he causes a scene. I gesture for him to come in, but the foyer is as far as we'll go.

I close the front door behind him, then cross my arms and wait in silence for Victor to speak. Until I figure out what to do, I don't want to give away the fact that I've regained my memory of that night.

Victor opts to dispense with the niceties as well. "I need the money, Luc," he says baldly, a tinge of fear and desperation lacing his words.

"As I've told you before, I'm not giving you more."

"You don't give me that money, I'll tell everyone that you killed your mother."

Finally. The moment I've been waiting for. I can't wait to see Victor's face when he realizes he's lost all power over me. "You go ahead and do that. Since you lied to the sheriff, you'll be going to jail along with me." I smile. "That's right. I remember everything now."

Victor freezes in shock for a moment before his expression turns smug. "Well, that's mighty convenient. Too bad you have no proof."

"I don't need proof. I just need the sheriff to reopen the case and give my investigators enough time to gather evidence."

Recognizing that he's lost this battle, Victor changes tactics again. "Look, I'm sorry about lying to you about the night your mama died. But remember that I also lied to protect you from being charged for beating me half to death."

"Because you were hurting my mother. Yeah, I remember that too. I remember all of it. As I said, I'll take my chances. It can't be worse than having to deal with you for the rest of my life."

"Let's see if you feel that way when I tell the world that you use steroids." Victor pivots with another ploy.

His new threat creates a moment of panic as I think of losing everything I worked so hard for—based on yet another lie. I push down the fear before he can see it and smile with a calm I don't feel. "You go right ahead and do that too, Victor."

My response shocks Victor, but he recovers quickly with a sneer. "What? You think you're too big a star, that everyone loves you now and won't believe it? I don't need evidence to ruin your reputation and career. I have a receipt for growth hormones, and I'll tell everyone you told me to get them for you. Once this is out there, people are always gonna doubt you got this far without a little help. Your name will be tainted forever."

I fold my arms across my chest and shrug. "I'll take my chances, especially if it means the money dries up and you'll never bother me again."

Quick as a flash, Victor's anger turns into desperation.

"Look, I'm sorry. Okay? Is that what you want me to say?"

"I don't need you to fucking say anything, Victor."

"Son, I just needed to make sure you wouldn't abandon me. You're all I had left."

"Really? The family card? After you tried to kill me too? It was pure luck that I didn't die too, so don't give me that bullshit." I give a mocking laugh.

Victor's expression doesn't change, but a fist tightens at his side. The calm I've been striving for settles over me, seeing how powerless Victor has become.

"Yeah, well, you didn't die, and we're still blood."

"You know, the problem with that, Victor, is you don't know a thing about family. After trying to kill me, you milk me for the past six years. And you mooched off your wife for years before that. I've seen you be a charming guy when you want to be. I've even heard you called handsome. You could have worked out a gig on TV or something when you left the game. But instead, you chose to be a leech."

I don't show my cards by revealing what Gabe uncovered about Victor's possible involvement in the deaths of my grandparents and his own father-in-law. I'm holding that close to my chest for now, because Victor's right. I don't have any evidence—of those suspected crimes or that he caused the car crash. I need to wait for Gabe to gather evidence that would put him away for good.

"What do you want me to say, son? I already said I'm sorry." Victor's voice is now tight with underlying anger, but he's holding his voice steady. He even manages a conciliatory smile.

"Are you? Really sorry? Or are you just trying to save your ass?" With my arms crossed and feet planted, I let him know I'm not going to budge for anything.

"Go ahead and spread your wild claims to the whole world," I say when Victor remains silent. "I can weather that storm financially, especially since I won't be giving you another dime. Sure, I'll lose endorsements, maybe have an asterisk by my stats, or never work in football again." I shrug. "But that's okay. You know why?" I lean toward him as if about to share a secret.

"Because I'll no longer have to put up with you. I earned every penny I had with my own blood and sweat. And I can do it again if I have to. I'm not afraid of hard work. I don't have addictions like you." I give a small laugh. "I might even have you to thank for that since it's my guilt that kept me away from all that stuff. And my fear of becoming like you."

I shake my head. "No, it's not thanks to you. It's because of my mother, a loving, beautiful woman who you tried to break. She taught me about working hard, never giving up."

Victor loses patience. "I don't give a fuck about her. She's long gone."

My own fists tighten now. It takes everything I have to not finish the job I started ten years ago. Carefully, I take a step back, but I bare my teeth, giving Victor an evil smile.

"My mother saved your life that night. She stopped me from beating you to death. You better leave, because she's not here now, and there's nothing I'd love to do more in this moment than to finish the job. Get the fuck out of my house."

I say it so calmly, Victor doesn't appear to understand the danger he's in, because he doesn't immediately move.

"Now!" I roar, my voice reverberating around the two-story tiled foyer. The calm and control evaporate in an instant, and I take a step forward, ready to pounce.

"You're going to regret this, motherfucker." The growled warning comes with a hate-filled glare before Victor hightails it out of the house.

I slam the door shut and lean over, hands on my knees, the adrenaline rushing through me now that he's gone. I try to breathe deeply to regain control as a cauldron of emotions roil inside me. Long moments later, when I can finally unfurl my tightly fisted fingers, I exhale once more to release the last of the tension in my body and stand straight.

I take a deep, cleansing breath and let it out and suddenly feel light, lighter than I have in years. Than ever. I might never play another professional football game again, I might lose my endorsements and become a pariah, but I don't care. I know what I'd rather do.

So I make some calls to start making it happen. First to Gabe to let him know about my conversation with Victor and my fear that he might try something.

"Make sure Daphne is watched at all times. Add more men if you have to," I tell him.

The next call is to my business team to get them rolling on updating an airtight trust for Daphne, and creating ones for Charlie and the baby to protect them financially if Victor does something to me or my reputation.

I video call Daphne to check in on her. As much as I want her here with me, I have to trust that she's safer at home in Mississippi. If she came to live with me, she'd be a prisoner in the house, between the paparazzi and the possibility of Victor trying something. At least in Mississippi, she can roam around the property and has the company of my aunt and uncle.

After she catches me up on the latest news in her life, I end the call and finally dial Charlie's number. I need to hear her voice.

32

Charlie

"**T**HAT MOTHERFUCKER," I GROWL through gritted teeth when Luc finishes telling me what he learned in his therapy session. My jaw is clenched partly because of what Victor has done to Luc, but mostly because my thighs are burning as I hold a wall squat. The hotel gym is closed for renovations so I'm doing calisthenics in my room. I figured being distracted by listening to Luc would help me forget how out of shape I've gotten since Mark has increased my workload.

"That he is."

I push off the wall to stand, my legs feeling like limp noodles. "You must be so relieved." When I feel like I can move without collapsing, I walk around the cramped room to loosen up my muscles.

"Yeah, it feels like a thousand pounds have fallen off my shoulders."

Despite the mixed emotions welling within me, I'm happy for him. I hope he'll now be able to move forward, but I also fear that moving forward might mean moving on—from me and the baby. He has years of normal life to make up for, and he can't do it if he makes a commitment to me. Not that I'm expecting a marriage proposal, but I do want more time with him, in every way, to see where this tentatively burgeoning relationship might lead.

Since the day of my ultrasound, we've been talking for hours on the phone. For the past couple of weeks, it's been our only form of communication. Our schedules haven't allowed for any time together.

In every conversation, whether it's about our families or our likes and dislikes, I find something more to love about him. And physically, I've never felt an attraction this intense with another man. I can't imagine ever feeling it with anyone else. Now that he's free from his guilt and self-punishment, maybe he'll be ready to make love for real. I just hope it's with me and only me.

To distract myself from my disturbing thoughts, I ask, "Did you talk to Victor, tell him that you remembered that night?"

I'm curious about how Luc will handle his father lying to him all these years.

"I did. You should have seen me kicking him out. You would—"

"Kick him out?"

"Yeah, he came over asking for more money."

"Again?" He told me about the two payments he already made since we met, and all the many times he's give Victor money over the years. "I hope you told him to fuck off."

Luc laughs. "I did."

How can he be so calm? I've only known about the payments for a short while, and it makes me boiling mad.

"I wish I'd done it long ago," Luc continues, "but I was afraid to risk it, for Daphne's sake. We'll see what he does now, but I have to admit I'm worried about him going after her."

My conscience pricks me at having contributed to his worry over his sister.

He sighs and continues. "Maybe telling him off wasn't such a good idea, after all. I should have thought this through some more, but I was just so...relieved to finally know the truth."

"Of course you were." I wish I'd been able to go with him to Dr. Vandermeyer's, to be there in the waiting room when he finished.

"Enough about me now. How are you doing? Still having morning sickness?"

"It's getting better. Still pops up every now and then."

"Poor baby."

My body tingles, hearing his voice drop to caress me through the phone. I stop my pacing and sit on the bed, crossing my legs to ease the throbbing between them.

"I miss seeing you in person," he murmurs.

"We can switch over to a video call." I lower my voice, hoping to sound as seductive as he does. "It'll almost be like we're together." I fall back onto the mattress and roll over, trying to relieve the pressure growing in my breasts. I hope pregnancy hormones are partly to blame for making me this horny. It can't be normal to be so turned on by just the sound of his voice, can it?

"Not even close."

"Well, I'll watch the game from my hotel room bed, so you'll be with me, even if it's virtually."

"I'd rather be in your bed in reality," he says huskily.

Oh boy. So do I.

"You think? Well, let me know when you're sure, and I'll be ready and waiting."

"I just might hold you to that soon, darling."

I smile, satisfied to hear Luc's breathing quicken. I'm glad I'm not the only one feeling raging, unfulfilled lust. We're making progress. Deciding a little more teasing might help move things along, I purr, "Oh yeah? You know, I'm in bed now, all warm and naked." Half-naked with my sports bra and leggings, but he doesn't need to know that.

He groans. "Jesus, darling. Are you trying to torture me?"

I laugh. "Actually, I was hoping for a little phone sex."

"Why don't you come over instead? I'll feed you...and then I'll—"

"Stop!" I groan, knowing where he's going with that thought. My thighs clench at the vision of his head between them, feasting on me. "Now *you're* trying to torture *me*. Besides, I can't, in case you missed the part about me being in a hotel right now."

"All I heard was 'bed' and 'naked.'" Luc mock growls when I laugh.

"Last chance for phone sex," I cajole.

"Enough, minx. It's late and you need to get some rest. I'll talk to you tomorrow. And remember to eat."

After I hang up, I think about how much I'm beginning to hate the travel already, months before the baby comes. It's nonstop now that basketball and hockey have started. It will get even crazier once the College Football Playoff begins, followed immediately by the NFL playoffs.

I'm exhausted just thinking about it. No way will I be able to keep up this pace for much longer. I'll have to tell Mark about my pregnancy soon and make a decision about the future of my career.

It takes another two weeks, but finally, Luc and I are able to align our schedules. I've missed him like crazy and am dying to see him again. We've talked on the phone almost every day, and I've seen him play on TV, but it isn't the same. I'm also dying to make love with him, and I'm going to his house hoping tonight will be the night it finally happens. Full of optimism at the prospect, I threw in a change of clothes in my oversize purse in anticipation of spending the night.

When the train arrives at Penn Station, I hurriedly gather my things. I've managed to do some paperwork on the ride and feel no guilt for leaving a little bit early to get to Luc as quickly as possible. Not that Mark has any reason to complain. I traveled for an interview at the beginning of the week and worked long hours the rest of it.

Seeing the long line for a cab, thanks to the rain, I go back down into the bowels of Manhattan and onto a subway train that will take me within just a few short blocks of Luc's house. It wasn't raining when I left work, so I'm unprepared, but I've always believed a little rain never hurt anybody.

I'm miserably rethinking that belief and Luc's offer to have Reggie pick me up as I stand shivering on his doorstep, waiting for him to let me in. The temperature has dropped, and the drizzling rain has turned into icy stinging pellets, making my hair and clothes dripping wet. The only good thing is that it's too dark, wet, and miserable for paps to be hanging around to see me or recognize me if they do.

Luc's smile of welcome changes to one of concern, and he quickly pulls me in and shuts the door. "You're soaked! You should have let Reggie drive you."

My teeth are chattering too much to answer.

He helps me pull off my lightweight quilted jacket, one that was perfectly warm earlier and not sticking to my skin. I toe my tennis shoes off, not wanting to drag water and anything else my soaked shoes picked up into his pristine house. Luc lets the jacket fall to the tiled floor by the door, along with my purse, and ushers me into the formal living room. He grabs a remote and points it at the fireplace.

"Stand here. The fireplace will turn on in a second. I'll go grab some towels."

I face the fireplace, with its perfectly placed fake logs that suddenly light up with a warm fire. I step closer to it, holding my hands out to the warmth that is beginning to seep toward me. Within moments, Luc is back. He rubs a soft towel along my arms, hair, and wherever he can see water streaming down me.

"You'll need to get these wet clothes off. You're not going to get dry otherwise."

Undress? Well, okay, if he insists. I smile at him and pull my damp cashmere sweater over my head and drop it onto the stone hearth.

It's Luc's turn to pause. He stares as I peel off my slacks and take another towel to dry myself off. I'm still wearing my bra and panties, just the slightest bit damp, but I keep them on for the moment. I'd much rather that he took those garments off me, and not because they're wet with rain.

I lean over at the waist to pull my hair forward to rub it dry.

"Jesus, Charlie."

Still hunched over, I glance behind me to see Luc staring at my ass, barely covered in lacy fabric. I hope the rubbing motion I'm making is causing my hips to shimmy. When I finally straighten and flip my hair back to run my fingers through the tangles, I notice he's looked away.

"Here's a throw for now. You can take a shower after you finish warming up a little."

"Luc," I chide him when he holds out the soft blanket to me. "I thought now that you knew the truth, you'd allow yourself to live a...normal life." I take a step closer and look up at him, invitation clear in my eyes.

Luc hesitates, his gaze sweeping my body, then shakes his head. "Charlie, I want to. Believe me, I do. But...after ten years believing one thing, I'm still trying to wrap my head around the truth."

When I don't take the throw, Luc puts it around my shoulders for me, but it begins to slide right off when he lets go. He holds the ends together under my jaw.

"You're afraid to believe it's for real." I can see the doubt and fear in his eyes, and feel my lust soften to tenderness. I finally take the ends of the blanket in my own fist and wait for him to continue.

"You ever have a really good dream that you don't want to wake up from?"

Since he's looking into the fire rather than at me, I don't answer.

He continues, "That's what it's like now. I'm finally free of the guilt, I have my memory back, I have you, and I'm going to have a kid soon. I'm afraid of feeling too much...joy. I'm afraid I'll jinx it, and I'll wake up and be back in my old life again."

He faces me again, and I can see the struggle reflected in his expression. I relent for the moment and nod. "Okay. I understand. Would you mind pulling that ottoman over here? The fire feels great. Let's just sit here for a few minutes."

Luc positions the large ottoman, and I sit on the edge of it. I motion for him to sit next to me. When he does, I lay my head on his shoulder, and we both stare into the fire.

"This is nice," he murmurs, putting his arm around me and kissing the top of my head.

"It is." I turn my head so my lips can place a soft kiss on his bicep. Though it's covered by a T-shirt, I can feel the strength and warmth of his muscles underneath.

Luc sighs against my temple, but before he can respond, my stomach grumbles loudly. We both laugh, Luc telling me, "Someone's hungry."

"Yeah, I think this little peanut is making up for the last couple of months of nausea. We're hungry all the time now."

"That's good. Come on," he says, standing and holding his hand out for mine. "Take a warm shower and put some dry clothes on while I put the pizza in the oven."

"Pizza?" My stomach grumbles again in anticipation.

"Homemade healthy pizza, though I'll admit I didn't make it. It's gluten free, loaded with—"

"That's sacrilegious. Pizza without gluten is like..."

Luc doesn't give me time to come up with a good comparison. "Trust me, you're gonna love it. You'll never know the difference."

"Then I wish you hadn't told me," I grouse. "Now I'll only be able to think about the fact that it's not real pizza."

Luc chuckles and gives me a nudge. "Go. You'll find a robe in the bathroom and T-shirts in my dresser. If you need anything, just give a shout."

"Good thing I have a big mouth; otherwise, you'd never hear me from up there." I walk away but look back over my shoulder when I hear a low groan. Luc's eyes go right to my mouth and they darken. Mine widen, wondering why he's suddenly feeling lust. I replay the last few moments, then smile naughtily.

I run my tongue along my upper lip, and he turns away with another groan.

"Go, you minx."

I chuckle and leave, grabbing my bag from the foyer on the way to the elevator.

33

Luc

I WAS BUSY ADMIRING her long, slim legs while she walked away but Charlie's comment about her big mouth brought my attention to her soft pink lips, as she intended. While I finish making dinner, I can't keep my thoughts off how that luscious mouth looked and felt wrapped around my cock.

My desire went from zero to a hundred in no time flat. Well, not zero, since I always feel desire around Charlie and have to keep it tamped down. If I confess my lusty thoughts, she'll redouble her efforts to seduce me, not that she'd need much effort at this point. My body is ready to give in to her, but my emotions are still a little raw.

I want to move forward with my life, but I want to do it slowly and carefully. Once I start making love to Charlie, I'm pretty sure I'll be a glutton and unable to stop. And she wouldn't either, based on the hungry look she gave me earlier, standing in her delicate matching underwear.

For right now, food will have to satisfy the one hunger, for both of us. When Charlie comes down, she's dressed in her own clothes, which she must have stowed in that giant bag of hers. I wonder if she always has an extra pair of clothes on her or if she brought them in case she ends up staying over, as she has before.

She's put on leggings and a long-sleeved sweatshirt-type top that's two sizes too big and covers the ass I was looking at earlier when she bent over to dry her hair. The soft blonde strands are now fully dry and fall around her face and shoulders. If she has on any makeup, it's subtle, but it doesn't matter. She doesn't need any. She's beautiful as she walks toward me, feet clad in black ankle socks.

"Okay, I have to admit the pizza smells delicious." She smiles at me.

"It tastes delicious too. Sit," I say, pulling out a chair for her at the table. When she settles in, I take a seat next to her. "There's salad, garlic knots made from sprouted—"

"No! Don't tell me. It looks and smells great. Just let me enjoy it without ruining it by telling me what it's made from."

I shake my head. "As slim as you are, you must eat pretty healthy."

"Looks are deceiving. I just have a fast metabolism. I eat like a teenage boy. Unfortunately, I look like one too."

The absurdity of her words makes me laugh.

"Okay, maybe I don't eat as much as a teenage boy, but the quality is definitely the same. Except for the last few months when I couldn't eat anything in the morning, my breakfast of champions was Froot Loops. On weekends, I'd go for pancakes or waffles."

"Charlie," I interrupt her rambling about junk food, "what the fuck are you talking about? You look nothing like a boy, of any age. You're fucking stunning."

She flushes, something she rarely does, unlike her best friend.

"I can't be the first person to tell you you're beautiful. You must hear it all the time."

"I was talking about my body."

I stare at her blankly.

"You know? Lanky, no hips, no breasts."

She looks at her food as she lists the features she clearly thinks make her less of a woman. And I'd bet everything I own that some man made her feel that way.

Hooking a finger under a chin, I turn her to face me and wait for her eyes to lift and meet mine.

"There is nothing boyish about you. Just because your body doesn't fit some bullshit superficial standard doesn't mean you're not every inch a woman. Every part of you is womanly and sexy."

She squirms uncomfortably, looking away as she says, "I have no breasts."

This might be the first time I've ever seen her insecure. If it's a guy who made her feel that way, I'd love a few minutes alone with him. I tug on her chin so she looks back at me. "You certainly do and I love them." I briefly lower my gaze to her breasts, but bring my eyes back to hers as I continue. "They're a perfect mouthful and so fucking sensitive. You respond so beautifully when I touch them, so honestly. I love hearing your breath quicken when I kiss them and—"

As if on cue, she gasps. Her mouth is slightly parted, her pupils dilated, and the pulse in her neck is jumping. But then, she must be mirroring me, because my cock is perking up as I talk about, and remember, that mouthful. I want to taste her again, tease her, until she's screaming my name and begging for release.

"It turns me on just thinking about making you come only by playing with your nipples. Can't wait to do that again."

She stands, almost knocking her chair over, and grabs my hand. "Let's go. No need to wait."

I laugh and pull her into my lap. "You have a one-track mind, minx."

"And it's going to stay right on this track until it reaches the final destination."

I give her a quick, hard kiss, then shift her to her chair.

"Eat first, darling."

Heaving a loud sigh and pouting, she begins to eat and continues her ramblings about food, describing her favorite meals.
I'm glad to see her enjoy her food, no longer thinking about what
it's made from, and I make sure to keep her plate full. She's even
drinking the plant-based milk I poured for both of us. When she
looks at it curiously after taking another sip, I quickly distract
her.

"How do you work off all the junk food you eat?"

"Fast metabolism, remember?" She points her fork at me. "I
don't have time for regular workouts, but I try to get to a spin
class when I can or use the gym and pool at home. If I'm traveling,
I'll either swim or do calisthenics at the hotel. And I do a lot of
walking at work since it makes me antsy to sit all the time. Instead
of calling or emailing someone at work, I'll go to them. Take the
stairs instead of the elevator. Park in the farthest spot as long as
it's not raining." She grins at me. "Though I'd do it even in the
rain if I knew you'd be waiting to dry me off and warm me up."

I shake my head and smile back. She's incredible. I love that
she's open about her desire for me instead of being coy. How she
remains so fun-loving after a difficult childhood, I don't know.
I have a feeling it has as much to do with her genetic makeup as
it does with the closeness she has with her mother and siblings.
I suspect Charlie wants a family like that of her own, and she
deserves one, but I'm not sure if I'm ready to give that to her.

"I'm not sure who I got my metabolism genes from," she
continues after taking another sip of milk. "My dad was a tall
man, like Brent, but not as built. And my mom has always been
slim, though that might be from running after five kids."

"Your face lights up when you talk about your family."

"I love them. They're everything to me."

"You all probably got a lot closer after your father and brother
died."

"Family was everything even before then. Speaking of family,
how is Daphne doing?"

"She's fine. Although according to her, her life is horrible because we won't allow her to download social media apps. During our last call, she cried, threatened to run away if we didn't give her permission."

Charlie laughs. "She wouldn't be a typical kid if she didn't threaten to run away at least once. Bobbie's more mature than most, probably the same as Daphne, since they are both surrounded by older family members and homeschooled, but she went through a phase where she threatened to run away almost weekly."

She takes a sip of milk before continuing. "Have you considered bringing Daphne here, to live with you? Now that Victor knows about her, there's no point in her hiding so far away from you. Maybe having her here will give you a little more peace of mind. And she can be better monitored in your home. She can go to one of the private schools in the city, one where the security is top-notch."

I consider her suggestion while I finish chewing the bite of pizza I'd just taken. "Hm. You may be right. Keeping her safe with me would be a lot easier. I'm just gone so much during the day and overnight sometimes." He sighs. "I could hire someone, but I don't know if Daphne would even want to leave the only home or people she's known to stay with me, never mind a stranger. Hell, I'm practically a stranger to her."

"I understand. Just something to think—"

Charlie gasps and her fork clatters onto the plate. "Oh!"

My heart skips a beat.

"What's the matter? Are you okay? Are you in pain?"

Charlie turns to me, her eyes wide. "I think it moved."

"What did?" Did we just have an earthquake? I didn't feel a thing.

"The baby. I know, it's terrible, calling the baby 'it.'" Charlie smiles. "Any guess as to whether it, the baby, is a he or she?"

"What are you talking about? I thought something was wrong with you." I don't mention the earthquake.

Charlie shakes her head. "I felt the baby move. Like a flutter deep inside. I read about it, but actually feeling it...It's amazing! Oh, Luc...There's a tiny human being inside me." Charlie's voice thickens and trails off. Her beautiful gray eyes glisten with joy. "I'm a mother." Her voice is husky with tears, one of which slips down her cheek.

I cup her face and rub the tear away with my thumb. What she says jives with my earlier thoughts. "And you're an amazing mother already." She is, her hand covering her abdomen protectively, the love for her child—our child—clear on her glowing face.

Our child. She's the mother of our baby, and I...I'm a father. I lay my hand over hers and she moves it, lifting her shirt and placing my hand back so that my palm presses against her still almost flat belly. She puts her hand back over mine. "The book said you won't be able to feel it from the outside for a while, but..." She looks at me and smiles. "He moved again."

I don't feel anything and am more disappointed than I thought possible.

"You'll be able to feel him move in a few weeks. Don't worry," she reassures me.

I'm not worried at the moment because my thoughts have redirected to the feel of her warm, soft skin under my hand. The elastic band of her leggings is at my fingertips, and I have the deepest urge to slide my hand under it and feel the softer, much warmer skin that lies below. She must have read my thoughts, because her smile slips and her breathing quickens.

Taking my hand, she helps it slide, not south, but instead upward in a slow glide, until it comes to the slight curve of her breast. She leans toward me until our mouths are just a breath away, eyes glued to mine. "Touch me," she whispers.

I allow my lips to touch hers. Charlie sighs against my mouth, and her eyes flutter closed. Unable to resist her another moment, I give in to the need to kiss her.

34

Charlie

I'VE NEVER HAD A man kiss me with such tenderness. As much as I love it, that's not what I need right now. Leaning closer to Luc, I try to deepen the kiss, but he pulls away.

"No," I protest.

He pushes his chair away from the table, then pulls me onto his lap. I have a second to see his eyes blaze before his mouth is on mine, devouring me. I wrap my arms around his shoulders, both to hold on and to get closer. With his hands free, he slides one under my shirt.

"Fuck, Charlie," he says when he finds my bare breast.

It's my turn to swear when he tweaks and rolls my nipple, making me whimper with need.

"I need to see you." He breaks our kiss to pull my top off. In the next second, his head lowers to take my breast in his mouth. I gasp and throw my head back at the sensation of his teeth and tongue on my nipple. But it's not enough. His kiss, his touch, have stoked the fire between my legs and I need more.

"Luc, please." I want to feel his erection against my sex. I *need* to feel him. He releases my breast and adjusts me so my back is against his chest, my legs spread over his.

"Kiss me, darling."

He turns my head to take my mouth, parting my lips, his tongue seeking mine. The kiss makes my toes curl and my insides clench with the need to be filled by him. But it's not his hot, hard length that fills my core. His fingers have slipped into my leggings to find my bare, weeping flesh. He wastes no time in sinking a finger deep inside me, curling it to find my G-spot, even as his thumb finds my clit. His other hand goes back to my breast to play with my nipple.

Yes. This is what I need. He knows exactly where to touch me, the right pressure. His fingers and thumbs work in tandem, taking me higher and higher until I'm practically giving him a lap dance.

"Fuck me, Luc," I gasp against his mouth. I'm about to come, but I don't want to, not until the thick length I feel under me is inside me.

"Not yet, baby. I'm not going to last if I come inside you now."

"Please. I need you. I'm so close. I want to come with you." I raise my hips off him so I can drag my leggings off. His finger slides out of me, moving under me to undo his pants. I hold myself up so he has room. When his hands go on my hips, I cover them with mine and lower myself, his silky hot erection gliding between my folds. He moves me over his length, my wetness coating him, until the next pull brings the head of his cock against my entrance. With a shallow thrust of his hips, accompanied by a harsh cry, he's inside me—at least the tip is. He freezes there, his breathing harsh and his body tense. I mewl in protest when he doesn't move. I need his entire length. I'm so wet that he should be able to glide right into me, but the angle isn't quite right. I take matter into my own hands and rise onto my toes before lowering myself.

"Oh fuck," he groans, still not moving.

I move up and down on his thick shaft several times, adjusting the angle, until he is fully embedded me. Once he is, he's all motion. His hips are thrusting, and his fingers are back on my breast and my clit. The sensations bombarding me bring me back to the edge again within seconds.

"Oh yes! Yes!" I lift a hand to hold his jaw as I turn my head to look at him. Our gazes meet and stay locked as he takes my mouth, adding another level of intimacy that has my body exploding into a million pieces. My eyes go blind and my body bows. I grab onto him, my arms raised behind me to grab his head. His mouth is buried at my neck, his breathing harsh and ragged against my skin. He locks his arms around me as he thrusts hard into me one last time before emptying himself inside me.

Just like the first time. Only this time, I'm able to soften and lie against him, with no sense of panic about what just happened. All I'm feeling now is satisfied and languid as his hands rove over my torso.

I kiss his cheek and whisper, "Even better than the first time. Definitely worth the wait."

He lifts his head to kiss me. "We're not done yet, darling. Give me a minute, and the next time will be even better."

"I'm not sure I can handle it if it gets much better."

As we cuddle in the chair, kissing softly, I soon realize a minute is all he needs. Having never even fully softened, he's already growing harder within me. The hands that were gently wandering over me stop at my breasts and play with the sensitive tips. Soon, I'm undulating over him, giving him another lap dance, this time with his cock filling me up.

"Hold onto me, baby."

My arms are still raised. I tighten them around his neck when he shifts in the chair so I'm facing the table. He shoves aside his empty plate.

"Lean over."

I yelp and slap my hands on the table when he stands, holding onto my hips so I'm standing with him, on my toes. When he starts driving into me, I almost pitch forward on my face, but Luc catches me.

"Fuck, darling, I'm sorry." He pulls out.

"No, don't stop!"

"I have no intention of stopping."

He turns me around and sits back on his chair. I shiver when his intense gaze runs over my body. When he's looked his fill, he kisses his way up my stomach to my breasts, pulling me onto his lap so I'm straddling him. He wastes no time sliding his cock back inside me, but then he doesn't move as he worships at my breasts...so I start another lap dance. I never realized I knew how to do it, but it comes naturally as my pelvis grinds against his.

I lose my rhythm when he takes a nipple between his teeth and lashes it with his tongue, sending shock waves directly to my clit. He takes over, his hands on my hips helping me with a simpler rhythm, up and down, one that matches his thrusts, but it's not enough.

He realizes it and grips my thighs before standing and placing me on the table.

"Lie back."

When I do as he says, he lifts my feet to his shoulders, grips my ass again, and drives into me, hard and fast. My fingers dig into his forearms, needing something to hold onto so I don't fly off into the stratosphere too soon. I want this to last forever...or for as long as I can hold off on my orgasm that's ready...to...barrel...through...

"Oh God! Oh Luc!"

My spine bows, forcing Luc to hold on tight to my hips as he hammers into me, chasing his own climax.

35

Luc

I WAKE UP WHEN a single ray of sun shines through the gap between the semi-sheer curtains and directly over my eyelids. I wish I'd remembered to close the light-blocking blinds before I went to bed. The exact time I finally fell asleep is a bit hazy. And blinds were the last thing on my mind last night. Or at any time during the night.

Charlie is still sleeping. Her slow, even breaths drift over my nipple, causing it to tighten. Her mouth is so close to it, I'm tempted to shift just the tiniest bit to get her lips on me. We should probably have a conversation about that first, because I'd love to wake her up in the future with my mouth on all the sweetest parts of her body. I'm definitely okay with her waking me with her mouth on my cock or in her tight pussy. The thought has me instantly hard against her thigh, which I didn't think would be possible. I'm surprised my dick hasn't fallen off by now.

I lost count of the number of times Charlie and I fucked during the night. Does it count as multiple times if I never even left her before starting again? I made love to her hard and fast—but not too hard even though she's assured me I wouldn't do any harm to the baby. After I sated myself in her several times downstairs, we rehydrated, showered, and continued taking our fill of each other. I made love to her with slow and gentle strokes, drawing out the pleasure for both of us. I'm pretty sure I fell asleep still inside her, her long limbs wrapped around me, both of us on our sides, facing each other.

Based on our positions now, we haven't moved much since. My erection is poking against Charlie's inner thigh as if seeking her entrance on its own. I brush my hand down my length and shift. *I hear you, buddy.* I want to be back in paradise again, too, but she has to be exhausted. Best to give her a little more rest.

Over the past ten years, I've had women throwing themselves at me. I'd never been tempted to fuck any of them, to break my vow of celibacy. So what is it about Charlie that made it so easy to fuck her within minutes of meeting her? And makes me unable to resist being intimate with her, even before I was ready to have sex again?

Was I able to have sex with her last night only because I no longer felt guilty over my mother's death? No, it had to be more than that. Right? I've wanted her like no other since I laid eyes on her.

And that first time in July wasn't just because I'd given myself permission for the night. Despite hiring prostitutes, I was nervous and not looking forward to the moment they arrived. I'd kicked myself for hiring them instead of just picking up a couple of women at a bar. It had made sense when I made the call to the agency, thinking of the privacy, the transactional nature of it. The lack of intimacy.

Sex with Charlie had been anything but that. And our time together since leaves me wanting more, rather than counting the minutes until I can get away as I do in the presence of other women. Even the moments when I wasn't eating her out felt intimate, like we were heading toward something deeper.

A muted, insistent vibration penetrates my contentment. My alarm. I have a team meeting this morning. My dick jumps when Charlie stirs and snuggles closer. Her movement lines my erection right up against her pussy. As tempted as I am to go one more round before I go to work, I gently pull away from her.

"Shh, it's okay," I whisper when she mumbles a protest. "Sleep." I kiss her forehead before I roll off the bed to reach my phone, which I find on the floor in my jeans pocket.

"Oh, shit!" I look at the time and see that the alarm went off for the first time almost a half hour ago. When I hadn't turned it off, it had auto-snoozed and gone off again twice more.

"What'sa matter?" she asks sleepily.

"I need to haul ass. You stay here and sleep. I've got to get to the stadium. It's a light day today, just meetings and film, so I'll be back by late afternoon." Thank God there's no practice. I'd get creamed on the field with the way I feel right now, like a limp noodle.

Since Charlie hasn't moved except to sprawl more loosely across the bed, that's probably how she feels too. I want nothing more than to crawl back into bed with her and hold her while we both sleep. But I have to get to work, so I pull the blanket off the floor and onto her, kissing her bare shoulder first. I pull the blinds closed so the room becomes dim, then head into the shower.

My stomach grumbles as I dress, and I realize Charlie must be starving too. She's said her nausea has eased, and she's able to eat light breakfasts again these days. But she has to eat better than those sugary cereals she likes. I usually make protein smoothies in the mornings before heading out, so I make one for myself to drink on the way, then a lighter version for Charlie, one without the protein powder. I don't know if all that protein and supplements are good for the baby, so I stick to fruit, Greek yogurt, almond butter, and almond milk. I put the blender in the fridge with a sticky note that says, "Drink me."

I'll text her in a couple of hours to make sure she gets up to eat. For now, she needs rest. Locking up behind me, I decide to set the alarm as a precaution via my cell phone once I get into the SUV where Reggie is waiting. Even though I don't think Victor knows anything about Charlie's personal connection to me—yet—I don't want to take any chances. She's in there, alone, vulnerable. The thought puts fear into me, making my heart pound. If anything happens to her...

No, nothing can happen to her. The thought of it makes me realize just how much she means to me. And it's not just because of the baby, because that's still hardly real to me.

I reach for the handle to go back inside, but Reggie pulls away from the curb, bringing me back to my senses. He'll come straight back after dropping me off. She'll be fine until then.

36

Charlie

I WAKE UP FEELING groggy and disoriented. Why is it so dark? I blink open my eyes, wondering what city and hotel I'm in. No, not a hotel. The bed is too big and comfortable for the kind of budget hotel that I usually stay in.

About the time my eyes adjust, I remember it's Luc's bed. Memories of the night before flood back, and I stretch in contentment. God, I'm sore all over. He made love to me in just about every position possible, and he was insatiable.

Well, he does have a lot of years to make up for. And I've been lucky enough to be the recipient of all that pent-up sexual energy. My brows furrow with a disturbing thought. Now that Luc has released himself from his self-imposed exile from sex, will he indulge himself anytime, with anyone?

I don't mind the anytime part, but I'd have a serious problem if he wants to do to someone else what he did to me throughout the night. The thought brings an ache to my chest. A part of me says I'm being ridiculous. It's not like he's a sex addict. He was a little...enthusiastic...because it had been so long for him. He's a healthy, young man with a libido to match. It's normal, what happened. Right?

The cynic in me scoffs. *Yeah, right.* The first time he goes out again to a club or comes across beautiful women throwing themselves at him, won't he feel the urge to make up for all the times he had to pass by them?

I've inadvertently become a permanent part of his life due to life-changing circumstances. But maybe he isn't ready to have his life changed in this way now that he's just gotten it back. Maybe he wants to catch up on all that he's missed out on these past ten years. Maybe he wants to go back to some of those women he kissed passionately in public and denied himself in private.

I fling back the blanket in annoyance at myself and get out of bed. *Why are you borrowing trouble?* I scold myself. I hear my mother's voice telling me not to worry about things I can't control. All I can do is hope for the best and plan for the worst.

So that's just what I'll do. If Luc decides this was a one-time thing, I'll have to find a way to deal with it. I'll be fine. The pang in my heart tells me I'm lying to myself. Yes, my heart has gotten irrevocably involved.

Sure, I respect him for the man he is, and I thought our relationship was based on friendship laced with a healthy dose of lust. But the thought of him moving on with his life without me makes my heart ache and my eyes sting with tears, proving my feelings for him are so much more. I've fallen for him, heart and soul.

While I shower, I make the decision to talk to him straight up about it when he gets back. Blunt is the only way I know how to be when something is bothering me, because I hate feeling uncertain. I'd rather just know than be tormented by the what-ifs. Feeling comfortable with that decision, I move on to what I'll do if Luc decides last night was fun but that's all it was.

In that case, I think I'll first kick him in the balls so he won't be able to have sex with another woman for a while, then...

I sigh. No, I won't do that. I will calmly discuss how he'd like to be kept informed about the pregnancy and what he'd like to do once the baby is born, if anything. I'm not sure if I'll still want him in and out of my life, feeling as I do about him, knowing that he's with other women.

Deciding to take things one step at a time, I get dressed and go downstairs to wait for Luc to get home.

Turning a corner, I see the shadow of a big man coming at me down the dim hallway, and I let out a short scream. Oh no! Someone has come in while I was sleeping. Victor? No, this guy is too big to be Luc's father. It must be some goon Victor has hired. But how did he know I'm here? No, he couldn't have known—this must be an intruder I've surprised.

My thoughts race even as my feet propel me toward the kitchen and the terrace doors. My breath is ragged, and I can't hear anything beyond the rush of fear in my head. I've just gotten the sophisticated latch undone and slid the door open an inch when piercing sounds, loud enough to raise the dead, start going off throughout the house.

What the hell? I look over my shoulder and realize I've set off the house alarm. Relief courses through me, knowing this will scare off the goon. But a second later, the sound ceases and all is quiet. Where is the man? Has he run out the front door? Should I go and check? I look out the glass door and hesitate to go that way, realizing I have no idea if there's an exit from the yard. The space back here is surrounded by buildings, shared by neighbors in the other properties. A private oasis for wealthy, private people.

I turn when I hear a noise from the hallway.

"No, it's fine. I scared her. Yeah, I'm going to check on her now."

That voice is familiar and so is the face that is visible now with the light shining through the glass doors and onto him.

"Reggie," I breathe in relief.

"Hi, Charlie. Sorry to scare you."

"It's okay. I'm just glad it's you."

"Yeah, yeah, hold on," he says into the phone. "She's right here." Reggie holds the phone out to me. "Luc."

I take the phone. "Hi."

"Are you okay, Charlie?" Luc's voice is laced with concern and lingering panic.

"I'm fine. Just had ten years scared off me. I wasn't expecting anyone else to be in the house."

"I know, I'm sorry. I didn't like leaving you, dead to the world, even though I set the alarm, so I told Reggie to come back and watch over you. I was probably just being paranoid, but I told him to reset the alarm once he was in. Jesus, I'm an idiot! I didn't think to leave you a note with the code. I'm sorry, baby. Are you okay?"

Warmth fills me at his concern, but I try not to read too much into it. He's a good man. Of course, he's going to be concerned about a woman he just fucked all night, who also happens to be the mother of his child, especially with the threat of Victor looming over us.

Dear God, I'm not sure if it's lack of sleep, lack of food, or the recent scare, but my thoughts are a tumbled mess.

"Charlie darling?"

How can I resist not reading anything into those words, that tone?

"I'm here. Don't worry, I'm fine."

"Okay, but I'm not. My heart's still racing. When my phone alerted me that the alarm had gone off at home, I panicked. I knocked over a couple of chairs—maybe a table or a person, I'm not sure—as I ran out of the room, trying to dial Reggie at the same time. I don't even know where I was running to since I don't have a car here."

"Well, you don't need to leave now. Finish what you need to do. It was just a false alarm."

"If you're sure. As much as I want to come back to you, to see for myself that you're safe, I really should go back. Coach is going to rip me a new one for running out without explanation, but to do it while he was talking..."

I smile at the dread in his voice. It's amusing to hear a grown man, successful and respected and earning way more than his coach, sounding like a kid about to face the principal.

"Well, you had good reason. You were afraid you were being robbed or your house was burning down."

"I wouldn't care about either of those things, as long as you weren't in there when it occurred. I was terrified something had happened to you."

"Say your damn goodbyes, Luc," Reggie mutters loud enough for Luc to hear. "Or call her back on her own phone. I want mine back so I don't have to listen to this sappy shit."

A little intimidated by Reggie, even knowing he would never harm me unless I was a threat to Luc, I hurriedly say bye to Luc, who is telling me to ignore Reggie.

Reggie takes the phone and hangs up without talking to Luc, whose cursing can be heard before the line goes dead.

"Come on, mamacita," he says in a completely different tone that tells me I have nothing to worry about from him. "Time for you to eat. Boss told me to make sure you ate as soon as you got up."

"You're fired, you son of a bitch," Luc growls bad-temperedly when he comes home, having gotten a ride from DeShawn, one of his teammates.

"Okay, boss. See you tomorrow. Bye, little mama." Reggie gets up from the big armchair he's been lounging in, watching TV with me, as I lay on the couch with a throw over me. The fire is going, the cold snap continuing though the rain has stopped.

I smile at their byplay and wave. "Bye, Reggie. Thanks for keeping me company."

He salutes Luc and leaves. I rise to a sitting position, feeling awkward suddenly. Time to deal with the morning after, delayed by his going to work. I play restlessly with the fringe on the throw, but I look directly at Luc. I might be feeling a little off-balance, but I'm not a shrinking violet or a coward.

"How were the meetings?"

"How was your day?"

We ask our questions simultaneously, and I laugh nervously at how domesticated we sound. Did Luc hear that too?

His smile has no hint of nerves, only happiness as walks over to sit next to me. I'm surprised when he leans in to kiss me lightly on my mouth and hold me in an affectionate hug.

"Did you get enough sleep? Drink that smoothie I left for you?"

"I slept for a couple of hours after you left. And yes, it took me an hour, but I drank that gigantic thing you left me. I'd ask what was in it, but I don't think I want to know. It tasted good, and that's all I need to know. Thanks for making it for me."

"You're welcome. I'll make it again for you next time."

I lean back in surprise. "Next time?"

Luc's tender gaze turns wary. "I'm hoping you'll stay over again soon."

He seems to have gone from zero to a hundred overnight. Okay, maybe thirty to a hundred. I had no idea last night would end the way it did, but I'd hoped. However, I hadn't expected it to affect me so deeply, and I don't think I can make a habit of this until I know where we stand.

Once you fall in love, can you fall in deeper? I'm afraid the answer is yes, and though I normally don't back away from risks, I'm standing at the edge of something I might not recover from if I fall over without some assurances. My doubts from last night come back full force.

"I...I don't know, Luc. Maybe. I think we need to talk first."

Luc leans back, putting distance between us, physically and...emotionally? I pick up his hand and hold it, needing some connection to him. I'm gratified when he links his fingers with mine and holds on.

"Okay." Luc doesn't say any more, letting me take the lead.

I smile nervously. How to ask a man what his intentions are?

"It's okay, darling. Just say what you have to say. I'll be fine." In fact, he seems braced for a blow.

I hurry to reassure him. "Oh, Luc. I want to stay. I do. I just...I don't know what you're...feeling...after last night."

Luc laughs softly. "Yeah, I'd give a million dollars right now to know what you're feeling. I was a little...overzealous last night, and I'm sorry for using you so hard."

"Were you?"

Luc looks puzzled at my question, so I clarify. "Were you using me?"

"Christ, Charlie, that's not what I meant! I meant your body—making love to you so often. I used your body like a sex-deprived—" Luc stops and blows out a breath in frustration. "Shit, how do I explain this without you thinking it was just about sex?"

"Was it more than sex?"

"Of course it was, darling. We may have been thrown into this thing fast and unexpectedly, but you're having my baby. Like you said before, we're linked forever."

I try not to let the disappointment show on my face. Based on Luc's frustrated expression, I haven't succeeded.

"Jesus, I'm making a mess of this." He takes a breath and meets my gaze. "Yes, this is all new to me, having a relationship for the first time in over ten years. With a woman I find not only incredibly beautiful and sexy, but who I've also spent time talking to and find that I actually enjoy being with. And I definitely have a hard time keeping my lust in check when I'm near you, but I also think you're smart and funny and a good person."

Luc doesn't seem to realize that his words are making me feel worse somehow, even though they're all nice things he's saying. But it's not what I want to hear, considering my own feelings for him.

"I love how close you are to your family, and I imagine you with a family like that of your own."

But not with him? Tears start to sting my eyes. I blink and look down at our clasped hands, not wanting him to see how his words are cutting thin slices across my heart.

"And I think about what a wonderful mother you're going to be. About how you'll look when our baby is feeding at your breast. *Our* baby. The thought just overwhelms me. And I want to be there by your side, with our baby. Our family."

He lifts our hands, and my eyes follow until he stops to kiss my hand. I raise my eyes the rest of the way to his. He's looking at me tenderly. My lungs expand with hope, but a random thought, zipping in out of nowhere, makes them collapse.

Is he looking for a ready-made family now that he's finally opened himself up to emotions again? Not only do I come with a baby but also a mother, a brother, and sisters.

And what about other women? That's my biggest concern. I'm happy to share my family, but I need to know that he wants me for *me*—first, last, and always. Is he ready for that?

Of course he isn't, I answer myself. How could he be? He was only eighteen when he cut himself off from living a full life. He's been without love and affection for ten years. Which basically means that he has the emotional maturity of a teenage boy. In other words, almost none. He doesn't know what he wants. I'm the first person he's had real, meaningful sex with, made more impactful by an emotional revelation that has him grasping for a foothold with all the feelings tumbling around him.

He's been an emotional virgin, and I've been his figurative first. But until he experiences life with an open heart again with other people, other women, can he possibly know for sure what he feels for me is real?

I slowly uncurl my fingers and draw my hand away.

37

Charlie

"J UST A FEW MORE measurements. You doing okay?" the ultrasound technician asks me as I lie on the cold exam table, trying not to cry. She turned the overhead lights off to see the images on the screen better, but she must have seen my expression from the glow of the monitor.

"I'm fine," I lie.

This has been the worst week I've had in a long time. I'm miserable with doubts about Luc's feelings for me—if he has any—swirling nonstop in my head. At work, since I told Mark exactly what I thought of what he'd done with the video, he's been punishing me by giving me assignments from hell. I can't wait for the day I tell him I quit.

And poor Joey has had a week too. The viciousness of social media trolls who have nothing better to do than comment on someone's appearance in one bad photo is appalling. In an effort to cheer ourselves up, we met up for gameday. Our tradition for away games is to watch from home with Mom and Bobbie and eat our favorite football-watching junk food the entire day.

Unfortunately, it went from bad to worse for Joey when my idiot of a brother did whatever he did to drive her away. She's back in New Jersey living with her old landlady, refusing my offers to come stay in Connecticut.

So here we are, two soul sisters in love with players on the same team and heartbroken because we're not with them.

It's been eight miserable days since I left Luc's house after the best night of my life. The doubts that crept in have only grown. Would he be with me if I wasn't the first woman he'd been with in ten years? What if he thinks he wants me now, but later feels he was forced into something he wasn't ready for?

There's no way to know the answers unless I talk to him again, but I haven't answered his calls and kept our texts brief.

Oh, how I'm tempted to call him back. But I need a little bit more time to steel my heart before I face him again and have the conversation we need to have.

The concerns I expressed to him the day after we made love still hold true. He doesn't need to hold himself away, at least physically, from other women now. I want to see what he would do if I wasn't in the picture, because I need to be sure that the chemistry between us wasn't a result of opportunity or convenience for him.

A part of me expects to see a tabloid photo of him, like the hundreds I saw when I was doing the segment on him. I'm surprised to realize I haven't seen one since the pre-season. Is it because of me? I scoff at my naivete. Maybe he always stops the photo ops with beautiful women once the season starts, using football as an excuse to not have to pretend anymore.

Adding to my confusion is Joey's unwitting endorsement of Luc. She'd told me about going to him after her breakup with Brent and how sweet he'd been to her.

"Would you like to know the sex of the baby?"

The technician's question brings me back to the present. She's been clicking away on her keyboard, taking measurements of the baby on the screen.

"Yes, absolutely." I've never been patient enough to wait for anything. Is that the problem between me and Luc? Am I rushing him?

"You're having a baby girl," she informs me with a smile. "I'll print out a couple of pictures for you to take with you."

"Thank you," I choke out through the lump in my throat.

A little girl. A daughter. No more referring to the baby as "it." My eyes fill with tears. I wish Luc had been here to share this special moment with me.

38

Luc

I DON'T KNOW WHAT the fuck happened with Charlie the other night. She left in a rush after pulling away and isn't answering my calls. She replies in short phrases to my texts. Usually the phrase is "Busy. Can't talk now."

Unfortunately, I've been busy too, or I would have camped out on her doorstep in Connecticut. The Firebirds have a compacted week, with a Thursday night game this week right after last Sunday's game. That means no days off for me to track down Charlie.

I find a quiet place while at work and leave another voicemail for her. "Hey, it's me. Again. I don't know if you're listening to these messages, but if you are, please call me back." I pause, taking a deep breath, not sure what to say. "Charlie...If I said or did something, I need to know so we can fix this. Whatever it is, I'm sorry. Please call me. Let's talk so we can hash this out, okay?" I exhale in annoyance. "At least call to let me know how you're doing. Is everything fine with the baby?" Softening my voice, I end with, "I'm worried about you, darling. Call me."

Hanging up, I go to the training room to work off the frustration and resentment building within me at Charlie's silence.

"Where you been hiding when you're not here, Saint?" CJ, my veteran wide receiver, asks as I sit on a bench nearby to do bicep curls. He puts his dumbbells away and waits for my answer. "How come you don't go out with us no more?"

"Miss me getting all the women for you, Horndog?" I ask.

"You kidding, man?" Hutch grunts as he lowers the loaded barbell to the floor and stands, breathing hard. "He finally has a chance to get a woman to notice him without you around." Hutch grins, then ducks to avoid the towel CJ throws at him. But he can't avoid the burn CJ sends his way.

"Yeah, that's probably why Joey even gave you a second look at the club. If Saint had still been there that night, she might be living with him instead of you."

Hutch scowls at that possibility, though it's remote as hell. The way those two looked at each other when she worked here...She didn't have eyes for anyone but Hutch. And yet, they broke up for some reason. I felt helpless when she came to my house right after, looking lost and heartbroken. Since Charlie hasn't been calling me back, I have yet to tell her about it. Maybe she's been busy with Joey and that's why she hasn't been able to call me back.

"Our QB probably found himself a girl and doesn't need to go out looking for company anymore," DeShawn suggests, getting in on the conversation as he lies down on the bench next to mine to do some presses. "Ain't that right, Saint? Yo, CJ. Spot me."

"Oh yeah?" Hutch asks. "You got a girl?"

"None of your business," I retort, keeping my voice light. "Besides, it's not like you told anyone you were dating Joey after she stopped working here."

"Just as well since she dumped his ass," comments CJ.

Hutch ignores him. "I was waiting for her to be ready to go public. She'd hate having public attention on her. You became buddies when she worked here." His frown turns into a scowl. He hated seeing us talk and eat meals together while he was trying to keep a professional distance from her. Needless to say, I enjoyed needling him and stoking his jealous streak.

"You saw how shy she is," he continues. "What's your excuse?"

I ignore him, continuing with my bicep curls though I've lost count of the reps.

"Who is it?"

His suspicious tone has my head jerking up. His narrow-eyed stare is boring a hole into me as he waits for my answer. *Fuck. Does he know? How?*

"It better not be Joey."

My mouth falls open for a second before I laugh in relief and at the hilarity of his words. The idiot thinks the woman who wore her heart on her sleeve every time she looked at him went out and immediately got a new boyfriend? And his teammate, no less?

"Wow, you really don't think a lot of Joey if you can even suggest that." I drop the dumbbell, my arm about to fall off. Good thing it's not my throwing arm.

"It's you I don't think a lot of, you fucker. It only crossed my mind because you look guilty as fuck. Like you did this morning when I asked if you'd talked to her."

It seems my poker face is about as bad as Joey's. I'm usually able to pull off Oscar-worthy performances. Whatever is going on with Charlie has me off-kilter.

How to get out of this? Which would be worse? For him to find out Joey came to my house immediately after they broke up, and I didn't tell him? Or that the girl I'm hiding is his sister...who's pregnant with my baby?

The way he's ready to tackle me, teammate or not, makes it an easy choice. He's bigger than me by at least thirty pounds of muscle.

"Okay, yes, I saw her. She came over, used my phone, then left." I don't try to lie again and tell him I don't know where she went, because I do know. But Joey is as much my friend as Hutch is my number one guy to get the ball to. He and I may not have reconnected as friends like we were when we played for the Sailors, but that's my fault. I've been worried about giving myself away somehow if we became closer. And feeling guiltier than I already do if he started confiding in me and I didn't reciprocate.

I probably could tell him about me and Charlie as long as he kept it between us because of Victor. But at this point, there's no easy way to tell him without him being pissed off that we kept it from him for this long. At the very least, it would be awkward as hell for the rest of the season. It could even impact the season itself if the tension between the two of us affects the rest of the team.

He'll be angry anyway when we do eventually tell him, but at least he'll have a few months to calm down before we have to work together next season.

"Hey, if you're not with Joey and Saint ain't with her, can I have her?" CJ asks.

Brent turns his pissed-off-ness to CJ. "You're a fucking pig, you know that? Maybe you'd have a better chance of getting a woman of your own if you didn't treat them like a piece of meat." He stalks away.

CJ turns to me and DeShawn, who's taking a pause from the next chest press. "What? I really like Joey's cooking."

I shake my head at him. The dude is clueless when it comes to women.

When I check my phone after practice, I find several missed calls from my aunt. I call her back from the car while Reggie drives. "Hello, Tati. Is everything all right?"

"Lucien, your sister is crying. She saw that video about you online. What is all this nonsense they are saying?" My aunt's Haitian Creole accent is strong, having been a teenager when she immigrated to the States with my grandparents. It gets thicker when she's upset, as she is now.

Shit. I didn't even think of Daphne coming across the video since her access to online content is limited. I sigh and pace around the room.

"I'm sorry. I should have warned you." I'd only told Tati to be more vigilant because Daphne's location had been leaked. Not wanting to worry her more, I hadn't mentioned the segment.

"It's not me you need to worry about. You need to talk to your sister. Hold on."

"Hello." Daphne's sad little voice, accompanied by a sniffle, breaks my heart. The misery in her voice eats at me. Poor baby. She's too young for all the crap she's had to suffer through in her short life. At least I had our mother my entire childhood, whereas Daphne was without her love and comfort. The injuries she suffered, the resulting physical pain was bad enough. But she lost her mother, and I went away to college. Our aunt and uncle had been virtual strangers to her, though they loved her and adopted her, having no kids of their own. And she can never know that her father is Victor, someone so vile. I'll do anything to spare her from knowing what kind of man he is.

"Hey, DeeDee. Don't cry, darling. It'll be all right."

"Is it true?" she whimpers.

"Is what true?" I ask, keeping my voice soft and gentle.

"That you're my father and you're ashamed of me?"

Oh fuck. She'd not only seen the video, she'd read the comments.

"No, darling, no. I'm your brother. And I'd never be ashamed of you. I promise you that's the truth."

"Then why can't I ever come there to visit you? You only come here and you never go with us on vacation." Another sniffle.

At least she's not asking me about who her father is. I dread the day she brings it up, something she hasn't done for years. At the time, we lied and kept it simple, saying only that her father was in heaven with Maman. I may regret it later, but I still think it was the right thing to do.

It never occurred to me she'd want to come to New York City, as introverted and self-conscious as she is about her scars. Would a twelve-year-old understand I kept her away for her own good? Not just to keep her safe from Victor, but to keep the attention of the media away from her?

Jesus, I sound like Victor, who used the public spotlight excuse not to claim me.

"Dee, of course you can come here." I'll work out security at the house with Gabe, but I don't know what she'll do if she wants to see the sights. I'll have to explain some of the danger Victor presents without telling her everything. She's old enough to understand my need to keep her safe, right?

"For a visit or to stay forever?"

Her question gives me pause, but I can't crush the hint of hope I hear. "Definitely for a visit, and if you like it here, and if Tati is okay with it, you can stay here with me forever." I'll have to figure out the logistics of school and security and the paparazzi, but I'll do whatever it takes to make her happy. Since Charlie had actually suggested Daphne come to live with me, maybe she'll have some ideas—if she'll ever call me back.

"Really? When?" Her voice doesn't sound so pitiful anymore. Thank God.

"I'll let you know as soon I make arrangements, okay?"

"Okay. Mama wants to talk to you."

I'll never get used to hearing her call our aunt "mama." Tati is the only mother that she remembers, which makes me sad every time I think of it. At least I don't feel the overwhelming guilt anymore since learning the truth.

Surprisingly, Tati is not upset about Daphne visiting me. I don't mention it might be a permanent move, not wanting to upset her. It's a conversation best to leave if and when the time comes.

When I hang up, I call Gabe.

"What's up, Luc?"

"I've invited Daphne up to visit me. You think you'll be able to watch her here as well as you did in Mississippi?"

"Probably better, since I'll have the same number of men but in one place. And it'll probably be harder for Victor to go unnoticed with more people around. Speaking of, any word from him? My guys say he's holed up at a motel in Atlantic City."

I was wondering where he'd run off to when I had the locks changed at the house in Vegas. When I told him I was done with him, I meant it.

"I haven't heard from him." And it worries me, though I'm relieved to have him off my back.

"Okay. We'll continue to keep an eye on him. Let me know when you're thinking and I'll check the schedule. I'll send Rafe and a female bodyguard along, so Daphne won't even go to the bathroom by herself. We'll bring her up on a chartered plane and get her into your house via the garage so neither Victor nor the paparazzi will see her." He pauses. "Ideally, it'd be better if you came along for the trip, but we shouldn't risk you being seen with her. You tend to attract attention," he says with amusement.

"I'll make sure I'm home when she arrives. Just make sure it's not game day."

"Okay. I'll get back to you once the arrangements are made," Gabe says before hanging up.

For the remainder of the drive, I think about how I'm going to deal with a twelve-year-old by myself. I haven't lived with anyone since my days of sharing a dorm with Reggie, and I never had to worry about taking care of him—or his feelings. Daphne is going to need the advice and companionship of another woman, and I wonder if the female bodyguard will be enough.

Charlie would be good for her. She'd know how to talk to a young girl. Not only because of her experience with her younger sister, but also because she's so warm and caring. Her friendly and open nature as well as her sense of humor would be good for Daphne. Too bad she won't pick up my calls.

My eyes narrow in thought, then I look up a number and dial. After getting bounced around by several people, I hear her voice. "Charlie Hutchinson."

Sweet relief fills me at finally hearing her voice again, though it hasn't even been a week. Why hadn't I thought to call her workplace sooner?

"Hi, Charlie. Haven't heard from you. Everything okay?"

"Just really busy at work. Which I need to get back to—"

"Please don't hang up," I say quickly. "I need help." I'm playing dirty, but I know those three words will get her. Since I can hear her breathing softly over the phone, it's working.

"Daphne is coming here for a visit. She saw the video and got upset after reading the comments. Thinks I'm embarrassed by her and don't want to be seen with her."

"Oh, shit, Luc. I'm so sorry. I never meant—"

"Don't, Charlie. It's not your fault. This is all my fault. If I had dealt with my guilt and Victor a long time ago, Daphne wouldn't need to hide out in the middle of nowhere."

"How can I help?"

I breathe out a sigh of relief.

"I was wondering if you could be with me, at my place, when she arrives. If she gets overwhelmed or upset, I have no idea how to handle that."

I hold my breath during the long pause that follows and exhale in relief when she finally answers.

"I don't see how me being there would help. I'm a stranger to her."

"But one who can relate to a young girl much better than I can. She's so shy as it is, and she's probably going to be a little scared of leaving the only home she knows." I hope I'm not laying it on too thick. "It would make her feel more comfortable to have you there. You'd be really good with her."

"Fine. When?"

"I don't have a date yet, but I'll know soon."

"Okay."

"Good. Can I see you tonight?" I'm exhausted with no day off this week due to tomorrow's game, but I need to see her. "Can you come over? I miss you, darling. And I don't know why you're avoiding me."

"I'm not—" She sighs. "Okay, I have been avoiding you. There's something I want to talk to you about, but I'm afraid to."

"Afraid? Charlie, you never have to be afraid with me. You can tell me anything."

"I guess we'll find out. I can't tonight and you have your game tomorrow, so the day after?"

"I have the day off, so anytime."

I have the entire weekend off, a rarity during the season, and if I have my way, I plan on spending every second with her.

39

Luc

"**O**UR DAUGHTER."

I tear my eyes away from Charlie to her out-stretched hand. She showed up on my doorstep, unsmiling and subdued, much earlier than I expected. These are the first words she's spoken since I invited her in and led her to the family room downstairs.

I take the photo she's holding and look at it. My eyes tear up at the image of what is clearly a baby. Not a collection of fuzzy shapes, like the first ultrasound image.

Charlie's expression softens when I raise my unashamedly wet gaze to her. I pull her into my arms and bury my face in her hair. She allows me to hold her, her stiff body yielding as she wraps her arms around me, one hand sliding up to gently rub my neck.

It feels so fucking good to have her in my arms again. The ten days without her have felt like a month, between playing two games in five days and not seeing her or even hearing her voice every night as I'd become accustomed to.

Much too soon, she pulls away and I'm left feeling bereft. But it's more than a physical distance she's put between us. There are deep thoughts going on behind those gray eyes, normally bright with the love of life. Right now, they're filled with anxiety, causing me to become anxious as well.

"Luc," she begins in a tone that lets me know exactly what's coming, "when we had sex last time, it wasn't very long after you relived your trauma from the night your mother died and found out the truth. It was a huge emotional upheaval for you. In a good way, but I'm sure it left you off-balance, turned around. It's natural you'd turn to me since I...well, for so many reasons. We became friends, and you were able to confide in me. And I'm the first woman in a decade you've had sex with. And, as you said, we're linked forever since I'm pregnant with your baby."

I listen to her ramble while I prepare myself for what's coming, knowing where this is going. She pauses, probably trying to figure out how best to let me down easy. But it doesn't make any sense that she would after the special night we had. Hell, after the last few weeks we've had, with or without the sex. Why is she doing this?

"But you've missed out on so much over the years you've held yourself closed off, physically and emotionally, from other women. You were just a teenager then, and you haven't had a chance to mature—"

I interrupt her with a disbelieving laugh, which I almost choke on when I realize she's serious. What the hell is she talking about? I'm almost twenty-nine years old, one of the best quarterbacks that ever played, a successful businessman...

She shakes her head. "I'm not explaining very well. What I mean to say is, you need to go out and experience life as you were meant to, with all the joy and happiness you haven't let yourself feel for so long. To see what you've missed out on. We'll still be friends. We'll still be connected because of the baby. But let's just see where the next few months take us."

I just stare at her as her words sink in. She thinks that I'm emotionally stunted and need to be with other women? Does she feel...*sorry* for me?

When she'd left in a rush last time, I'd been trying to put into words how I feel about her, that I was falling for her...working up to an emotional commitment to her with my outpouring of feelings...She must not feel the same way. It's why she's been avoiding me. And now she's cutting me loose. God, how fucking humiliating!

I feel like an idiot. I don't even know how to respond to her pitying words. So I do what any emotionally stunted man would do and go on the offensive.

"Charlie, I don't know what the hell you're talking about. If you think a relationship with me would be like being with a horny teenager because of the other night—"

"That's not what I'm say—"

I don't let her finish. "Since you never said no—hell, you were always pushing me to fuck you, remember that? I just thought we could try to make this work, for the sake of the kid. I saw how important family is to you, and I wanted to do the right thing by you, by seeing if we could make us work, that's all. I'm sorry if I made you uncomfortable, if you thought I was about to declare my undying love or something."

She stares at me, eyes wide and unblinking.

I pause, then go in for the killing blow. My pride won't allow for mercy. "But I'm glad to see that you'd also rather we just stay friends. Like you said, I have a lot of catching up to do on life." I force a grin, falling back on my long experience of pretending with women. "Now that I know you're okay with how things are between us, I don't have to feel guilty for finally dating other women for real. I'm done with feeling guilty!" I fake laugh with fake exultation. "I'm free, Charlie. I'm free!"

I fling my arms wide and laugh even though I want to howl and throw something. "God, that feels unbelievable."

I tell myself to stop talking, but demons named Pride and Ego egg me on. "Thank you, Charlie. Seriously." I bring her stiff body closer and hug her to me, kissing her on the temple, surreptitiously breathing in her scent. I force myself to let go of her. A quick look at her face shows she's still a little stunned by my words. I hope they were convincing enough to drive out any feelings of pity she has for me.

"I'm happy for you, Luc."

The smile she sends my way is as tight as her voice, as if she's forcing down strong emotion. Have I hurt her feelings? How? She's the one who's pushing me to move on with my life. So that's what I'm going to do.

Someday.

She turns and heads out of the room. I watch her, frozen, wondering how the conversation devolved so quickly. It's never been in my nature to be cruel, and I especially wouldn't be that way to someone I...*love.*

Fuck, I love her.

I can't let her leave with these ugly words between us, especially since I don't even mean any of them. I have to fix this. I race after her and find her halfway up the stairs, leaning against the wall with her eyes closed, hand on her stomach and half slumped over, her face twisted in pain.

Oh shit. The baby.

She straightens abruptly when I reach her and faces away from me, but not before I see a tear fall. I take her arm when she tries to move up the stairs.

"What's the matter? Are you in pain? Is it the baby?"

Did I cause something to happen?

"Nothing's wrong." She clears the huskiness from her voice, keeping her face turned away. "I'm just leaving so you can enjoy your freedom." Her voice hardens on the last word.

I wince. Even as I was saying those stupid words, I knew they'd come back to bite me. Regret fills me. "Charlie, I didn't mean that. Don't go. Let me explain."

She ignores me, trying to yank her arm from my hold. Unwilling to risk her falling on the stairs, I let her go, staying close behind.

When we reach the top, I allow her to take a few steps away before I practically leap in front of her to stop her from leaving.

Her eyes are angry and dark with thunderclouds, ready to throw lightning bolts at me. My own ire rises. She's the one who put distance between us this last week. She's the one who's pushing me away, telling me to go out and experience life. So why is she mad at me?

But I'm not stupid enough to say that. I've already been dumb enough today.

"You don't need to explain a thing, Luc. Now move."

I want her to let me have it, not hold in the hurt and anger I've somehow caused. She's not the type to hold back, and I love that about her. Why isn't she letting me have it now?

"Please," I say softly, desperately, taking a step closer to her.

I am not above begging. Pride and Ego shriveled and died a quick death when I saw her walking away, because nothing matters but her. I'll get on my knees if I have to, clinging to her like a toddler to keep her from walking out the door.

Thankfully, I don't have to, because she crosses her arms and says, "Fine. Talk."

So what if her voice is as unwelcoming as her expression? I blow out a breath and rub the back of my neck, trying to come up with the words to make this right.

"I wish I could take back what I said, Charlie. I didn't mean any of it. Not one word."

"So why did you say it?"

Her expression hasn't softened even a little, but at least she's still standing in front of me and listening.

"You caught me off guard, talking about my emotional immaturity and feeling sorry for me. Last week, just as I was about to admit my feelings to you, you pulled away and couldn't leave fast enough. And today, you're practically telling me to go out and fuck other women, to get it out of my system. As if it wouldn't matter to you. Because it sure as hell would matter to me if another man even looked at you like he was thinking about fucking you."

"Are you saying it's my fault you said those awful things?"

"What?" Shit, I'm making a mess of it again. Taking a deep breath, I try again. "I'm saying it hurt to have you pushing me away, and I lashed out at you in self-defense. Let me finish"—I raise one hand when she opens her mouth to speak—"before you say anything. I may not have had sex or relationships with other women for ten years, but I did before the accident. And I never felt about them the way I felt about you from the start, or what I've been feeling more recently. Since I made my vow, I've never even been tempted to break it for any other woman. Not until you."

"Luc, I didn't mean—" She takes a deep breath of her own, seeming to choose her words as carefully as I've been trying to do. "I never meant to hurt you by suggesting you...explore...other women. In fact, it was killing me to even think of you doing that. But I needed you to be sure you wanted to be with me for *me* and no other reason. Not even the baby."

She finally takes my hand and the band around my heart loosens so I can breathe fully again.

"Because I've been falling in love with you," she continues, "and I wouldn't be able to bear it if you looked around one day and realized what you were missing out on. To see all the possibilities out there, ones you'd closed yourself off from for so many years."

I turn my hand in hers and hold it with both of mine, needing to touch her. "Charlie, darling. I've always seen the possibilities, but they held no temptation for me. I was having a hard time resisting you even before I learned the truth and was freed from the guilt. I've never had difficulty resisting before."

I raise her hand to my mouth and kiss the back of it, then the palm before bringing our joined hands to rest against my heart.

"I love you, my darling Charlie. You made my heart beat again from the moment I saw you on my doorstep. You've brought me back to life, with your warmth and strength and zest for living."

All her stiffness melts away as she stares at me wide-eyed, the storm clouds turning to rain as tears well up.

"Oh, Luc," she breathes. "Are you sure?"

"I've never been more sure of anything in my life." I take a step closer so we're inches apart, cupping her head with my free hand, my lips a breath away from hers. "I'm so fucking in love with you, Charlotte Hutchinson."

I close the millimeter of distance between our lips, pressing tender kisses against her mouth, each one becoming firmer, deeper. Finally, I dip my tongue between her parted lips, and I'm lost.

I don't know how long we kiss, but it isn't nearly long enough when an insistent buzzing in my pocket forces me to stop and untangle myself from her.

"Sorry, baby." I pull the phone out of my pocket just as it stops ringing. It's Gabe. "I have to return this call. Let's go sit."

Thankfully, she agrees with a nod.

I sit on the sofa in the large parlor and hold on to her when she tries to let go of my hand and walk away.

"Where are you going?"

"To give you privacy."

"I don't need privacy. Sit."

"Yes, sir!" She salutes me, then sits. I pull her flush against my side.

"Sir, huh?" I kiss the top of her head. "We can try that out later."

She laughs, but I'm completely serious. I would fucking love to see if this bold and sassy woman would allow me to dominate her in bed. Would she let me call her a girl, as in *good girl*? It's hard for me to picture her being submissive. I can see her flipping roles and taking over. My dick stirs, waking up at the images going through my mind.

"Your wheels are turning, Luc. Hurry up and make your call so you can tell me what you're thinking. Or better yet, do whatever it is you're thinking about."

I quickly call Gabe back, who tells me arrangements have been made for Daphne to arrive tomorrow.

When I finish my call, my beautiful minx demands, "Tell me what you were thinking before."

"Later. First, we need to have good old-fashioned makeup sex."

"God, yes!" She throws herself at me, straddling me and cupping my face. "I love you, Lucien Saint."

My heart rolls over at hearing her say those words for the first time. They're music to my ears and I'll never get tired of the tune, no matter how many times Charlie plays it.

40

Charlie

"OH GOD YES, LUC! I love you! I love you!"

My cry echoes around Luc's massive bedroom. I'm overwhelmed by his assault on my most erogenous areas—his mouth on my clit, two fingers inside me rubbing my G-spot, and his other hand rolling my nipple.

With a flick of his tongue and a pinch of my nipple, I'm done for. I scream, my hips off the bed and undulating against his mouth as I clasp his head against me. The vibration of his groan against my clit as he laps at me from entrance to clit sets off another explosion.

I've barely recovered, still pulsing, when he slides up my body. He pauses to suck each of my breasts into his mouth, making my core clench in response. Then he's at my mouth, kissing me like his life depends on it, even as his cock slips inside me, his hands cupping my buttocks. My overstimulated nerve endings cause my walls to tighten around him, making his entry almost painful. I force myself to loosen my grip around him, allowing him to drive into me to reach his own climax. I'm confused when he doesn't move.

"Luc?" I whisper against his hungry mouth, circling my hips to let him know I'm ready for him.

His cock swells inside me, causing me to squeeze around him in automatic response. He tightens his hold on my ass. "No, baby, don't move. I don't want this to end." One hand moves from my hip, travels up my side, over my breast, to cup my cheek. "You feel so fucking good. So perfect." He kisses me softly, then whispers, "I love you, darling."

I mirror his hold and cup his jaw. "I love you too."

Keeping his gaze on mine, he slowly begins to move. Tiny movements, in and out, that gradually get longer, deeper, harder. Soon we're both breathing hard. He lifts one of my thighs to hold it against his shoulder. I moan as he hits that spot inside me, again and again, hurtling me toward another orgasm. My hands grip his ass, frantic to reach the pinnacle with him. I can tell by the clenching and unclenching of the muscles beneath my fingers that's he's close.

"Luc..." I plead, needing something more, unable to keep up with him after my recent explosive orgasm.

"I got you, baby," he murmurs. He releases my leg so he can lean down and catch my breast in his mouth.

"Yes! Yes!" My legs cross around his back, and my hands are on his buttocks again, my nails digging into him. He hooks his arms under me and speeds up, pistoning into me like a jackhammer. The sound of our flesh slapping together competes with our moans and harsh breathing. He pushes in deep one last time with a hoarse shout, swelling impossibly bigger inside me. I mewl, disappointed to be left behind, but he scrapes his teeth over my nipple and bites just hard enough to take me to that point between pleasure and pain. The jolt of it goes straight to my sex, taking me over the edge with him.

By the time our bodies stop jerking and pulsing, we're panting into each other's necks.

"You're going to be the death of me, darling, if it keeps getting better every time," Luc murmurs into my hair.

"It's all you, my love. I'm just along for the ride." I kiss the pulse at his throat that's still fluttering madly, running my tongue over the damp skin above it. It jumps against my lips, so I do it again and suck the spot. He groans when I bite lightly, then soothe it with another stroke of my tongue.

"No, it's definitely you. Look at you, getting me hard again when I'm still inside you."

His words make me conscious of his cock expanding within me, bringing a bit of discomfort. I kiss him in apology. "I don't think I can again."

"I know, baby." He kisses my temple and gently disengages before rolling over to lie beside me.

"But my hand and mouth still can." I turn onto my side and reach my hand down to wrap it around his hot, half-hard length. One stroke and it's fully erect. He groans and covers my hand with his. Instead of guiding my grip to touch him the way he likes, he takes my hand away and brings it to his mouth for a kiss on my knuckles.

"Not yet. First, I want to give you something and then I want to feed you."

I grin and try to go for his erection. "That's just what I'm thinking."

He laughs. "Minx." He nips my fingers, then lets go to roll over and grab something out of his nightstand drawer. He rolls back over and drags himself up to lean against the headboard. "Sit up here with me. I have a present for you."

I scramble up. I love surprise gifts. "What is it?" I'm practically bouncing on my knees.

When he holds out a jewelry box, I almost lose my breath until I realize it's too square and flat to be a ring box. I release my breath with a self-conscious laugh.

"Open it."

Without taking the box from him, I open the lid. A thumb-sized locket lies in the middle, heart-shaped and sparkly with tiny diamonds encrusted throughout. It's attached to a delicate chain, its twisty design making it sparkle with the light's reflection. Both are made of a white metal, and my gut tells me it's not silver. I'd bet a month's pay they're made of platinum.

"I'd like to make a miniature of the ultrasound and put it inside the locket, if that's okay," he continues.

"It's beautiful, Luc. Thank you." I smile at him, my mouth trembling with pure emotion.

"Take it out, darling. Look at the back."

I carefully remove the necklace. Holding the chain draped over the fingers of one hand, I turn over the locket with my other.

Thank you for bringing joy to my life.

"You have, you know. Brought joy into my life. And it's not just because of the baby. It's you, your zest for life, your humor and curiosity and integrity and boldness, your shining spirit. It's everything you are that makes me so happy to be alive and by your side."

Blind with tears, I rub my thumb over the engraving as he speaks. My throat is too thick with happy tears to voice everything he means to me.

He takes it from my hand and draws it carefully over my head. The pendant rests against my sternum, perfect to hide under my shirt while at work.

I swallow hard so I can speak. "Watching you come alive since we first met, learning to live life to the fullest and accept all the love you deserve, is what gives me joy. I love you so much."

It's his turn to get choked up with tears.

"Nice to meet you, Daphne. Welcome to the Big Apple." I smile at the shy, beautiful young girl standing in Luc's family room. I stayed overnight to be available for her arrival.

The girl whispers a quiet thank-you. Her curly light brown hair covers one side of her face, but I can see hazel eyes peeking through in the brief instant she looks up, as well as some faint scars along her neck.

My heart melts for her. She's already been through so much in her short life. And now she'd traveled to New York, coming alone with the bodyguards. Their aunt, Luc explained, had to stay behind to care for their uncle, whose health wasn't conducive to traveling.

After a quiet, awkward lunch of baked mac and cheese, one of the dishes I can make pretty well, I motion for Daphne to sit next to me on the couch. "I have some pictures on my phone I'd like to show you. I have a sister who's fourteen." I continue talking cheerfully while Daphne makes her way slowly to sit next to me, leaving a good two feet between us. I scoot over, holding my phone tilted in her direction so she can see the screen.

"This is Roberta. We call her Bobbie. She's a brainiac. My mom homeschooled her because she was in the hospital so much. Since she couldn't go out and play with other kids, she learned to read really early, and she used to spend all her time reading books. Do you like to read?"

Daphne nods and asks softly, "Why was she in the hospital?"

"She was born with a heart defect, and she had to have a bunch of surgeries."

"Me too."

I look at Daphne's serious face and widen my eyes in exaggeration. "You had heart surgeries too?"

Daphne shakes her head quickly, still serious. "No. Mine were to fix my leg and my...face."

I grimace in sympathy. "I bet that sucked big time." I smile when Daphne's eyes widen. She's obviously not used to hearing someone talk like that since almost all her time is spent with her older aunt and uncle.

"Did you milk it for months afterward and have everyone wait on you, hand and foot?"

Another shake of the head, this one accompanied by a small smile.

"No? You missed out then. Bobbie once watched a show where a kid got to eat ice cream after getting his tonsils removed. For a long time afterward, she would pretend her throat hurt whenever she came home from the doctor's and insist she could only eat ice cream."

Daphne giggles, a sweet sound. I look at Luc, who stands by the fireplace, watching us. He gives me a smile of thanks, then says to his sister, "Let me show you around, Dee, and then you can get settled in your room and rest for a little bit."

When Daphne looks at me, I smile and stand up. I beckon to the young girl, saying, "Let's go. I've only been on the tour once. It's so big, I don't remember half of it."

Daphne and I follow Luc to the stairs. I keep up a running commentary, interjecting questions for the brother and sister in an attempt to get them comfortable with their new dynamic. They don't seem to know how to behave with each other in a different environment than the one they've always met in.

Finally, we leave Daphne to rest in her bedroom on the fourth level. Luc and I take the elevator back down to the lower floor, neither of us saying anything though we stand close in the confined space.

When the doors open, I hasten out and finally speak. "She's a sweet girl. If it's okay, I'll bring Bobbie by to visit her one day so she doesn't feel so alone, and I'll call her later."

"Later? You're leaving?"

"Yes. I thought you'd want to spend some time with her." I look at the panic in his face and laugh. "Don't worry. You'll both be fine. It'll just take some getting used to, for both of you. Let her know she can call me anytime, and I'll be back in a few days."

"I think you're forgetting something."

I stare at him blankly. I only came with my coat and purse, which are waiting for me by the front door. I'm even wearing the same clothes, having washed them this morning while wearing one of his shirts.

He strides over and takes me in his arm. "You forgot this," he says and kisses me. His mouth is hot and desperate.

I wrap my arms around him, ready to stay for as long as he needs, when he pulls away suddenly. Not just from my mouth but from me. I blink my eyes open and see him standing several feet away, his back to me.

"I'm thirsty."

Daphne's voice from the other side of Luc clues me in to the fact that he pulled away in embarrassment at having his baby sister catch him making out. I laugh, and he turns to me, scowling.

I walk toward Daphne, but Luc catches my hand as I pass him. "I have to go home now, but I'll call you later, Daphne, okay? Oh! And when you have dinner later, don't ask him what's in it, whatever you do. It'll taste delicious, but trust me, you don't want to know."

When a soft giggle escapes her, Luc squeezes my hand. Love and gratitude shine in his eyes, and my heart swells with happiness.

"Hello, Charlotte."

"Nice to see you again," I reply to Luc, aware of Brent and Joey standing with us.

I hope the look and nod I give him are nothing more than polite, because inside, I'm drooling over how sexy and gorgeous he looks in a tuxedo.

My gaze falls to his hand entwined in Joey's. I quirk an eyebrow at him, causing him to squirm. I smile and watch as he carefully releases her hand. Joey is too busy to notice, her focus on Brent as they stare at each other.

I shake my head at them. What a mess. Brent and Joey are still not back together. I asked Luc to bring Joey as his date to the charity gala, hoping it will make Brent jealous and speed things along in getting them back together. Since I can't be Luc's date, I thought it would be a good way for me to be near him, without it seeming suspicious.

Luc is attending the event because it's a fundraiser for youth sports in underserved communities. Mark shocked the hell out of me when he asked me to attend in order to schmooze and try to bring in more high-profile guests to the show. He probably thinks Brent could introduce me to them. Fat chance. I have no intention of asking him to make introductions for me.

Not that he'd do it, not tonight anyway. His full attention is on Joey—and I can see from his face that tonight's ruse is working. Though I love my brother, he deserves this torture for making her miserable.

And if Luc hadn't declared his love to me, and if Joey wasn't my best friend whom I trust to the ends of the earth, I might have been green with jealousy. She and Luc make a stunningly beautiful couple.

She's wearing a halter-top gown Andi designed to show off her statuesque figure. Where Joey's dress is bold and sexy, my royal blue gown with flowy layers of blue and silver material is more understated, though the desire in Luc's eyes makes me feel as if I'm the sexiest woman in the room, especially when his gaze travels over my body.

I still haven't started to show, though I've noticed a slight thickening of my waist when I try to button up my skinny jeans. The dress was designed a month ago with the expectation it would need to hide a baby bump. Since I lost weight in the first couple of months and am just now gaining that weight back, the precaution was unnecessary. Nevertheless, it's a beautiful dress, and I uncharacteristically enjoy feeling like a princess.

Sneaking another look at Luc, I catch the heat in his eyes as he tries not to stare at my chest. It isn't my breasts he's looking at, though the cleavage magically formed by the crisscrossing material over my chest is a rare sight.

No, he's looking at the gift he gave me, the locket. I touch it, smoothing my finger over it in a silent signal to him.

When the lights flicker, telling us to take our seats, I head over to my table. I'm kicking myself for not figuring out a way to sit at the same table as Luc.

By the time the lights come back on after the endless number of speeches, I'm impatient to find Luc. Unfortunately, Mark has also sent my colleague Tom to the event, and he drags me around to talk to various agents and athletes. Finally, I'm able to get away with the excuse of having to visit the ladies' room. Unable to see Luc or Joey and unwilling to believe either would leave without letting me know, I head for the lobby, but see Luc as he re-enters the ballroom, sans my bestie.

"Where's Joey?"

He shakes his head, frowning. "She and Brent had an ugly fight. She went up to the room."

"I should go to her." I turn to go to the elevators. Joey and I decided to get a room here to get ready in and stay the night.

"She asked me to tell you she'd like a little time alone and no need to rush back on her account."

He looks around, then takes my arm. "Come on. Let's go to the bar." People are starting to filter out of the ballroom as the event wraps up. He leads me to the bar and asks what I want.

"I'll have seltzer with lime please," I tell the bartender.

"I'll have the same," Luc says.

"Was Joey okay?"

"I don't know."

The bartender puts our drinks in front of us and we drift further down the bar for more privacy. I take a sip while Luc continues, "She and Brent were throwing some poisoned darts at each other. I'm not really sure what it was all about."

"Probably my brother being dense and letting the past get in the way of the future."

"I can see how that could happen," he says with wry amusement.

I smile. "Yes, I suppose. But you were smart enough to apologize before I could get away," I tease.

He shrugs. "I said some pretty stupid things first. Luckily, I realized it right away. Brent will realize it soon too."

"I don't know. Brent can be pretty hard-headed." I fish my phone out of my clutch when it vibrates. "Although he's come a long way since he and Joey got together, so I suppose there's hope for him."

Checking my phone, I see a text from Joey.

I got another room. I'll see you in the morning.

She's put her phone on Do Not Disturb but I text her back anyway. *Call me if you want to talk or need anything.* I hit Notify Anyway, but she doesn't read or reply.

"Everything okay?" Luc asks.

"Joey is staying by herself in another room." As terrible as I feel for her, there's nothing I can do if she doesn't want to talk tonight. I give Luc a coy smile. "Which means..."

He drains his drink and pulls out a bill from his wallet. He slaps it on the bar and says, "Let's go."

I come to my senses and ask, "Wait, what about Daphne?"

"I checked in already. She's in bed. The alarms are set and there's a bodyguard in the house with her as well as Reggie. But I do have practice in the morning so I can't stay too long."

Since we decided to hold off on me spending my nights at Luc's while Daphne was visiting, going back to his place was not an option. But my hotel room is empty, and it's been a long few days since we've made love.

"Then we better hurry," I say over my shoulder as I head for the elevators.

41

Charlie

I sigh as I slip behind the steering wheel to head home after work. I went in to the studio for a few hours after coming back from another work trip, once again on the red-eye, so I can take tomorrow off to go see Luc and Daphne. Between my travel and Luc's schedule, we don't get to see each other as often as we'd like. It doesn't help that we live an hour and a half away from each other.

Since Daphne decided to extend her visit, Luc and I agreed to come clean and tell her we were dating and that she'd be an aunt soon. She was so excited about the baby, I don't think she registered the dating part.

When he returned in the middle of the night after his game, he snuck into the guest room where I was staying and we spent the hours until dawn making love. He left the bed before Daphne woke up, assuring me it was because he was still trying to figure out what kind of role model he was supposed to be for his impressionable, sheltered sister. I kissed him, telling him it was sweet, but it was a little too late for that. He'd already sex with a woman the first time he met her, didn't use a condom, and got her pregnant.

"Fuck, you're right. I'm a terrible role model."

I tried not to laugh at his distress, assuring him it was okay for her to not know all the messy details. His behavior since has been exemplary. Mostly.

As much as I miss Luc, I'll go home tonight to check on Mom and Bobbie and pack some clean work clothes before going to his house tomorrow to stay for a couple of days.

"Charlie, I wish you'd been here to watch the game with me instead of Reggie," Daphne told me on the phone last night. "He grunts and jumps around in front of the TV like he's out there playing on the field with Luc."

Since Daphne's arrival, I've talked to her every day and even stayed with her last weekend when Luc had to leave her overnight for his away game. Joey, my mother, and Bobbie—who I swore to secrecy when she asked if Luc was my baby daddy—came over to watch the game on TV.

I've become quite fond of Daphne, and so have Mom and Bobbie, who FaceTime with her at least once a day while Luc is at work. We begged him to let us take her with us to the home game, but he adamantly refused, saying it's too crowded to properly protect her. Victor hasn't called again since Luc threw him out of his house, but that makes him more worried. He said he'd be putting my family in danger if Victor connected us to him, and Brent would have his head if anything happened to any one of us, especially Joey.

Thinking of Joey, I call her from my car's Bluetooth to see how things are going with Brent. The morning after the charity gala, Joey and I went to Brent's penthouse so Joey could apologize for whatever she'd said to him during their argument at the gala. In the end, due to tabloid stories that suggested Joey was pregnant and Luc might be the father, I ended up revealing to Brent that I was the one pregnant, not her. I still held back the information that Luc was the father. Since Brent wasn't happy with Luc bringing Joey as his date, I decided it was best to leave that little tidbit out for the moment, though I did tell Joey the truth.

When she called me later to say that she and Brent had worked things out and gotten back together, I was so happy for the two of them. They both deserve to be happy, and they are so good together. And it doesn't suck that my best friend and soul sister will one day be my sister by marriage.

"Hi, Charlie!" Joey's voice comes through the speaker, bright and chipper. "Are you back from your trip?"

"This morning. Just going home from work now."

"Have you told your boss yet that you're cooking a bun in the oven and you'll need to cut down on your traveling?"

"I'm going to have to soon. I've grown an entire pant size since the gala. Andi would have to let out the seams if I had to wear the gown now."

I've started my fifth month and have been lucky to hold off having to say anything due to my lack of belly expansion, but that's quickly changing. Loose tops and blazers aren't going to cut it for much longer.

"If I wait just a little longer, I don't think I'll have to say anything. My belly can do the talking for me." I'm only half joking. I'm not looking forward to the conversation with my boss, even if I'm very much looking forward to traveling less. I don't even care if he demotes me, as long as I keep my health insurance.

"Or maybe they'll think my metabolism is finally catching up with me, and I'm just gaining weight."

"When the rest of you stays the same?"

"What are you talking about? Wait until you see my boobs. If they keep growing, you and I might finally be the same bra size."

"Ha! I doubt that. Not unless you're having quadruplets and breasts grow according to the number of babies you're having. By the way, you're on speaker and—"

"Size doesn't matter to you know who." I talk over her. "He loves my boobs, even when I barely had any. As long as they stay sensitive, I—"

"For the love of God!" Brent roars in the background.

Joey giggles. "Sorry. I tried to tell you Brent just walked in."

"Get over it, Brent. It's basic biology," I yell through the phone.

"I'm not listening. La-la-la..."

Joey and I laugh as his voice fades away and a door slams.

"Have you made a decision about what you're going to do after the peanut arrives?" Joey asks.

"Yes. I'm applying for a master's program. Just trying to decide between social work and psychology."

I'll eventually figure out what I want. I'm extraordinarily fortunate to have choices, thanks to financial security from my savings and Luc if needed, and emotional support from him and my family.

"That's amazing. I can put you in touch with Dr. Vandermeyer if you want to talk about the program where she teaches and the career prospects in the different areas. When I took her class, I briefly considered becoming a therapist. Then I realized I'd need therapy to help me deal with everyone else's trauma."

Trauma therapy. Yes, that's it. Assuming I can get into a program nearby.

"I think that might be the field for me. Thanks."

Joey laughs. "You're welcome. I'm glad my incisive question helped you figure it out so fast. Maybe I should change careers and help others like you. Oh, wait. Then I wouldn't be able to get my hands on perfect bodies like Brent's and Luc's."

This time, I laugh.

"Um, while we're on the subject of Luc's body, I have a confession to make," Joey says.

Confident in what I have with Luc, even though it isn't defined yet, I tease, "Did he get turned on while you were working on him?"

"What? No, never. At least, not that I could see. Not that I was looking."

I laugh at Joey's flustered assurance.

"Okay, so you were turned on?"

"No. I kissed him. On the mouth."

That gets my attention, though I still am not worried. Joey loves Brent and no one else. And Luc is not the type to poach another man's woman or cheat on his own.

She continues hastily, "But I swear I felt nothing. And poor Luc was frozen in shock. I was only trying to make Brent jealous."

It seems to have worked because Joey sounds deliriously happy again as she recounts everything Brent has been doing to make up for his idiocy. My word, not hers.

Since I travel this road almost every day, I drive on autopilot while I talk. I barely notice the flurry of early season snowflakes. Snow usually doesn't start this early in southern New England, but it's known to happen every once in a while. There isn't supposed to be more than a dusting, but there's a layer of white sticking to the pavement now that I'm on the less-traveled road off the highway.

I slow down when my tires slip slightly around a curve, making me realize I should probably get my tires checked before winter really gets going. This road is usually pretty quiet, and with the weather, there's only one vehicle a bit ahead of me and one not too far behind.

When the tires slip again, I slow down some more. Unfortunately, the car behind me doesn't. It has its brights on, blinding me. It's almost on my ass now, ticking me off. No one gets annoyed by slow drivers more than me, but even I give them a pass during bad weather. What's this guy's problem?

"Hold on a second, Joey. There's an asshole on my butt."

While Joey laughs at the unintended wordplay, I tune her out and focus on my driving. I hit my brakes lightly as another curve approaches. The car behind me slows down and backs off, and I breathe a little easier. Taking one hand off the steering wheel, I turn the lever for the wipers to increase their speed. Just as I turn the knob, I hear a roar behind me and then feel the sudden impact from behind. I cry out in surprise and slam on my brakes, but they do nothing as my tires slide across the icy, slick surface of the road.

"What was that, Charlie?"

Unable to control the steering, I helplessly watch as the trees come rushing at me. Thankfully, the car slows down just before I reach the trees, but another roar and then a crushing sound come as I'm rear-ended again. What the hell? Is the guy drunk?

I have no more time to think before my car slams into the trees and my head slams into something. Darkness consumes me.

42

Luc

"**I** TOLD YOU YOU'D be sorry."

I stop dead in my tracks in the locker room, where I'm putting my stuff away before going into a team meeting.

"Send me the money by midnight or you'll be even sorrier."

The line goes dead before I can release my fury on the devil that spawned me. I'd be sorry? I don't know what he's talking about, but I check on Daphne and breathe a sigh of relief when she answers. Not wanting to worry her, I ask her what she wants for dinner tonight. I ask her to hand the phone to Reggie and tell him to notify the security at my house to be extra vigilant.

My next instinct is to check on Charlie, but there's no reason to think he would know about her. We've been very careful, having her and her family coming and going at my place through the garage entrance. I call her anyway and get her voicemail.

My anxiety ratcheting up, I call Gabe but get his voicemail too. I leave him a message, telling him about Victor's cryptic message.

I call Charlie again, but it goes directly to voicemail. While I text her, Brent comes rushing in and grabs his phone which he starts tapping on one-handed while he fishes his car keys out of his duffel bag with the other.

"Everything okay?" I ask, praying the anxiety rolling off him is not for the same reason as mine.

"My sister Charlie was in an accident."

My heart stops. *No, please no. Not again.* Charlie. The baby. "Is she...?"

I can't finish the question, but it doesn't matter. Brent is on the phone. I barely register the words helicopter and hospital. I grab my own things and rush after him to the player parking lot.

"I'll drive you, Hutch. My car is right here."

He's heading for his Ferrari, eyes on his phone as he punches buttons on it. He pauses at my words.

I point to my Corvette, needing to stay with Brent so I can find out what's going on and get to wherever Charlie is.

"You can make your calls while I drive," I offer. I'm glad I drove myself today so Reggie could keep Daphne company.

"Yeah, that'd be great. Thanks."

"Where to?" I ask when we both lower ourselves into my car. Brent has to lean his seat back so that his head doesn't brush against the roof.

"The helipad, in the lot on the other side of the stadium. Niko is sending his helicopter there to take me to Connecticut."

Niko Anastasios is majority owner of the team and a billionaire, so it makes sense he would have a helicopter with a helipad at the Firebirds facility. It also helps that Brent is a neighbor, business partner, and friend of his.

I take off with a screech of tires. I focus on driving while he talks to his mother. From what I hear on his end of the conversation, Charlie was in a car accident on her way home. She's at the hospital, and they're running tests to check for head trauma, because she's in and out of consciousness.

Please, please, please, I pray. *Please let her be okay. Please let it not be a repeat of what happened to Mama.*

I can't help but think that she's hurt because of me, because I dared to be happy.

When we get to the helipad, Brent is still on the phone. He gets out of the car to wait for the helicopter. I stay inside and call Gabe again.

"Hey, Luc. I got your message," he says as soon as he answers. "I was going to call you back once I had more information, but don't worry, Daphne's covered. I've been busy trying to track down Victor. He rear-ended someone, then took off. My guy stayed back to check on the driver and call for help. By the time he was able to follow the tracker to the rest stop where Victor was supposed to be, the car was there, but no sign of Victor. We've scoured the place so he either stole another vehicle or hitched a ride."

"Where did this happen? Who was the driver?" I ask, afraid of the answer.

"It was in Connecticut, near—"

My heart races with fear and anger. "Fuck! I'm going to kill that asshole when I get my hands on him. But right now, I need you to check on Charlie...Charlotte Hutchinson. She's at—"

"How do you know—"

"It was Charlie that Victor rear-ended. I'm on my way to the hospital now with her brother."

I give him the name of the hospital and tell him to send someone there right away to keep an eye on her.

I cut off his questions and exit the car when I hear the whir of blades. A big black and red helicopter with the Anastasios logo swoops down to land on the helipad.

I bend low and follow Brent to the chopper. When he realizes I'm following behind him, he turns to me and shouts over the noise, "Thanks, man. I'm good from here."

"I'm coming with you!" I climb in and settle into a seat across from him. No way am I staying back while the woman I love is lying in a hospital bed.

It's too loud to carry on further conversation without headsets, though Brent gives me a look. He doesn't say anything, but he's probably wondering what my interest is in a family matter. We pick up Joey from the rooftop of the building where both Brent and Niko live. Once belted in, she takes my hand and tries to give me a reassuring smile, though her trembling mouth betrays her own worry over Charlie. Brent's expression is a mix of confusion and irritation as he takes Joey's hand from mine and clasps it in his own.

Less than half an hour later, we slam through the doors of the hospital. My heart is racing in time with my rushed footfalls. I hope to God I don't have a heart attack before I get to Charlie.

I'm on Brent's heels when we walk into the hospital room, where Sandra and Bobbie are sitting near the bed.

"Mom." Brent leans over to give his mother a kiss and an affectionate pat on Bobbie's head. "How is she?"

I'm already at Charlie's side but tear my gaze away from her pale face to glance at Sandra for her response.

Returning my look, she assures me, "The doctors say she has no broken bones or internal bleeding. There's no swelling in the brain, but she does have a big gash on her head and most likely a concussion."

I almost wilt in relief. Concussions are no small matter, but the rest is good news.

"And the baby?" Joey asks as she walks over to stand opposite me and hold Charlie's limp hand.

"So far, so good, but there's still some risk something could go wrong. When she wakes up, she'll have to be on bed rest for at least a few days," Sandra says.

Joey leans over and kisses Charlie's cheek and whispers something. I pick up the hand closest to me and hold it gently. Brent stands next to Joey and looks from me to our joined hands and back to me, his eyebrow raised.

"Something you want to tell me?"

Ignoring Brent, I focus on the woman who has become my life. She looks so pale, and the huge bandage near her temple makes her appear fragile. I gently smooth a palm over the uninjured side of her head before cupping her cheek. I lean over to whisper in her ear, "Come on, darling. Wake up. I need you."

"Why do I feel like everyone knows what the hell is going on here except for me?" Brent growls.

I continue to ignore him. Tuning out the whispering behind me, I focus on Charlie, murmuring my own words to her, smoothing her hair, and kissing her uninjured temple.

"I want to see you in the hallway, Luc. Now." Brent's voice brooks no argument, but I don't want to leave Charlie's side.

Joey comes to stand beside me again, her hand rubbing my back in comfort. "Go on. I'll stay right here with her and call you as soon as she wakes up. I promise." She smiles at me reassuringly.

Reluctantly, I follow Brent out of the room. With the fury I feel at Victor for trying to repeat history, my worry for Charlie and the baby, and the guilt for not keeping them safe threatening to suck me back into a dark void, this is probably not a good time to hash things out with him. But he's her brother, and I intentionally kept it a secret from him—and forced Charlie to do so as well. It's time to make up for that.

As soon as I clear the doorway, Brent turns and demands, "What the hell is going on?"

I hold up a palm and gesture to him to follow me. We go to the nurse's station and ask if there's a private place to talk. She directs me to a consultation room at the end of the hall, next to the family waiting room.

I close the door to the tiny room and turn to Brent. "Listen, man. I'm sorry we didn't tell you before. I had personal reasons to keep our relationship quiet, as we just found out."

"Are you telling me you know why this happened to my sister?"

As Brent bares his teeth at me, I'm pretty sure I'd be able to hold my own against the bigger man, but I sure as hell hope I won't be tested on that anytime soon—or ever.

"I think so, but I have no idea how my father found out about me and Charlie."

"What the fuck does your father have to do with this?"

I sigh. I really don't want to go into all this now. It would take too long, and I want to get back to Charlie. "Suffice it to say, he's a fucking opportunistic, greedy bastard. He threatened that I'd be sorry, but I thought he meant me or my sister. I had no idea he'd found out about Charlie."

"What does he want?"

"Millions."

"Money? You have it. Why didn't you just loan him some?"

"Because he doesn't want a loan. And I've already given him millions over the years, but he keeps coming back for more. I finally told him no, and he didn't take it very well."

"Fucker."

Brent stares at me, but I'm not sure if the invective is meant for me or Victor. He narrows his eyes and asks, "Is that your baby my sister is carrying?"

I nod, bracing myself. I'm not sure if he's going to come at me with words or fists.

"How long has this been going on?"

Relieved he's staying calm, I let out the breath I was holding. Unwilling to get into the details now—or ever, I stick with the simple semi-truth. "I met her when she interviewed me over the summer."

Brent must have decided he doesn't want to go into the details either, because after a moment, he nods once. "Okay. Now tell me how the fuck Charlie ended up hurt."

There's no simple answer to this. "I don't know for sure it's my father, but he's been making all sorts of threats since I refused to give him more money. I swear I didn't—"

I turn in surprise when Gabe walks into the room.

"What are you doing here?" Brent asks him.

"How the hell did you get here so fast?" I ask at the same time.

"I was at the training compound, not too far from here. Hey, Brent."

My head swivels between the two of them as they shake hands and slap each other on the shoulder in a half-hug. I feel like I've entered an alternate reality, where two separate worlds are colliding.

"You two know each other?"

"Since we were kids," Gabe answers. "Which leads me to ask how the fuck Charlie got on Victor's radar. How is she involved in all this?"

"That's what I was just trying to find out," Brent growls.

"Charlie and I are...dating."

"The fucker got her pregnant," Brent adds.

Okay, maybe he *was* referring to me earlier.

Gabe shoots me a look of surprise that turns into disappointment and annoyance. "I thought we were past the point of keeping secrets. How am I supposed to keep everyone safe if I don't know about them?"

How is it that two men, not much older than I am, can make me, an accomplished and revered NFL quarterback, feel like a kid getting lectured?

Wanting nothing more than to get back to Charlie, I admit, "This is all my fault. I thought we were being so careful, even the paparazzi didn't catch us. But, yes, I should have told you and put protection on her as well. Trust me, no one regrets it more than me."

Gabe sighs. "It's no one's fault but Victor's that she's hurt."

"So it was definitely Victor who did this?" I ask.

"Yeah. He rear-ended her, running her off the road. My guy called me right after he called nine-one-one and again at the rest stop. Without the tracker, we have no idea where he is, but there's a BOLO out on him and the stolen vehicle, so we hope to find him soon."

"I want round-the-clock protection for Charlie while she's at the hospital. And double whatever you've got at my house. I'm not taking any chances. I'll take her there when she's discharged."

When Brent looks like he's about to argue, I add, "It'll be easier to keep an eye on her there. If Sandra wants to be with Charlie, she's welcome to stay also. Hell, I've got enough room for whoever in your family wants to stay. In fact, Daphne would love that since she and Bobbie are becoming friends."

"At some point," Brent says, narrowing his eyes at me, "we'll get back to the fact that everyone in my family seems to know about you and Charlie except me. But are you sure you want all these women under your roof?"

Ignoring him, I tell Gabe, "Make sure everyone is safe and protected every minute. Whatever you need, I'm on board. Now I'm going back to check on Charlie."

I catch the doctor outside of Charlie's room, telling him I'm her fiancé. Is it a lie if I plan on making it the truth at the first opportunity? He recognizes me and falls all over himself to give me a full update on her condition. When I walk into her room afterward, it's to find her sitting up, looking pale and groggy.

"Hey, darling. You're awake." I rush to her side and place a soft kiss on her head, taking her hand and holding it gently. It guts me to see the fear and confusion in her eyes. "How are you feeling? Do you hurt?"

"I'm okay. How's the baby?"

"Sweetie, I told you, the baby is fine," Joey says from the other side of the bed, a calming hand on Charlie's shoulder.

Charlie doesn't look away from my face. She wants to hear it from me.

"Our daughter is a fighter, like you. She's just fine," I assure her, gently squeezing her hand.

"But the doctor is putting me on bed rest."

"Just to be safe," I reassure her. "You got jolted pretty good, and you might have a concussion. You wouldn't want to get dizzy and fall, would you?"

Charlie shakes her head and winces. Lying back on her pillow, she closes her eyes. "Head hurts."

I lean over and kiss the skin next to the bandage. "I'm sorry, darling. If I could take the pain for you, I would."

"I know." She blinks open her eyes and tries to focus on me.

"Marry me, Charlotte," I ask, unable to wait another minute to tell her how much she means to me.

"Okay," Charlie replies softly, her eyes drifting close.

"I hope you're planning on doing that right, young man," Sandra says, "when she's awake and lucid. Otherwise, she's not going to be happy she missed her own marriage proposal."

I turn to my future mother-in-law, who's smiling and shaking her head at me from the end of Charlie's bed. She's right. What a romantic I am. Asking the woman I love to marry me while she's barely conscious. Hopefully, she won't remember this proposal, and I can do it properly when she's healed—and lucid, as Sandra suggested.

A corner of Charlie's mouth curls up in the slightest bit of a smile, but she doesn't open her eyes. I look at the monitors in alarm, though I have no idea what any of the numbers or waves mean. The thought of anything happening to her, of losing her, causes a fist to tighten around my heart, making it impossible to breathe.

"She's sleeping," Sandra reassures me, coming to stand beside Joey. "The doctor came in to check on her and she was responding fine. She just needs rest."

I nod but don't look away from Charlie's pale face. She has come to mean everything to me in such a short time. She tore down the walls I'd put up around my heart, walls that had helped me survive the guilt all these years. I wish they were still there, guarding the vulnerable organ, because it hurts so much right now. The overwhelming emotions I feel for her—and the fear of almost losing her...

What would I do if anything happened to her?

43

Charlie

"Now I know how the president and his family must feel," I comment after my mother and I are settled into Luc's house, surrounded by big men I'm sure are armed under their suits. They won't all be staying here at the same time, but Gabe and Rafe wanted to go over security with them before they split up for the shifts.

"Yes, put on some dark sunglasses and you boys could pass for the Secret Service," Sandra notes.

"Gabe and Rafe are not boys anymore," Brent protests on behalf of his childhood friends.

"No, they're not," I say. "They are all grown up and way hotter." I grin at Rafe.

He winks at me. "Back at you, Charlie. Who knew the tomboy who followed us around everywhere would grow up to be—"

"Okay, if we're done with the mutual admiration society, can we get on with it here?" Luc snaps.

I smile and hold my hand out to him. His face softens with tenderness, and he crosses to where I'm lying on the sofa in his family room. He insisted on carrying me inside despite my protests that the doctor didn't mean I had to literally lie down all the time. He perches next to me and brings my hand to his lips.

"You two look pretty blissful considering you have men with guns in your house and a crowd of paparazzi on your sidewalk."

"Stevie!" I crane my neck around Luc to see my big sister coming toward me. "You didn't have to come home." I hold my arms out, and Luc moves out of the way to make room for her.

"You're dumber than you look, blondie, if you thought I wouldn't come back to check on you and my baby niece or nephew." Stevie gives me a hug and kiss despite my pout. I don't reveal that I'm having a girl. Not wanting to be inundated with pink if everyone knew, I asked Luc to keep the news to ourselves. I may not like to wait for surprises, but I love the anticipation of surprising others.

Stevie introduces herself to Luc and gives him a hug as well.

"Luc, everything's all set. Team's in place. I'm going to take off, and I'll check—"

My sister freezes at the sound of Gabe's voice, which had stopped in mid-sentence.

"Oh. Hey, Stevie." The temperature in his voice is as Arctic as his expression.

Stevie pastes on a fake smile before she turns to face her former high school boyfriend. "Hello, Gabe."

Awkward. They broke up when he went into the military, but I'd thought it was mutual because of the long-distance issue. Based on the ice between the two, there seems to be more to it.

"Thanks, man, for everything," Luc interjects into the silence.

Gabe drags his gaze away from Stevie, who busies herself with hugs for the rest of our family gathered in Luc's family room. He manages to grin at Luc. "Remember that when I send you the bill." He flicks brief glances at everyone else around the room. "See you around, ladies. Brent." With a casual salute, he leaves.

"So," Stevie says, her voice overly bright, "what's with the paps out there? Did you guys put out a press release or something?"

"Probably has something to do with everyone wanting to know who Luc's new girlfriend is," Brent comments, kissing Joey on her forehead. They finally stopped hiding their relationship after they reconciled, which meant cameras often followed them when they went out together. She hates having random pictures taken of her ever since an unflattering candid of her went semi-viral.

"Maybe you should just go out there and tell them so they're not salivating over what they think might be a juicy story," Stevie suggests.

"That's not a bad idea," Luc says, surprising the hell out of me. "Maybe we should." He lifts me in his arms and then sits down again, cradling me in his lap. This seems to prompt everyone in the room to move to the kitchen area to give us privacy.

"Are you sure you want to do that, with Victor still missing?" I ask.

"That's exactly why. Because Stevie is wrong about them going away after they get their story. They'll just start following you around, at least the local papers and the fans. They already do that to me. If there are more eyes on us, there's less chance of Victor getting near us. Since he already knows about you, there's no point in hiding it from the public anymore." He places a kiss on my forehead near my bandage. "What do you think, darling?"

With both hands, I cup his face, matching his tenderness. "I think you're right. You deserve to live freely in the open. So...what? Are you really thinking of going out there to address them? Or maybe you can do a press release or a social media post...?"

"Well now, let's not go crazy," he says in mock horror. "I was thinking more along the lines of going out for dinner and holding your hand in public. Maybe even kissing that sexy mouth of yours without caring if anyone is watching."

I laugh. "You do any of that and it's as good as a press release. We'll be all over social media the first time we're seen together, with rumors flying."

He looks at me with concern. "Will you be okay with that? Having a spotlight on you because of me?"

I look at Joey, who is still trying to get used to it, but Brent is helping her overcome her self-consciousness. With my mouth a breath from Luc's, I say, "I'm okay with anything as long as I have you."

He closes the distance and kisses me with sweet tenderness.

"Alright, that's enough, you two," Stevie calls out as our kiss soon becomes heated. She comes over and plops beside us on the sofa, the others following her back to the family room.

"Stevie, have you heard from Georgie yet?" Sandra asks, both concern and annoyance in her voice.

"No, but I need to talk to you about that. I'm worried about her."

"She texted me this morning," I say. "Said she's trying to co-ordinate things so she can get away. She seemed really stressed about it, though, so I told her it was okay." Not wanting to add to my mother's worry, I don't voice my own concerns. Giving her a reassuring smile, I add, "I'm sure she'll come when the baby is born. Besides, I'm fine, and there's nothing she could do here anyway. I'll be back on my feet in a few days."

Luc frowns at me. "I don't think so. You need to rest for a week, at least. After that, you're not going to be able to jump right back into your hectic work schedule, especially with Victor still out there. As far as I'm concerned, you don't need to go back at all."

He is not a fan of Mark. He told me he knew Mark was an asshole as soon as he heard him call me "little superstar."

Mom agrees with him. "He's right, honey. Do you really want to risk the baby by pushing things too soon?"

I smile back at both of them. "Trust me, I've already been planning my exit strategy from this job."

"Not so dumb after all," Stevie teases, poking me in the arm.

I stick out my tongue at her before clarifying, "I'll call Mark and see if I can coordinate things by phone and video calls once I get the all-clear from the doctor. And tell him no more traveling for interviews once I'm able to go back to the studio."

My most important job right now is to do all I can to deliver a healthy baby.

44

Luc

I SPEND AS MUCH time as possible over the next few days with Charlie, much of it also in the company of her family and my sister, who wants to stay in New York until Charlie goes back to work. It makes things easier for Gabe to have her here where his men can protect us all together.

The sudden chaos in my house, which had been silent and empty for so long, should have been overwhelming, but I'm enjoying it. I love how Charlie's family enfolds me and Daphne into their warm circle. I'm happy to see my sister smiling more and even laughing. She doesn't say much, and she's still self-conscious when she does speak, but it's good to see her enjoying herself.

It's with regret that I leave Charlie for the Firebirds' away game. I'll be gone for the night and won't return home until late tomorrow.

She walks me to the door, but unable to give her a proper goodbye kiss in the house with her mother, Daphne, and Bobbie wandering around, I settle for a quick but heartfelt press of my mouth against hers. But Charlie puts a hand on my head and pulls me back for a longer, deeper kiss. It takes all I have to keep my hands light on her waist when what I really want is to slide them down to her perfect ass and pull her tightly against my growing erection.

I reluctantly pull away, echoing her groan of disappointment. "I know, darling. But this can't go anywhere and it's going to be harder if we don't stop now."

She flicks her gaze down my body. I grin. "Yes, that too is becoming much harder."

My beautiful minx gives me a sexy, naughty look. "Hurry home so we can do something about that."

Her words are echoing in my head as the team buses pull into the Firebirds' parking lot the next night. I'm the first one off the bus, running to the SUV waiting for me with one of Gabe's men inside. Charlie insisted I also have a trained bodyguard at all times. Reggie is able to fend off reporters and fans by his sheer size, but he is not equipped to handle anything more serious. Due to the late hour, there's no traffic and I'm able to reach home in record time.

"Great game," Charlie murmurs, her voice soft with sleep, when I slip into bed beside her.

"Thanks, but it was a little too close for comfort." I pull her warm body against me, wrapping myself around her.

She gives me a congratulatory kiss, which turns into so much more as I take her mouth in a desperate kiss. I am soon on her like a starving man, slowing down only when I'm ready to enter her. Despite the doctor's assurance that normal activities, including sex, are safe to resume, I've refrained from making love to her, frustrating Charlie with my overabundance of caution. I can't resist anymore.

Later, lying in bed behind her with her back against my chest, I let my hand wander over the curved tight mound of her belly. It's the size of a basketball now, no longer just a bump. She seems to be growing so fast these days. Probably proper rest and nutrition have played a big part in that, her mother helping me ensure Charlie gets plenty of both despite her protests that she feels fine.

Her belly isn't all that has expanded. Her breasts have grown too, almost a handful now, and still as sensitive as ever.

A slight movement under my hand startles me. I go up on one elbow to look at Charlie to see if she felt it, but she's asleep. Her breathing is soft and even, her hands under her cheek.

Her belly jumps again. Is that the baby? I hold my hand still, barely breathing, waiting for the movement again, but nothing happens. I stroke her belly, circling my big palm over the mound, massaging it gently, encouraging my baby girl to move again.

There it is.

"Charlie," I whisper, full of wonder.

She shifts in her sleep. I have to share this moment with her. I kiss her softly on her forehead, her jaw, her mouth, which turns toward me, her lips parting. Pressing a quick kiss to them, I pull away and turn on the bedside light.

"Charlie, darling."

She moans slightly, rolling closer to me. Her eyes open and look at me sleepily. "Again?" she asks with a smile when my hand resumes stroking her belly.

"I think the baby moved," I say softly, in awe.

"Yeah, our daughter seems to be a night owl."

Our daughter.

Charlie snuggles close, putting her hand over mine and moving it so that it's right above where the baby is moving. "Feel that?"

I slide under the covers and place a kiss on the spot where I feel the movement. Moving the covers so I can peer up at Charlie, I stare at her with utter reverence. Her eyes blur with tears. No, wait. It's my vision that's blurred. I close my eyes before I embarrass myself. Her hands cup my face and tug lightly to pull me back up to her, silently demanding a kiss.

I concede by giving her a soft, short kiss. When she protests, wanting more, I place a finger on her lips. Resting my head on my palm, I ask, "Charlie, do you remember the first night you were in the hospital?"

I proposed to her on impulse, and since then, I've wrestled with my guilt over her accident. Doubts filled me about whether I deserved to have her and the baby and all the happiness that came with it. Desperate for guidance, I went to Dr. Vandermeyer, who helped me understand I didn't need to pay the price for someone else's actions. Her words were similar to what Charlie had told me when I confessed everything to her.

Charlie looks at me now, her eyes wary. Does she not remember?

"Some," she finally answers.

"Okay. Well, forget whatever you remember. I didn't mean…"

I stop when Charlie pulls away, looking devastated.

Shit.

"You do remember." And thought I was rescinding my proposal. My nervousness eases. I smooth the back of my hand over her cheek and laugh dryly. "Wow, I really need to work on this. You were practically unconscious the first time, and I just bungled my second attempt. Let's see if third time's the charm."

I sit up and lean over to pull a small box from the back of my nightstand drawer. Twisting back to face her, I bring my hand up to her line of vision so she can see the black velvet ring box I'm holding.

She scrambles up onto her knees to face me. Her position is similar to when I gave her the locket, but she's not bouncing in excitement this time. Her gray eyes are wide and serious, her fingers over her mouth. I hadn't planned on proposing in the middle of the night, but I can't wait another minute to put my ring on her finger.

"You've already given me the greatest gift in life. You've given me joy and opened up my heart when I thought I'd never feel anything again. All I can offer you in return is my love and my promise that I will do everything in my power to make you happy every day for the rest of our lives. I love you, my darling Charlie. Will you marry me?"

I open the ring box one-handed to reveal a heart-shaped diamond in a stunning setting of more hearts formed by smaller diamonds. But it can't compare to the brilliance in Charlie's shining eyes when she raises them from the ring to my face.

She cups my jaw and kisses me, deeply, desperately, giving me her answer. But I still need to hear it.

"Is that a yes, my love?"

"Yes. Yes, yes, yes!" she exclaims, bouncing on her knees now. "God, I love you, Luc. So much."

I take out the ring and let the box drop onto the covers. "Give me your hand, darling."

She holds out her left hand and watches me slide the ring onto her finger. When the ring is in place, I give her a moment to admire the sight before bringing her hand up to press a kiss to her fingers.

"I love you," I murmur past the lump in my throat, then help her back under the covers. Settling in behind her, I tuck her head under my chin and hold her close against my body, laying one hand lovingly, protectively, over our baby daughter.

I close my eyes, my entire being filled with gratitude for the two lives I hold close to me.

My family. My life. My joy.

Epilogue

"**A**M I DOING THE right thing?" I ask Luc as we stare down at our cherubic sleeping daughter, Evangeline Joy Saint. I'm filled with doubts about the path I'm about to embark on tomorrow, going to my first day of classes for my master's degree in psychology. While I'm excited about taking the first step in a long journey to become a trauma therapist, I'm likely to miss some of her biggest moments while I'm in classes. Is it worth it? And what if she forms a close attachment to the live-in nanny we hired?

Ugh. I sigh in disgust at myself. Of course I want her to love her nanny. Okay, maybe *like* her, not *love* her.

"Darling, you're doing what you need to—for yourself and for our daughter, being an amazing role model for her."

He's said various versions of this over the past few weeks, assuring me every time I voice my hesitation at leaving her at home with a nanny.

"Then why do I feel like I'm being selfish? It's not like we need the money or will in this lifetime, thanks to your hard work."

"And thanks to Victor being out of our lives forever."

His voice is matter-of-fact, but I take his hand and squeeze it. Victor is dead and no longer a threat. After he was killed, I encouraged Luc to have a session or two with Dr. Vandermeyer. He needed to know it was okay to feel whatever he was feeling, whether he was sad or glad or nothing but relieved at his father's death.

"Go to your classes," he continues "see how you feel this semester. You can always change your mind. But I have a feeling you're going to remember why you're doing this, and it has nothing to do with money or security."

He's right. I want to do this to help people like Luc, my siblings, and anyone who's gone through trauma and needs assistance processing it and figuring out how to cope and move forward with their lives.

"She'll be fine, darling. Now let's go to bed."

I look at my baby girl's sweet chubby face, a bit of drool at the corner of her mouth as she sleeps the sleep of the innocent. Leaning down to kiss her as lightly as a whisper so as not to wake her, I take a moment to breathe in her special baby scent. I wait for Luc to do the same before raising the side of the crib and locking it in place. He brushes a hand over her wispy curls before putting an arm around my shoulders and leading me out of the nursery. Evangeline is sleeping through the night, but her nanny is in the next room in case she awakens.

Once in our bedroom, Luc takes me in his arms and sighs into my hair. "Have I told you today how much I fucking love you?"

"Hm, I'm not sure," I tease. "But I clearly remember you telling me this morning how much you love fucking me."

I giggle when he nips my neck.

"Minx." He kisses me, conveying so much more than desire with his lips and tongue. "I love you so much."

"I love you more," I whisper against his mouth.

"Is that so?" He cups my face and kisses me tenderly. "I guess I'll have to show you that can't possibly be true."

He carries me to our bed and shows me for the next hour—just like I know he will for the rest of our lives—how much he loves me.

Ready For More?

Deleted Content, Bonus Scenes & Upcoming Titles

I HOPE YOU ENJOYED Luc and Charlie's story as much as I did writing it. Their journey continues as part of the next book, Ready to Risk. While it is Stevie's story, you'll learn how Victor meets his end and get to meet Luc and Charlie's daughter. And if you sign up for my newsletter, you'll be notified of bonus scenes. You can sign up at:

http://www.shefaliprem.com

My newsletter will also have information about giveaways and sneak peeks of upcoming titles in the Ready For Love series that will include the Hutchinsons and their friends. If you have not read Brent and Joey's story, you can read it in **Ready to Play**. Please visit my website for book blurbs and links to order the books as they are released.

Reviews are so important for new indie authors like me. It would mean the world to me if you took a quick moment to leave a review on Amazon and/or Goodreadsand of course, any other platform.

Acknowledgements

THANK YOU ONCE AGAIN to my editors, Kristi Yanta, Peter Senftleben, and especially Kristen Tate, for helping me make this book one I can be truly proud of.

I have to give a shout out to my proofreader Gennifer Ulmen for catching things when I couldn't stand to look at the manuscript anymore.

A special thank you to my beta readers.

A huge thanks to my readers for your lovely reviews that bring me to tears. Your kind words and enthusiasm keep me going when I wonder why I do this.

And lots of love to my family for supporting me and putting up with my crazy writing schedule and all the ramblings about my characters as if they're my friends in real life.

About the author

S HEFALI PREM IS INDIAN-BORN and American-raised. She has lived on both coasts and traveled to—or at least passed through—almost every state in the US. She loves to read and write heartfelt emotional romances with a lot of heat and a guaranteed happily-ever-after.

Sign up at to be notified of bonus content, upcoming releases, sneak peeks, and giveaways. And don't forget to follow her on social media:

Get all the social media links:
https://linktr.ee/shefalipremromance

Scan Me

www.ingramcontent.com/pod-product-compliance
Lightning Source LLC
Chambersburg PA
CBHW050021120726
47903CB00006B/1860